No-One Ever Has Sex

IN THE

SUBURBS

Also by Tracy Bloom

No-One Ever Has Sex on a Tuesday
Single Woman Seeks Revenge
I Will Marry George Clooney (By Christmas)

No-One Ever Has Sex

in the

Suburbs

BY

Tracy Bloom

ISBN-13: 9781514225110

For the people and parties of Loughborough Road.
The absolute best of times . . . in the suburbs.

PROLOGUE

September – Leeds General Maternity Ward

Ben took her hand and looked her straight in the eye. 'I love you, I always have.'

'I love you too, you know,' Katy replied.

'You don't have to say that just because I did.'

'No, I do, I really do, and I will marry you – if you meant it, that is.'

'Of course I meant it. But I do have one condition.'

'What's that?' asked Katy, fearing the worst.

'That we never become one of those boring married couples. You know, like the ones who sit in pubs and don't talk to each other and probably never have sex.'

'I promise,' said Katy, knowing that life with Ben could never be boring. 'Tell you what. We'll even have sex on a Tuesday.'

CHAPTER ONE

Six weeks later

'You have to be kidding me?' gasped Katy, overwhelmed by the audacity of the man.

'No,' he replied gravely. 'We really need to discuss contraception.'

'Contraception!' she screeched.

He looked nervously at the door as though concerned that the people gathered outside might hear her outrage.

'Contraception!' she screeched again. 'Are you out of your mind? How can you even mention it?'

'I can assure you, it's a very routine question.'

'I–do–not–need–contraception,' Katy stated.

'I see, but—'

'I am certain of that,' she interrupted, 'because I currently have cabbage leaves stuffed down my bra. Can you imagine a more effective passion killer than breasts that smell like a compost heap and are prone to leakage?'

The doctor turned back to his computer screen, showing little reaction to what Katy thought was a reasonable question. He started tapping something into his keyboard. 'I can give you antibiotics if you are suffering from mastitis,' he muttered, staring intently at the screen.

'And,' she continued, feeling the need to further justify her absolute rejection of the mention of contraception just six weeks after she had given birth. 'And, I've had eighteen stitches in my vagina.' She folded her arms and leaned back, feeling smug. Now see if he dared raise the subject of contraception again. My, she'd come a long way since she'd given birth a few weeks ago. She never would have would have used the V-word with anyone – including a doctor – before. Her dignity, however, had been left on the labour room floor and she no longer felt any compulsion to keep her vagina and its injuries to herself.

The doctor appeared unfazed by her declaration. 'I need to make you aware,' he said, 'that just because you've recently had a baby, it doesn't mean you can't get pregnant if you have unprotected sex.'

'And when exactly do you imagine this unprotected sex will be occurring?' she asked. 'Would that be at night when our daughter chooses to celebrate the dawning of a new day in the southern hemisphere by refusing to go to sleep, or would that be during the day when my fiancé is at work and I'm exhausting myself by trying to keep her awake to convince her that Greenwich Mean Time is the way to go?'

The doctor looked at her as he must have looked at a thousand first-time mums.

'It will get better,' he said calmly.

'Or maybe,' she continued, 'I'll be in the mood just at that point when I haven't been near a shower in days, I'm reduced to using Sudacrem to style my hair and Millie has just projectile pooed all over me.'

The doctor held her accusing stare. 'I understand,' he said gently.

'Do you?' she cried. 'The fact you have four kids would indicate to me that you do not understand in the slightest.' She nodded at the framed photo of the doctor surrounded by his wife and tribe of sons, sitting behind him on the window ledge. 'You've put some poor woman through this four times. You clearly have no idea.'

Katy leaned back in her chair and tried to control her rapid breathing. She was in no mood to have her love life interrogated. To be perfectly honest, sex was the last thing on her mind since the hand grenade of a new baby had landed in their lives. However, she had to admit it was bothering her that it also appeared to be the last thing on Ben's mind. She was very aware that he'd made no move whatsoever to instigate lovemaking since their new arrival. Previously a post-pub snog would easily fall into a happy tumble on the sofa or under the sheets, and Ben had even been known to set his alarm in order to sneak in some early morning passion before work. But now they were a total sex-free zone. She hoped it was down to Ben being considerate and as overwhelmed by everything as she was, but what really chewed at her was that they actually hadn't made love since Ben had discovered she'd had sex with Matthew. Maybe he hadn't totally forgiven her after all for her stupid one-night stand with her childhood sweetheart. She certainly hadn't forgiven herself, and she doubted she ever would. But he'd still asked her to marry him, hadn't he? Said he loved her when he'd returned, just in the nick of time, to the delivery room, not only to forgive, but also to propose.

Their engagement had lasted for a whole four hours and twenty-three minutes before they became parents. Their relationship barely mended, healing time had taken a back seat to baby demands, and their promise of betrothal had got lost somewhere in a sea of tiredness and Pampers. Any desire to consummate Ben's proposal was crushed by the need for a moment's peace, or worse, as Katy feared, by unresolved resentment that she'd fucked everything up by shagging her ex. Either way, being interrogated by the doctor on this sensitive subject was not going down well.

'I see you haven't had a smear test for over three years.' The doctor looked at her over his glasses. 'You really need one soon.'

Katy stared back at him. Could he really be that insensitive?

'I have two words for you,' she said. 'Eighteen. Stitches.'

'I'll make sure you're sent a reminder in three months,' he replied, typing again. 'Now, let me ask, how are *you* feeling?' he said, changing the expression on his face from slightly frustrated to a mock caring one.

'Fine,' she muttered, worried it was some kind of trick question.

'Have you felt down at all since giving birth? Have there been any times when you've had a sense of hopelessness, like you couldn't cope?'

'Hourly,' she replied deadpan, then laughed nervously. She thought of the chaos she'd left her designer flat in that morning. Before the baby she couldn't bear to leave the place in a state, as she loved the calm feeling of arriving home to its tidy perfection. Now she woke up surrounded by chaos, lived in chaos, shut the door on chaos, arrived home to chaos. She thought of the hanging files in her old office at the advertising agency. An account director must always appear in control, and her alphabetical, colour-coded files were the bedrock of a system that allowed her to organise with a ruthless efficiency renowned throughout the agency. She had no system for the baby. She just couldn't find the system, however hard she tried.

'Are you often tearful, or emotional for no obvious reason?' the doctor continued.

Katy thought about her reaction to having discovered there was no coffee in the house that morning. Mild hysterics. Her response to the takeaway pizza arriving without extra mushrooms. Mass tantrum. News that Take That were going on tour again and all the tickets were sold out already. Literally floods of tears. She was constantly emotional and on the brink of falling apart. She wasn't coping at all well with motherhood and she had no idea why. She was a smart, intelligent, successful woman who didn't have a clue how to look after a baby. She felt like a failure, and that was something she just wasn't used to.

'I'm fine,' she insisted,' fighting the urge to burst into tears. 'Everything is fine.'

'Good, good,' the doctor said, apparently satisfied with her answer. 'And are you getting help from your partner with the baby?'

'Oh yes,' she nodded. He was outside now, looking after Millie in the waiting room. No doubt Millie would be gurgling at him happily as all the oldies told him how good he was with her. No-one ever told her that. Ben picked her up and she instantly calmed, mesmerised by his big blue eyes and shock of ginger hair. Katy picked her up and she looked disgusted at the imposition. Babies must be like dogs, she thought. They knew when you were scared. Millie had already worked out she was a rubbish mum, she just knew it. She could tell by the look on her face.

'Her daddy is very good with her,' she informed the doctor. 'She really is a daddy's girl.' Her stomach clenched as she said the words. She still couldn't bear to think about what she'd put Ben through regarding Millie's parentage. The timing of her stupid one-night stand had proved potentially catastrophic when she'd realised it had coincided with when she'd conceived. Knowing there was even a tiny chance that Matthew could be the father of her child had led to months of anxiety until Millie appeared, sporting a shock of ginger hair identical to Ben's as well as his cute, slightly turned-up nose, dispelling any doubt whatsoever that Ben was her father. He was in fact waiting outside with her now so they could all go to the registry office and get Millie's birth registered. Katy had been avoiding it, dreading the awkwardness and recriminations might get raked over. But now she wished she'd got it over and done with straight away so they could have moved on weeks ago. Still, it would all be done today, and once they'd completed that task then she really should get around to having sex with Ben. She realised that they needed to have sex. Soon. Perhaps when they were both less tired.

CHAPTER TWO

Leeds Registry Office had the look of a building more suited to registering the misery of death than the joy of a new life, with its looming, grimy stone walls and double-height doors guarded by iron gates. Ben bounded up the endless steps at the entrance with all the ease of a twenty-nine-year-old who spent his days tearing around a school sports field with teenagers. Katy meanwhile took it more slowly, feeling every one of her extra eight years on Ben as well as her lack of gym attendance since pregnancy, which had given her the welcome excuse to end her membership. Ben waited at the top of the steps, swinging Millie in her car seat like it was a ride at the funfair until Katy reached him. He put Millie down and started punching the air.

'What *are* you doing?' asked Katy.

'Pretending I'm Rocky,' Ben grinned. 'It's impossible to come up a massive set of steps like that and not sing the theme tune to *Rocky* and then do this at the top.'

'Even Millie is looking at you as though you are deranged,' Katy pointed out.

'The minute she's old enough I'll be sharing the joys of *Rocky* with the Millster *and* I will bring her to these very steps, and we shall sing and run and pretend-fight together, and she will understand that it is the right thing to do whenever you see a long set of stone steps.'

'So glad you have her education close to your heart, Ben,' Katy said dryly.

'Important life lessons, Katy. What to do on seeing a large flight of stone steps and how to handle the utter depression of being a Leeds United fan. These things are all on my essential list of teachings for Millie.'

'Glad to hear it,' smiled Katy. And she was. She stepped forward to kiss him on the cheek. It was at moments like this that she knew exactly why Ben was the perfect man for her. Whatever crap was going on in her life, whatever inner turmoil she was feeling, it was Ben who reminded her not to take life so seriously. To have fun. She sincerely hoped it was a trait Millie would inherit from her father.

He held her gaze for a moment as she pulled away.

'You ready for this?' he asked, looking serious for a moment.

'Oh yes,' she replied. She held her breath, fearful that Ben might say something to remind her how lucky she was that he was standing there at all, given what had happened. But he said nothing, just looked at her with his big grin and twinkly eyes, then wrapped her in his arms in a hug so generous and committed that it brought tears of joy to her eyes.

'Right,' he said when he finally released her and bent to pick up Millie in her car seat. 'Shall we go and agree to keep her then? I've got used to her now, and I don't think you can get a refund after twenty-eight days.'

A council worker in polyester and NHS glasses directed them to a waiting room lined with worn-looking chairs and worn-looking people. Clearly it was an exhausting business being related to the newly born or the newly dead. There was no hint of tiredness, however, on the faces of the two girls in their late teens who were sitting right opposite the entrance. One of them leapt out of her seat and flung herself at Katy the minute she walked in, her mass of blonde hair smothering Katy's face.

'Oh my God, look who it is!' she screeched. She was gripping Katy so tightly that she thought her breasts might explode, whilst her spiky false nails cut into her arms.

'Hi, Charlene,' she said, once she'd been allowed to come up for air.

Charlene bounced up and down in front of Katy with excitement.

'Wow, Ben!' she shrieked, catching sight of him behind Katy. 'This is brilliant. It's like a reunion. Abby, look,' she said, turning to the girl she was with, who was openly staring at Ben through make-up of the shovel variety and over the top of a cleavage that was demanding attention like an emerging new talent. 'It's Katy and Ben from our antenatal class. Remember? They came to our wedding party. Ben was the guy who knocked out that bloke in the middle of the dance floor.'

Abby stood up from her chair and took a step forward, still openly gaping at Ben.

'Oh, I remember,' she said, looking him up and down very slowly.

'How's Luke?' Ben asked Charlene, trying to draw his eyes away from Abby's cleavage but failing.

'Fine,' replied Charlene. 'He's at work, so Abby said she'd come with me to get Rocco registered. Can you believe it? No-one told us we had to come and register him ourselves, did they? We thought the hospital sent a form or something, and we were in the pub the other night, weren't we, Abby, and I was telling this bloke who was trying to chat me up to get lost because I had a baby and he wouldn't believe me. Anyway, he thought I was messing with him and asked if I had his birth certificate to prove it and I suddenly went, fuck me, didn't I, Abby? Fuck me, we haven't got Rocco a birth certificate. So as I said to

Luke when I got home, it's a bloody good job that that bloke tried to chat me up or else baby Rocco might not exist.'

Katy stared at Charlene, open-mouthed, before saying feebly, 'We just never seemed to have had the time before now.'

'Is that why you haven't come along when the antenatal class meets up, then?' demanded Charlene.

'Er . . . yeah,' Katy replied, looking over at Ben, who raised his eyebrows. He took an empty seat next to where Charlene had been sitting and began to get Millie out of her car seat. 'Just been too busy,' she said to Charlene. 'You know how it is.'

'You not coping?' asked Charlene. 'Because we're all in it together, you know. You should come along. And you should see Alison and Matthew's house. It's amaaaaaaaazing.'

Nooooooo, Katy wanted to scream. The last place she wanted to hear Matthew's name mentioned was here. Not now, just as they were about to officially declare that Ben was Millie's dad. Neither Ben nor Katy had let his name pass their lips since Ben had proposed. It had been such a ridiculous piece of bad luck that they'd ended up in the same antenatal class as Matthew and his pregnant wife Alison. Traumatised, Katy had realised she could no longer avoid the niggling doubt that Matthew could be the father of her unborn child. Secret meetings between the two of them had led to an agreement to ignore the slim possibility. But then it had all started to unravel when Ben had twigged that Katy and Matthew had been childhood sweethearts.

'Are you not coming because Ben twatted Matthew at our wedding reception?' demanded Charlene.

'No,' Katy said, too quickly.

'Because Alison's not bothered, you know. She knows he only did it because he was jealous of how successful Matthew is,' stated Charlene.

So that was how Matthew had explained away the fisticuffs to his wife. That it was over money jealousy, not because Matthew had just told Ben that he and Katy had had a one-night stand at that damned school reunion. Katy looked over to Ben, who thankfully seemed to have zoned out of the conversation and was desperately trying to settle a fraught Millie.

'We're meeting next Monday, actually,' Charlene persisted. 'I'll pick you up, shall I?'

'No,' cried Katy, thinking quickly. 'I can't. I go to a music class with Millie on Mondays.'

'Oh, which one?'

'At the Community Centre. Music, Mummy and Me.'

'Coolio. I'll come with you to that instead. Tell Alison to move the meeting. Actually, Mondays tend to be a bit boring. I'll come every week. Brilliant.'

'What?' exclaimed Katy, but before she could stop Charlene from becoming her new mummy stalker friend, Millie let out a piercing wail from where she was lying in Ben's arms. Katy knew the signs. Millie needed feeding. It was a disaster of epic proportions. They were in a public place and she had vegetation down her bra. Ben leaned towards her to whisper in her ear.

'Do you think you need to get your tits out?' he said.

'Ben!' gasped Katy, horrified. Sometimes the eight-year age gap between them was so evident it took her breath away. She tried hard to ignore these moments in favour of the ones that had her in fits of giggles at some inappropriate comment he'd made about one of his school colleagues, or his unique ability to make her see the funny side of the ridiculous world of advertising, preventing her from being the workaholic, nightmare career bitch she could have become without him.

She noticed that the cleavage with a name was still openly gawping at the buff body of her twenty-nine-year-old football-playing PE teacher boyfriend. She didn't know whether to feel proud or petrified.

'Well, do you?' asked Ben, offering up a wailing Millie.

'Just give me a minute.' Katy shot off to find a loo so she could deposit her cabbage leaves in the bin. By the time she'd returned, Millie was beside herself. Katy began the tricky manoeuvre of unhooking a maternity bra and latching on a screaming baby whilst revealing the smallest amount of flesh possible. She'd tried and failed the nonchalant use of muslin draped over the shoulder, but it always fell off, and so she was reduced to the odd pointing of shoulders into the corners of rooms in an effort to maintain some dignity.

Silence descended on the room suddenly as Millie found her food. Katy looked up, grateful for the peace. Charlene and Abby were openly staring at her.

'I couldn't do that,' pronounced Charlene.

'It's not that bad,' Katy lied, wincing.

'But how do you go out at night?' asked Charlene.

Katy cast her mind back over the last six weeks. She didn't know why – she knew she hadn't been out at all during that time.

'And you can't drink, can you?' said Charlene.

'Seriously?' said Abby, finally deigning to look at Katy. '*Seriously?*'

'Oh yeah,' replied Charlene. 'That's right. They expect you to spend nine months hardly drinking and then if you breastfeed you still can't go out on the lash. We wouldn't be going down the Pink Coconut every Friday and Saturday night if my mum couldn't give Rocco a bottle.'

'Friday and Saturday?' said Katy, her jaw dropping open.

'Yeah,' nodded Charlene.

'But,' said Katy, 'aren't you, like, knackered?'

'Not really.'

Katy felt every day of her thirty-seven years.

'But . . . but . . . night feeds?' she asked.

Charlene shrugged.

'We're living at Mum's, so we take it in turns during the week and Mum does weekends.'

Katy thought of the night before when she'd felt like screaming as Ben slept next to her whilst she battled the tiredness to give Millie her feed. She didn't blame him – there was nothing he could do – but it didn't make it any easier.

'Very well organised,' she muttered. She looked away, not trusting herself to not let an exhausted tear slip down her cheek.

'You should come out with us,' said Abby.

Katy snapped her head back up, shocked at the ludicrous request. She realised immediately, however, that the suggestion wasn't directed at her; it was aimed at Ben. Abby was blushing slightly, and she appeared to be opening and closing her eyes very fast in a fluttering motion.

'I mean, if she can't,' she continued, nodding her head at Katy without looking at her.

Un-fucking believable, thought Katy angrily. This *child* was hitting on her boyfriend whilst she was sitting next to him breastfeeding their baby.

'I don't think that would be fair on Katy,' said Ben.

Katy smiled at Ben before turning smugly to Abby.

'The Pink Coconut isn't really my scene either,' he added.

'Shame,' said Abby, licking her lips. 'I really think you'd have a good time.'

'Perhaps when Katy's finished breastfeeding and we can get a babysitter, then maybe we could all go,' said Ben diplomatically.

'Awesome idea,' said Charlene, bouncing up and down in her chair. 'That'll give you the chance to lose the rest of your baby weight as well, Katy.'

Katy turned to stare at Charlene, her mouth open.

'I've been so lucky,' Charlene continued. 'It's just dropped straight off me.'

Abby smirked at Katy. She could have sworn the girl leaned forward just a fraction to give a better view of the cleavage.

'And how many children have you got, Abby?' asked Katy.

Abby threw her head back and laughed, then fixed Katy with a steady stare.

'I'm way too young,' she said. 'Besides which, I haven't met the right man yet.'

Katy held her stare.

'We got engaged,' she said after a long pause. She took hold of Ben's hand and smiled at Abby.

'Wow!' shrieked Charlene. 'That is so cool. When did that happen?'

'Ben asked me in the labour room,' Katy told her.

'Amaaaaazing,' said Charlene. 'Show me the ring.' She held out her hand. 'I bet it's massive,' she whispered loudly to Abby. 'Katy is loaded.'

'Oh, we haven't got round to buying one yet,' said Katy.

'What!' exclaimed Charlene. 'You've had ages.'

Katy looked at Ben, who stared blankly back.

'We want to take our time,' said Katy. 'I've no idea what kind of ring I want and my fingers are still like sausages at the moment, and I just want to plan, you know, get it right, but we haven't had the time with the baby. And we need to save up, don't we, Ben?'

Ben screwed his face up and said nothing.

'Okay,' nodded Charlene. 'So when *will* you get married? We'll come, won't we, Abby?'

Abby looked down at her knee-high black leather boots.

'Oh God, not yet,' said Katy. 'I can't think about planning a wedding at the moment. Maybe the end of next year when Millie's a bit older.'

'Well, don't leave it too long,' said Charlene. 'The minute Luke asked me I was on the phone to the Social Club booking our reception in. I didn't want him changing his mind, did I? You know what men are like.'

Katy looked over at Ben. His head was bent, checking football scores on his phone, ignoring the female battlefield going on next to him. There was plenty of time to get married. There was no rush. They had enough to deal with at the moment being parents, never mind becoming husband and wife. Ben was happy to wait until the time was right. She was sure of it.

'So can you give me the full name of your child, please?' said the registrar, who had the gentlest voice Katy had ever heard. She had talked them both through what registering a birth entailed in super calm tones, and now they were actually doing it. Registering their daughter with the world. Ben looked at Katy.

'You tell her,' she said, taking his hand.

'Millie Freya Annie Chapman,' Ben announced.

Katy gasped. 'That wasn't what we agreed,' she told the very calm registrar. She felt like crying. This wasn't supposed to be the tough bit.

'It is!' exclaimed Ben. 'Millie, because that's what we call her. Freya Annie because we wanted to name her after your gran, but you can't call the poor girl Fanny, so I came up with the idea of Freya Annie, then she can always sign herself Millie F. Annie Chapman, so very cleverly we have hidden the name Fanny in there. Genius, if you ask me.'

Katy didn't know where to start. She looked at the registrar in desperation.

'Would you like to come back when you have agreed on a name?' she asked, showing early signs of exasperation.

'No,' cried Katy. She couldn't go through all this again. 'Just give us one moment.' She turned to Ben and attempted a private conversation, with the registrar sitting right in front of them.

'We talked about this last night,' she said through gritted teeth. 'It's Amelia, not Millie. I know we call her Millie for short, but having Amelia gives her the option.'

'But I don't like the name Amelia,' said Ben. 'I told you that. It's just a bit poncey.'

'But you can call her Millie.'

'So what's her name, then?'

'Amelia.'

'What's the point in giving her a name we're not going to use?'

'So she can choose.'

'She can't speak. She can't choose. We get to choose, that's the whole point. Besides which, I have Ben on my birth certificate. It could have been Benjamin. Can you imagine? Do I look like a Benjamin? I'd have disowned my parents if they'd landed me with a name like Benjamin.'

Katy glanced back at the registrar, who was pretending to write something.

'I thought you were joking about the Freya Annie thing?' she continued.

'Why? It's genius. You get to honour your gran without having to call her Fanny, and you wanted Freya as her middle name anyway. So all we're doing is adding Annie, which was also on our list.'

Katy decided to try a slightly different tack.

'She should really take your surname, not mine.'

'Really?'

'Yes. Of course. When we get married we all want the same surname, don't we, so we might as well start her off with yours. I'm keeping my maiden name as my professional name, though.'

Ben looked stunned for a moment. He took her hand and swallowed before he managed to get any words out.

'I just thought . . . I don't know . . . I just thought, because we're not married yet, that she'd have your name.'

'No. I want her to have your name.'

'So you've come in here thinking we're calling her Amelia Freya King and I think it's Millie Freya Annie Chapman,' he said.

Katy nodded.

'What about Amelia Freya Annie King?' he said.

Katy thought for a moment. Then nodded. She turned to the registrar. 'Please can you write down Amelia Freya Annie King?'

'Are you sure?' the registrar asked.

'Yes,' they both replied.

'Just write it down,' urged Katy as she watched the pen hover painfully above the paper.

'You can always go away and come back when you've had the chance to talk it through properly. This is a very big decision. I would hate that you might do something either of you might regret.'

'Write, it, down,' said Katy firmly. She was beginning to feel claustrophobic. The sooner they got out of there the better.

She watched, mesmerised, as the registrar wrote the name out slowly and carefully, checking for spelling as she went along.

'So can you now give me the full name of the father?' the woman asked, glancing up and directing her question at Ben. Ben hesitated and Katy felt as though time stood still. She nudged Ben, who looked over to her, panic clouding his face. She couldn't ask him what was wrong. She knew exactly what the problem was. They were about to make it official that Ben was Millie's dad, and given everything that had happened during the lead-up to her arrival, that was a pretty big deal.

'I've just realised something,' Ben said to Katy.

'What?' she gasped. What could he possibly have only just realised at this very moment?

'I've never told you my middle name before.'

'Oh,' she said, confused and relieved.

He turned back to the registrar, looking a little pale.

'It's Ben Barry King,' he said quickly.

'Can you repeat that?' the registrar asked. 'I'm sorry, I missed it.'

'Ben Barry King,' he said again, turning back to Katy, looking slightly flushed.

'It's okay,' she shrugged. 'So your mum and dad were big B.B. King fans. That's pretty cool, actually.'

Ben shook his head. 'Barry Manilow, I'm afraid. The B.B. King thing was an accident.'

Katy couldn't help but start to laugh.

'You're named after Barry Manilow?' she managed to splutter out.

'Yes,' he nodded, trying desperately to hold on to his mortified expression but eventually forced into joining in with Katy's mirth. Soon they were both roaring with laughter, until tears were rolling down their faces.

The registrar gave them a few moments, then stepped in. 'Shall we continue?'

'Let's,' said Katy, taking a huge breath and looking away from Ben to stop herself laughing. 'Sorry,' she muttered as the woman gave her a stern look.

'So could you tell me the father's occupation next?' the registrar asked.

Ben cleared his throat and forced a serious expression onto his face.

'Singer at the Copacabana,' he replied. Katy collapsed into giggles again. Ben fixed his serious eyes on the registrar, who was eventually forced to crack a smile. Katy leaned over and took Ben's hand in hers. She should have known that he would turn the whole potential nightmare of registering Millie's parentage into a comedy showcase.

'Why don't we just book ourselves in?' said Ben later as they passed through the reception for the second time. Fortunately, Charlene and Abby were nowhere to be seen.

'What for?' asked Katy.

'To get married,' he replied. 'Let's just see when they've got a slot free, shall we?'

It was all too much for Katy. Registering Millie had been more fun than she'd ever dreamed possible, but now she just wanted to get out.

'We're not getting married here,' she announced, casting a disparaging glance around the shabby interior. 'Somewhere more fitting, more official. More… more a sense of occasion.'

'Oh. Right,' said Ben, obviously confused. 'I see.'

'You want that too, don't you?'

'Well, yeah,' he shrugged. 'Kind of. If that's what you want, then yeah, that's what we'll go for. Of course.'

He didn't look convinced.

'We don't need to decide now, do we?' she said, brushing past him to open the door, eager to get home. 'Anyway, we need to save up first. We can't afford to get married anywhere at the moment. Not whilst I'm on maternity leave.'

'I know,' said Ben. 'I know.'

CHAPTER THREE

'I mean, really, Matthew, how insensitive can a man be?'

Alison was sitting on the sofa, a pillow wedged on each knee, nestling her twin babies as they efficiently tucked into their evening snack of breast milk.

'He suggested the pill!' she continued as Matthew took off his suit jacket and draped it over the back of a dining chair. 'He clearly hadn't consulted my notes properly. Why would you ever suggest a drug to prevent pregnancy to a woman who's spent the last five years of her life taking every drug available to *encourage* pregnancy? Why, Matthew, why?'

'I don't know, Alison,' he replied wearily.

'I said to him,' she continued, 'I said, we have fertility problems – a major contraceptive in itself – and we have six-week-old twins. When exactly does he expect we'll be having sex anyway?' The kitchen timer, balanced on the sofa arm, suddenly sprung to life. Alison carefully lifted George and placed him on her shoulder to wind him as Rebecca continued to feed. Checking her watch, she reached over and with one hand reset the digital timer. 'Another eight minutes should do it,' she said, adjusting Rebecca slightly to make her more comfortable.

Matthew watched Alison in her calm, ruthless efficiency as advocated by the baby-rearing guru Gina Ford. Eight minutes would be fine, he thought to himself. Eight minutes would do. Five minutes, actually, would probably be more than enough.

'Does Gina's regime not timetable sex?' he muttered. 'Surely she's thought of that in her grand plan.'

'She covers that in a different book,' Alison told him. 'I've not ordered it yet.'

'I'll get it if you like,' he offered. 'Let you know what she says.'

'No, it's okay,' she replied. 'I'll get round to it. Do you want to take George upstairs and start to run the bath? I'll be up in a minute with Rebecca.'

Matthew took George from her, gently planting a kiss on top of his head, feeling the fine hair tickling his nostrils.

'I'll bath them and put them both down if you like,' he offered. 'Seeing as I'm off out later. You have a break.'

Alison looked up at him.

'You won't manage it on your own. Not with two of them.'

'I'll work it out.'

'But . . . but what will you do with Rebecca whilst George is in the bath?'

'I'll work it out. She can lie on a towel or something.'

'But you don't know how to use the temperature gauge for the water.'

'I'll work it out, Alison.'

'But what if you let it get too hot?'

'I am not going to burn our children.'

Alison looked down at Rebecca and stroked her head.

'There's really no need,' she said, looking back up at Matthew. 'We can do it together. It'll be quicker, then you won't be late for meeting Ian at the pub.'

Matthew sighed. Only he could be married to a woman who could organise herself into not requiring any help from her husband with their twins.

'Are you sure you don't mind me going out?' he asked, secretly hoping she might beg him to stay home. He missed the long evenings they used to spend together over her delightful home-cooked food and great wine, when they would talk about each other's days and then plot and plan their future together. Alison was so preoccupied with the twins that her ability to focus on a conversation that didn't involve nappies or sleep routines was non-existent. He dreamed of one evening having a conversation with his wife rather than just the mother of his children. He missed his wife terribly.

'Of course I don't mind you going out,' she said.

'I don't have to, you know.'

'Matthew, it's the first time you've been out since the babies arrived. It's fine, really. There's nothing you can do here anyway. Everything is under control.'

'So what do you reckon, then?' asked Ian as they sat in the Green Man later that evening.

'About what?' asked Matthew, his chin resting on his hand as he stared at the bottom of his empty pint glass.

'Her?' replied Ian, nodding after Becki, who had just excused herself from the table to go to the bathroom. Matthew hadn't expected that Ian would bring his latest girlfriend along on their first night out together in weeks. He'd actually been looking forward to man talk: sport, and possibly some work gossip, given that they both worked for the same financial advisory company. What he hadn't expected was to be sharing his evening with Becki, a strapping twenty-five-year-old blonde call centre worker, who for some unbelievable reason thought that the sun shone out of Ian's forty-two-year-old saggy, divorced backside.

'She's fucking unbelievable,' said Ian. 'I tell you, she cannot get enough of me. And I mean *enough* of me. I seriously think she might actually be trying to wear it out.' He winked at Matthew. Ian's abundance of sex with a twenty-five-year-old was certainly not what Matthew needed to hear right now. Ian leaned towards him and whispered in his ear. 'She rang me at work yesterday. Told me what she was going to do to me that night. I couldn't get up from my desk until I had stared at the HM Revenue and Customs self-assessment page for at least ten minutes.'

'Where on earth did you find her?' asked Matthew as he watched Becki shimmy her way back across the pub, barely staying in control of her towering spike heels.

'Online, mate,' Ian declared. 'Finally the internet comes up with something truly useful. A way of disseminating signals from women before you even have to meet them. Saves so much time. And they have to put them in black and white, so it gets rid of all the guesswork. Becki's profile clearly states that she prefers good-looking older men with life experience who can keep up with her energetic lifestyle. I think I fit that bill to a T, don't you?'

'What you sayin'?' giggled Becki as she slid into her seat next to Ian.

'I was just telling my good friend here that I knew instantly that we were going to be totally compatible . . . in every way.' Ian raised his eyebrows at her.

To Becki's credit, she blushed slightly. Ian put his arm around her and looked smugly over at Matthew.

'I've bought a waterbed,' he said, grinning proudly.

Matthew stared back.

'Why?' was all he could find to ask.

Becki's eyes grew big and round.

'Have you never done it on a waterbed?' she exclaimed.

Ian and Becki's eyes bored into him.

'No,' he replied.

'Oh my God!' cried Becki. 'It is the best, seriously. We went away last weekend, didn't we, Ian, just to Blackpool, and Ian booked a room with a waterbed.'

Ian was still grinning smugly.

'It was amaaazing,' continued Becki. 'Honestly unbelievable. Anyway, Ian said we have to get one of these, and now he's bought one. It's coming next week. I'm so excited.'

Matthew nodded at Becki and Ian.

'I'm very happy for both of you,' he said sarcastically.

'You can so borrow it, can't he, Ian?' cried Becki. 'You have to try it, seriously.'

'Alison would be well up for it, I reckon,' Ian offered.

'Alison has just given birth to twins. Having sex on a waterbed is not high up on her list of priorities at the moment, I can assure you.'

'Oh, come on,' said Ian. 'Might be just the thing to get her back in the saddle again.'

'Look,' said Matthew, slamming his fist on the table and making Becki jump so violently that her breasts threatened to break out of her too-tight top. 'Can we get off the sex talk, please?'

An elderly gentleman stared over from the next table and tutted.

'Calm down, mate,' said Ian. 'Just because you're going through a dry spell, there's no need to get angry. I remember what it's like when kids arrive; I've been through it, remember. My advice is to get back in the swing of it as soon as you can before one of you forgets how to do it.'

'You have no idea what it's like with the twins in the house,' said Matthew. 'It's fine. I'll wait until Alison's ready.'

'When was the last time, mate?' asked Ian.

'What?'

'When was the last time?'

'You can't ask me that,' said Matthew, looking nervously at Becki.

'I just did.'

Matthew thought for a minute, though he didn't really need to. He knew exactly when the last time he'd had sex was.

'With Katy,' he muttered. He picked up his pint glass and went for a swig until he realised it was empty.

'You have got to be kidding me!' exclaimed Ian, leaning back in his chair, his eyes wide in amazement.

'Katy?' said Becki. 'I thought you said your wife's name was Alison?'

'It is,' said Ian, raising his eyebrows at Becki.

'So . . . er . . . who's Katy?' asked Becki, looking from Ian to Matthew. Matthew slumped back in his chair and debated whether to make a run for it.

'You've not had sex with Alison since that almighty cock-up with Katy?' demanded Ian.

'Well,' said Matthew, running his fingers through his hair. 'Alison realised she was pregnant

31

just after . . . you know . . . me and Katy slept together, and she was so focused on that, and I guess I was all screwed up and feeling guilty about Katy, and then the twins arrived, so we sort of never got round to it.'

'Fuck me, mate,' declared Ian, for once looking genuinely concerned. 'That's bloody tragic.'

Becki was staring at Matthew open-mouthed.

'It's not what it seems,' he somehow felt compelled to tell her. 'It was just a one-night stand, that's all. At a school reunion. I'd not seen her since we went out together as teenagers. It should never have happened.'

Becki continued to stare at him.

'That's nearly a year,' she eventually breathed. 'You haven't had sex in nearly a year!'

'And the last time wasn't even with your wife,' added Ian.

Matthew had nothing to say on the state of his sex life.

'You have to sort that out,' declared Ian, shaking his head. 'I mean, seriously concerning.'

CHAPTER FOUR

'So when's Katy going to start coming to the pub again?' Braindead asked, as Ben placed three pints on their usual table in the Whitlocks pub. 'I miss her.' He stuck out his bottom lip. 'I need her to tell me what to say to that new woman bouncer at the Blessington Carriage. My usual chat-up lines aren't working.'

'You've got chat-up lines?' exclaimed Ben. 'Really?' That's as likely as Rick not wanting to spend all night showing off about how amazing his honeymoon in the Maldives was.'

'Wasn't going to mention it, actually,' muttered Rick, gulping his pint in the fashion of a man who'd endured cocktails for a solid three weeks.

'Good,' said Ben. 'So you coming to the pub on a cold, wet, miserable Leeds night wearing cut-offs and a white T-shirt is nothing to do with showing off that disgusting brown colour you've turned, then?'

Rick licked his lips. 'Only thing that was clean,' he grinned.

Ben sat down and picked up his pint.

'Cheers,' he announced, holding up the glass. 'Good to have you back.' And it was. Although it all felt a bit awkward. It was the first time the three of them had been together properly since Ben had become a dad, Ricky had become a husband and Braindead . . . well, Braindead hadn't changed, that was something you could always rely on. And it was the first time in a while that they were in a pub together without Katy.

'It was like a gift from God, wasn't it, really?' asked Braindead, picking up his pint. 'Katy getting pregnant.'

'Not sure God actually had anything to do with it,' Ben said.

'I know, but having someone in your crowd of mates who couldn't drink and therefore *had* to drive. How amazing was that? We could literally go to any pub in the whole of Yorkshire. It was like a dream come true, really, wasn't it?'

'Good times,' Rick nodded.

'We have seriously been looking for a mate like that for years,' Braindead declared. 'Little did we know that all we had to do was get Ben to knock someone up, and hey presto, pub crawl heaven every weekend.'

'Yeah, Katy's fine, thanks for asking,' Ben responded.

'But I don't just miss her for her driving prowess,' Braindead continued. 'I actually miss *her*.' He shook his head in bewilderment, as if he couldn't believe what he was saying. Braindead had come to treat Katy like an older sister, while she had attempted to give him some insight into the female perspective. In his opinion, his inability to grasp the inner workings of a woman's mind was the only thing stopping him from getting a girlfriend. Everyone else knew his total lack of a filter when he spoke had more to do with it.

'She'll be able to come out soon, hopefully,' said Ben. 'She's finally decided to ditch the breastfeeding, so the Millster is going on the bottle, which will give her a bit more freedom. As long as we can get a baby-sitter, of course.'

'Breast . . . feeeeeeding,' Braindead pronounced slowly.

'Yeah, what about it?' said Ben.

'I was just thinking . . .' Braindead started.

'You had a brain transplant since I went on hon-eymoon?' asked Rick.

'Will you stop going on about your honeymoon?' said Ben.

Ricky thumped him on the arm.

'I was just thinking that we only ever say *breast*-feeding. Never boob-feeding or bosom-feeding or tits-feeding or even jubbly-feeding. Why is that?'

Ben and Rick stared back at Braindead.

'Well,' sighed Ben, knowing he needed to nip this in the bud quickly or else Braindead would be stuck on the subject for hours. 'Because it doesn't sound right, does it? They're words you might use when talking about sex, I guess. And believe me, there's nothing sexy about breastfeeding.'

Braindead furrowed his brow. Ben knew they were on dangerous territory. Braindead's lack of sensitivity on such matters could prove disturbing. For once he was glad that Katy wasn't with them in the pub.

'So is there, like, an off switch, then, or something?' asked Braindead.

'For what?'

'The milk stuff. How does the milk know not to come out when you're, you know, doing it?'

Ben looked over to Rick, who grinned inanely back at him.

'Would you like me to tell you about my honeymoon now?' he offered.

'No, seriously,' continued Braindead. 'How?'

'I didn't get any of these questions on my absolutely brilliant honeymoon in the Maldives where I got this blinding tan,' Rick interrupted.

'I need to know,' continued Braindead, ignoring Rick completely. 'What stops breasts leaking during sex?'

'I don't know,' Ben finally shrugged.

'So they just go back to normal when you're having sex, despite the fact they create enough milk to fill an entire baby every day.'

'I said I don't know,' Ben repeated. 'We haven't got around to testing if they're leak-proof during sex yet. Okay?'

'Oh,' said Braindead.

'Shall we drop it now?' said Ben.

'But you'll let me know,' Braindead persisted.

'Let you know what?'

'When you find out?' Like you said. If they leak or not?'

'No,' replied Ben.

'Why not?'

'Because no-one ever has sex when they breast-feed . . . probably.'

'Oh,' said Braindead. 'Right.'

'We had lots of sex on our honeymoon,' said Rick.

'That's just brilliant, Rick,' said Ben. 'Thanks for that.'

'You're welcome,' Rick grinned, slapping Ben on the back 'Anyway, won't you be getting hitched soon? You'll be all right then. Normal service resumed.'

Ben picked up his pint and took another slug.

'Doesn't look like it will be anytime soon,' he sighed, nursing his glass in his lap. 'Katy's too exhausted with looking after Millie to even think about organising a wedding. She barely gets round to getting out of her pyjamas these days. Reckons she's flat out all day.'

'Doing what?' asked Braindead.

Ben shrugged.

'You know, baby stuff. Feeding, nappies, washing. I go to work and she's sat in front of breakfast telly feeding Millie, and I get home and she's sat in exactly the same spot, watching reruns of *Location, Location, Location* and feeding Millie.'

'Sounds like a doddle,' said Braindead. 'I could happily spend all day watching Kirstie Allsopp get stroppy.'

'Didn't you actually do that once?' asked Rick.

'Oh yeah,' said Braindead. 'You're right. I did attempt a whole day of Kirsty Allsopp once. Unfortunately she didn't appear to be on anything between two and three p.m. Had to resort to Sarah Beeny.'

'I think I'd call that welcome relief,' said Rick.

'So if I had a baby I could have Kirsty Allsopp all day every day if I wanted,' Braindead said to Ben. 'That's like the best job in the world.'

'I think there's a bit more to it than that,' said Ben.

'Like what?' asked Braindead. 'They can't talk, they just dribble. They can't go anywhere. In fact, they're the perfect audience for daytime telly. And you have to be there with them because they can't be left on their own. This is a genius plan dreamed up by women to be able to have a legitimate excuse to watch continuous reruns of *Bargain Hunt*.'

'I think if Katy were here she'd have something to say about that,' said Ben. 'She's certainly not acting as though spending the day with Kirstie Allsopp day in, day out is the best thing that's ever happened to her.'

'Do you know what I'd do if I had to be at home every day looking after a baby?' said Rick, slowly nodding his head as if he'd been contemplating how he would handle the issue for some time.

'I'm not sure I want to know,' Ben replied.

'Online poker,' Rick announced. 'I got into it on honeymoon.'

'That's a crap honeymoon if you spent it playing cards with a computer,' said Ben.

'Actually, there was a casino attached to our resort. I went a few times to watch the high rollers play, but I didn't dare join in myself, so I thought I'd have a go online to get some practice in. I'm so addicted now, I can't tell you. I actually won some money last week. Imagine being able to stay home all day and play poker? Awesome.'

'Mmm,' Ben nodded. 'Maybe I should suggest it. We could do with a windfall. We're supposed to be saving up for the wedding, but I don't know how. Katy's maternity allowance is so much lower than the whopping wage she was getting paid at the agency. Not sure how we're going to pay the mortgage, never mind a wedding. And I know she'd really like to move out of the flat and buy a house with a garden, you know, for Millie when she's older. Somewhere like Chapstead, but we're never going to be able to afford a place there on the pittance I get paid.'

'Chapstead,' said Braindead, screwing up his nose. 'You're going to live in Chapstead?'

'Not if I can't work out how to win the lottery.'

'You can't live in Chapstead, mate,' said Braindead, looking agitated. 'You may as well give up. Nothing happens in Chapstead. There's nothing in Chapstead apart from rows and rows of dull, boring houses where dull, boring people live. Ben . . . it's the suburbs!'

'I know,' said Ben. 'But that's what happens when you have kids. You move out of the city into the suburbs so you can afford a garden. That's just how it is.'

'You've changed,' declared Braindead.

'How do you work that one out?'

'The old Ben would never live in Chapstead.'

'I'm a dad now. I'm going to get married. My priorities have changed, that's all. Back me up, eh, Rick?'

'No-one ever has sex in the suburbs,' said Rick, shaking his head. 'It will not help your lack of sex issue, believe me, if you move to the suburbs.'

'Yes, they do.'

'Have you seen the people walking round Chapstead?' asked Rick. 'They're not getting any, you can tell. It's full of knackered parents and pensioners. Stay in the city, mate. Give yourself half a chance.'

'Well, we won't be moving anywhere at this rate,' said Ben. 'We can't afford to move or get married. I'm actually thinking of taking on some extra coaching so I can bring some more money in.'

'Oh yeah,' said Rick. 'Where? Footie coaching would be perfect.'

'It's tennis coaching, actually,' said Ben.

Braindead nearly choked on his beer.

'You *hate* tennis,' he exclaimed. 'You bunked off every tennis lesson we ever had at school.'

'I know,' Ben nodded. 'It's the stupidest game known to man, but the tennis club in Henshall are desperate for someone in the evenings and the weekends, and it pays really well.'

'Henshall!' exclaimed Rick.

'Yeah,' said Ben. 'What about it?'

'Talk about suburbia. Henshall is bloody gold-plated suburbia. You'll be coaching spoilt brats and bored housewives who have nothing to do but organise cleaners to tidy up after them in their six-bed mansions.'

'Bored housewives,' muttered Braindead. 'Sounds good to me.'

'You're right,' said Rick. 'They definitely have sex in Henshall. They've got much more time for that sort of thing. Some desperate housewife is going to have you as her toy boy before you know it.' Rick put his free hand up to his cheek, pretending to hold a phone. 'Hi, Georgina, daaaaarling, just ringing to tell you the latest goss'. Yes, it's true, I'm leaving David. Oh, you've heard, have you? Yes, all the rumours are true. I've been shagging the tennis coach. Can you believe it, daaaarling? Such a hoot. I'm moving him into the mansion next week.'

'That's not funny,' said Ben.

'But a tennis coach!' cried Rick. 'I repeat. You hate tennis.'

'It's not ideal,' Ben admitted. 'But we're really struggling without Katy's wage. I need to do something.'

'Have you told Katy about this?' asked Rick.

'No,' Ben sighed. 'Not yet. Not sure she's going to like the idea, either. She has a fit if I'm more than five minutes late home as it is. She's often waiting at the door with Millie in her arms, ready to hand her over the minute I get through the door. Not sure how she's going to react if I tell her I'll be home even later and not around at weekends. But I don't know what else to do.'

'So Katy was a catch, then?' asked Braindead.

'What do you mean?' said Ben.

'She earned a packet at that advertising agency?'

'Yeah. As I said, beats my job any day of the week.'

'Fucking obvious, isn't it?' Braindead shrugged.

'What is?' said Ben and Rick in unison.

'The answer.'

'The answer to what?' asked Ben.

'All this money stuff and not being able to get married and online poker and Kirstie Allsopp.'

'You're making no sense, Braindead,' said Ben. 'Which I know is no major insight, but needs pointing out most times I see you.'

'Katy goes back to work. You spend your days with Kirstie Allsopp.'

There was silence around the small table in the corner of the pub underneath a random framed picture of some fruit.

Rick spoke first.

'I can teach you how to play online poker,' he said.

Ben didn't reply. His mind was grappling with Braindead's idea.

'She does say she misses work,' he muttered finally. 'I know she phones Daniel every week to see what's happening and to check up on her clients.'

'And I can teach you how to play online poker.'

'I think she'd like to go back to work,' said Ben, to no-one in particular.

'It's really easy once you get the hang of it.'

'Looking after a baby?' Ben asked.

'No. Online poker.'

'But do you think I could look after Millie full-time?'

'You're a natural,' said Braindead. 'I could never beat you at snap when we were kids.'

'I could do it, you know,' Ben continued, leaning back in his chair. 'Actually, I think Katy lets her hormones get in the way sometimes. She gets all uptight and emotional about it. Whenever I look after Millie she's fine, she's great. She just lies on my belly while I watch the footie. It's the best feeling in the world, guys, honestly.' He stopped, looking slightly embarrassed. 'You've just got to relax and then they will relax. I've thought about telling Katy – that she just needs to chill a bit, then Millie will, but I think she'd bite my head off. She's . . . she's just not herself at the moment,' he said, looking away.

'It would save you having an affair with a wrinkly orange housewife,' Rick said helpfully.

'This could be the answer,' Ben muttered. 'Katy goes back to the job she loves whilst I stay at home with Millie. We can afford the mortgage on the flat and start saving to get married or even a house, *and* I don't have to be out of the house all hours tennis coaching.' He paused, turning his gaze to the framed fruit on the wall. 'And maybe Katy will be more herself again,' he muttered to no-one in particular. 'We just need to figure out how to convince her it's a good idea.'

CHAPTER FIVE

K aty gave herself one last once-over as she stood outside her former workplace. Shoulders puke-free – check. Leopard-print wool coat bought in the Harvey Nichols sale three years ago, and carefully selected for today to show she had not turned into a dowdy-ville mum – check. First time in heels, chosen for the same reason as the coat despite the fact they were crippling her – check. Cath Kidston cowboy nappy bag, bought to show Daniel that baby accessories could be cool and didn't have to be dominated by primary colours – check. Millie fast asleep following strategically timed mammoth feed in the café next door in the hope that she would stay asleep for the entire duration of the obligatory take-your-baby-to-work visit, when everyone pretends to be overjoyed to meet your offspring but secretly is just delighted for the distraction and a gossip – check.

Katy could feel her heart pounding with nerves, which was ridiculous. She'd walked into the building a thousand times before, so why the big deal today? She knew exactly why. The last time she'd walked through those doors she'd known who she was. She was their best Account Director, whose opinion was respected and sought after to the extent that last year she'd been made an Associate Director, earning the right to have an opinion on the entire business. She was an award winner. She could see the trophies earned for some of the campaigns she'd worked on, lining the far wall of the reception area. She was a colleague, a mentor, a lunch companion, an after work drinks buddy, a water cooler gossiper. She had been all of those things and now she was none of them. Just eight weeks ago her life had been full of work. Her work had defined how she lived and who she was. Since then it felt like she'd not only had a baby but also been through some strange time machine, entering a new zone entirely, and was revisiting her former life as an alien. She wanted to run away. She wasn't sure if she could handle the inevitable scrutiny from her former colleagues as they judged how she was handling her new self. She didn't feel up to facing the out-of-body experience of being in her former workplace as an outsider, a foreigner, someone who had to wear a sticker on their lapel that shrieked VISITOR – be careful what you say.

She took a deep breath and leaned forward over the pram to push the door open, but it was too heavy for her to move with one hand. She attempted to jam the pram at it, but even that was no match for the heavy, sleek, all glass door. She could feel her cheeks start to turn red as she noticed a receptionist observe her battle with the door. She was getting flustered now. This was not the entrance she wanted to make. Cool, calm and in control was the image she intended to leave behind, not blind panic because she couldn't manoeuvre a pram through a door.

The receptionist, who was different to the one who normally worked there, was gesticulating at her, pointing vigorously at something to her left. She looked over to where the woman was indicating. There was another door that to Katy's recollection she had never used in her entire seven years working at the agency. Tucked away in the corner, a gentle slope led up to a door with a disabled entrance sticker on it. As she looked, it automatically glided open. Katy didn't want to go through the disabled entrance. She'd never been through it before and she wasn't about to go through it now. She was Katy, Account Director at this fine establishment, temporarily on maternity leave. She would use the door she always used. She reversed the pram slightly, awkwardly spun it around then shoved her back into the glass, forcing it ajar just enough to squeeze herself through. Unfortunately, its heavy bulk started to swing back immediately, trapping the pram and forcing Katy yet again to attempt to budge it using just one hand.

'There you go,' said the receptionist, appearing at her side and pulling the door back for her. 'You could have used the disabled entrance, you know.'

'*I don't have a disability*,' Katy wanted to scream. '*I have a baby, that's all*.' Instead she turned on a forced smile and said, 'Thank you,' through gritted teeth. She turned her back on the woman and headed for the lift.

'Are you visiting someone?' the receptionist called, just as she pressed the button. 'I have to sign you in first.'

Katy stared back at her. It wasn't that long ago that Katy had held a set of keys for the entire building, and now some woman was asking her to sign in.

'Do you know who I am?' she said before she could stop herself.

'No,' replied the receptionist. 'Should I?'

'I work here, I don't need to sign in,' said Katy as firmly as she could without shouting. She jabbed the lift call button again. She couldn't bear the sight of this woman who didn't recognise her. She could also sense a couple of clients perched on the bright red, deeply uncomfortable designer sofas trying desperately hard not to be seen to be watching the altercation.

'Do you?' the receptionist said. 'Have you been off sick or something?'

'Maternity leave,' said Katy. 'Or do you think I've stolen this baby? Why is this lift taking so long?' she said, stabbing the button, desperate to remove herself from the reception area and away from the embarrassment of not being recognised at her own workplace.

'Don't you have a pass?' asked the receptionist.

'A pass for what?'

'The lift.'

'I don't need a pass for the lift.'

'You do.'

'Since when?'

'Since a tramp wandered in a couple of weeks ago and got all the way up to the top floor then fell asleep in the boardroom, just before a big presentation. They've put a new system in.'

'I see,' said Katy. 'Please may I have a pass then?'

'I'm afraid not.'

'Why not?'

'Visitors aren't allowed passes.'

'I'm not a visitor, I work here. Haven't you been listening?'

'Then you should already have a pass.'

The woman folded her arms, a hint of a satisfied smile on her face.

'Where's Dawn?' asked Katy. If Dawn had been on reception like she usually was then this would not be happening.

'She was let go because of the tramp incident,' the woman continued. 'And I have a Post-it note stuck to my computer saying NO UNAUTHORISED ACCESS in capital letters.'

'Well, if it's on a Post-it note then who I am I to argue,' said Katy, beginning to lose it. 'Call Daniel in Creative Services. He'll come down and tell you who I am.'

The woman turned and walked back behind her desk, then tapped something on a keyboard before speaking into a headset.

'Hello. It's Sue on reception. I have a lady down-stairs with a baby who claims to work here but she doesn't have a lift pass and she refuses to sign in. She asked me to call you.'

Sue went silent for a moment listening to the reply.

'Is that what you'd like me to tell her?' she said. 'In those exact words?'

She turned to Katy and shouted across reception. 'Daniel says to tell that drama queen bitch to put her child-bearing thighs on the visitor couch and he'll be down after he's finished doing her job for her.' She punctuated the sentence with a smug smile.

'What on earth are you doing to the Crispy Bix cam-paign?' demanded Katy, striding into Daniel's office. She'd already been round the entire office to have her baby manhandled. Millie for the moment appeared to be grateful to be lying back in her pram, so Katy hovered in the doorway rocking her backwards and forwards.

'And what business is it of yours these days?' replied Daniel, looking up from behind his desk.

'I know what's happening, Daniel,' said Katy. 'I'm not here, and you've seized your chance to let your creative juices run riot.'

'That's my job, Katy. I'm the Creative Director of the agency. It's what I'm paid for, in case you'd forgotten.'

'Yes, but as I've said to you many times before, you are not here to create art, Daniel, you are here to sell stuff.'

'People buy beautiful things, Katy. You should give the general public more credit for their appreciation of beauty.'

'But that's the whole point, isn't it? It's not their idea of beauty; it's *your* idea of beauty. Crispy Bix is a kids' cereal. A poster campaign based on extracts from Shakespeare sonnets isn't going to attract your average six-year-old.'

'So this is what having a baby does for you.' Daniel stood up and waved a cursory arm at the pram. 'You're going all low-brow on me.'

'Don't you dare bring the baby into this argument,' cried Katy. 'You know I'm right. Shakespeare doesn't fit in with the brand values for Crispy Bix.'

'Fuck the brand values!' Daniel shouted back, banging his fist on the desk. 'The posters are stunning. Award winning. They'll stop traffic, I'm telling you.'

'And sell precisely zero packets of Crispy Bix.'

'God, I've missed this,' he declared, striding from behind the desk and taking Katy in his arms.

'Me too,' she muttered into his shoulder.

'So how was it out there?' he asked.

'Oh, fine really,' she sighed. 'Apart from the fact I couldn't help noticing bits of campaigns everywhere, and what was wrong with them.'

'Not your job any more. This is your job.' Daniel nodded down at Millie. 'You going to stand there pushing that thing backwards and forwards like a trained budgie, or are you going to sit down? I can't talk to you whilst you're doing that.'

'But she may explode if I stop,' said Katy. 'Stopping is a high-risk strategy.'

'Come on. Sit down, she won't notice.'

'Oh, she will,' Katy said. 'She reminds me a lot of you, actually. If she doesn't have loads of attention and constant flattery, she throws a tantrum and chucks all her toys out of the cot.'

'I like her style,' Daniel said approvingly.

'Eeeeugh!' A young man had barged into Daniel's office, nearly falling over Millie's pram in the process. 'What is *that*?'

'Ahhh, Freddie,' said Daniel. 'Let me introduce you to a baby.'

'What is a baby doing in your office, Dan?'

'This baby has arrived with Katy, who I guess you will not have met before. Freddie, meet Katy. Katy, this is Freddie. He's on loan from the London office as an Account Director to cover your clients whilst you're on baby watch.'

'Oh. Hi,' said Katy awkwardly.

'Hi,' replied Freddie, his eyes raking her up and down. Having completed his appraisal he switched his focus straight back to Daniel.

'Crispy Bix don't like the Shakespeare campaign,' he told Daniel. 'You were right, the Brand Manager is a cultural desert. I told her it was ground-breaking and would disrupt the entire under-sevens, low-sugar, high-iron, low-salt, semi-natural cereal category, but she wouldn't listen. She insists we roll out Crispy Casper again and use him.'

'Not the chipmunk!' cried Daniel, putting his head in his hands. 'Please tell me she doesn't mean the chipmunk?'

'Yep,' replied Freddie. 'She'd rather have a chipmunk than Shakespeare. How do these people get these jobs?'

'When Casper was introduced, Crispy Bix sales increased by over fifteen percent,' muttered Katy.

Daniel and Freddie just looked at her.

'Just saying,' she shrugged.

'I'll go back to her,' Freddie told Daniel. 'Tell her that the brand needs fresh innovation, not tired old, lacking-inspiration cartoon animals that have been done to death.'

'That's my boy,' said Daniel, slapping Freddie on the back. 'You ask her. Does she want to be a brand pioneer, famous for her foresight and guts, or a brand follower who will never be recognised for the great work which she's capable of?'

'Gosh,' said Freddie. 'Dan, that's brilliant. Say it again so I can write it down.'

'You'll remember it,' said Daniel. 'Now off you go and sell my Shakespeare campaign in.'

Freddie backed out of the doorway without even saying goodbye to Katy.

'You are such a twat sometimes,' she told Daniel once they were alone.

'Freddie is the Account Director, not you. He believes in the campaign.'

'So he's a twat as well, then.'

Millie chose this moment to throw a tantrum and hurl her toys out of the pram. Katy bent to pick her up.

'See, just like you,' she said to Daniel. 'Always demanding attention. Do you want a hold?'

'No.'

'Fair enough,' Katy shrugged. 'I'd better go back home anyway. Let you get on with destroying our relationship with Crispy Bix.'

'I thought it must be you when I heard a baby cry,' said the Managing Director, poking his head around the door. 'There's nothing that sounds quite the same as a new baby crying, is there? Hand her over then.' He took Millie from Katy, throwing her easily over his shoulder, and she instantly went quiet. 'It's so good to see you, Katy,' he continued. 'We're really missing you.'

Katy beamed back. This was the best news she'd had all day.

'Daniel, could you pop up to my office and—'

'Of course,' replied Daniel. 'Totally in baby over-load now. Ciao, Katy.' He kissed her on the head. 'Call me.'

'Bye,' she said, watching him leave as fast as he could before the boss closed the door behind him.

'I was hoping I'd catch you,' Andrew said, sitting down with Millie still cooing gently on his shoulder. Katy prayed she didn't chuck down the shoulder of his expensive suit. 'I know I really shouldn't ask you this, but is there any chance you could give me an indication of when you might be coming back?'

'Er, well, I'm not really sure yet,' she admitted. 'You said I should come in at three months and discuss it with you.'

'Yes, I know, but, well . . .' Andrew paused, looking nervously at the door. 'Between you and me, Daniel is slightly out of control without you to hold him back.'

'Well, I did see the Shakespeare Crispy Bix campaign . . .' Katy shook her head.

'Exactly. He can't help himself. And Freddie, your stand-in, thinks the sun shines out of his arse so is doing nothing to stand in his way. I never realised what a fantastic job you did of guiding his talent. I just wanted you to know that as soon as you want to come back you would be very, very, welcome. Like as soon as possible would not be soon enough.' He looked nervously at the door again. Katy knew he was taking a big risk talking to her like this. She'd be well within her rights to make some kind of compliant involving discrimination or harassment or something. But she didn't feel harassed. She felt enormously flattered.

'Well . . . as you can see, it's not that simple,' she sighed, nodding at Millie.

'Just think about it,' he pleaded, putting his hand on Katy's. 'Please. Call me in a week and tell me what you think.'

Chapter Six

Katy's eyes flashed open as soon as she heard the front door bang. She thought she'd been asleep. She must have been asleep. She squinted across the bed to Ben's Darth Vader alarm clock and saw it read 11.23. She'd fed Millie, she thought, around ten-ish, so she must have slept since then. A few precious hours that needed to be filled with sleep or else Katy knew she would be unable to function at all. She winced in dismay as she heard a cupboard door slam in the kitchen. Her precious sleep interrupted by Ben's arrival home from the pub. She held her breath, knowing that it wouldn't be long before Ben would arrive in the bedroom about as quietly as a herd of baby elephants and risk waking Millie, at which point Katy would quite possibly kill him with her bare hands. She tried to keep her breathing low and calm as she awaited his arrival. He'd only been out once since Millie's arrival to wet the baby's head with some colleagues. He'd come back slightly worse for wear and put *Match of the Day* on at full blast, totally forgetting there was a baby in the flat. This time she'd left a trail of reminders such as cuddly toys and nappies, hoping he'd remember to be quiet.

After a few minutes the door to the bedroom slid open and she watched as he tentatively crept around the room going about the business of getting ready for bed. His glass of water was successfully placed on his bedside table without too much fuss and he even managed to extract his pyjamas from under the pillow without sound effects. Failure struck, however, once he'd got himself into the en-suite, shutting the door behind him and putting the light on. There were a few moments of quiet rustling before the delicate silence was ripped apart by a massive fart.

Katy shook her head in despair, waiting for Millie to protest at the interruption created by her father's backside. Thankfully, despite the fact that the noise still felt like it was echoing around the entire flat, Millie continued to sleep and Katy allowed herself to breathe again. Ben emerged shortly afterwards and slid into bed next to her. She was wide awake now and for a moment they looked at each other, their faces illuminated by the glow-in-the-dark room thermometer.

'If the room gets too hot, does Tom Cruise drop down from the ceiling on a wire and blast everything with a freeze gun?' Ben had asked when he'd unwrapped the gift from Dennis, a fellow teacher from school.

'Given how much my wife said she paid for it, I'd want at least Cameron Diaz dropping from my ceiling, not Tom bloody Cruise,' Dennis had replied.

The thermometer was thankfully glowing an acceptable yellow, giving them both a slightly jaundiced appearance as they continued to look at each other, neither daring to speak as Millie slept soundly next to them. Ben smiled, a contented, slightly drunken smile. Katy smiled, an exhausted, just-let-me sleep smile. Ben moved his hand up to rest on Katy's waist. Katy felt herself tense. She knew what usually followed the post-pub contented smile and hand-on-waist routine.

'I've got a great idea,' whispered Ben, leaning towards her. Katy did a rapid mental inventory.

Legs – stubbly and dry. No shaving or moisturising in at least two months.

Underarms – hairy – not evacuated since Millie had been born.

Attire – pyjama's that hadn't left her body in possibly over twenty-four hours.

Underwear – maternity bra that contained breast pads.

Fragrance – faintly of cabbage.

Hair – dirty and containing Vaseline from when she'd raked her fingers through her hair earlier after attending to some dry skin on Millie's leg.

Atmosphere – mood lighting courtesy of baby room thermometer, sleeping baby right next to them.

Fit for Purpose – stretch marks and eighteen stitches in her vagina for goodness' sake!

There was nothing about their circumstances that was conducive to sex.

Ben leaned forward again and squeezed her waist.

'Did you hear me?' he whispered in her ear. 'I've had a brilliant idea.'

Katy could have wept. She wanted to want to have sex with Ben, she really did, but she just didn't see how. The woman who used to be only too happy to have a quick romp when Ben came home like this was gone. She didn't exist any more. This hairy, stubbly, smelly monster had replaced her.

'I think you'll like it,' whispered Ben.

She pushed him away.

'I can't,' she said, failing to stop the tears falling down her cheeks as tiredness and disappointment got the better of her.

'What is it?' asked Ben, raising his hand to gently brush away her tears. 'This isn't like you.'

Well, he was right there. It wasn't like her. But then again, she didn't know who she was any more. Her body no longer felt as if it belonged to her, her brain was away with the fairies and her emotions were totally out of control. It felt as though Katy was no more, a shadow she couldn't quite grasp hold of. The only time she'd caught a glimpse of her had been that morning when she'd been arguing with Daniel about the Crispy Bix campaign. The old Katy had re-emerged for a moment then disappeared when Millie woke, dismissing old Katy as useless to her existence. It had been a mistake going to work. All she'd thought about that morning was old Katy, and how she missed her, and the impossible dream her boss had tempted her with of being old Katy again whenever she wanted.

Ben leaned in again. She had to put a stop to this. She couldn't stand it.

'Why don't we go into the kitchen?' he said gently.

He wanted to do it in the kitchen? Under halogen spotlights and on hard granite? Was he insane?

'Come on,' he said, getting out of bed. He crept through the door, leaving it ajar. Reluctantly, she heaved herself up and grabbed a tissue before following him.

'Are you insane?' was all Katy could gasp once Ben had revealed his brilliant idea that had nothing remotely to do with sex.

'I think it could work,' he said, nodding vigorously. 'It makes absolute sense as long as you think you could cope with not being at home with Millie every day.'

'How much have you had to drink?' Katy asked.

'Adequate,' replied Ben.

'What does adequate mean?'

'Enough to have made a night of it without having made a big night of it.'

Katy moved to get up from the kitchen table.

'I think we should talk about this tomorrow when you understand exactly what you're saying.'

Ben caught her arm and forced her to sit down.

'I know exactly what I'm saying,' he said firmly. 'I'm offering to swap roles. I'll stay home and take care of the Millster and you go back to work.'

'But . . . but . . . you love your job,' said Katy, desperately trying to get her head around what Ben was saying.

'I do,' he replied, 'and believe me, I've been racking my brains as to how I can earn more money to keep you both in the manner to which you've become accustomed, but teaching is never going to pay as well as what you do. The only thing I came up with was tennis coaching. I can start down at Henshall whenever I want, but it's all evenings and weekends.'

'But you *hate* tennis,' Katy exclaimed.

'Correct, but . . . but if it meant we could afford the mortgage on this flat . . .'

'You'd do that for me?' said Katy.

Ben nodded, then looked down at his hands.

'I hate the idea of you having to make sacrifices because I don't earn as much money as you.'

Katy closed her eyes. They'd been here before. She knew Ben was insecure about the fact she earned more money than he did. In fact, he'd assumed that she'd slept with Matthew because he was as successful as she was, not just some lowly PE teacher like him. But now Ben did have a point. Financially it did make sense. Katy had been worrying about the mortgage, and if she went back to work it wouldn't be a problem; they might even be able to save for a house . . .

with a garden. But she couldn't stand the thought of Ben feeling bad because he earned less.

'I'm very proud of what you do,' she said, taking his hand. 'Which is why I could never ask you to give it up.'

'I teach PE,' said Ben, shaking his head. 'I'm not changing the world.'

Katy didn't know what to say. Ben looked sad, like he'd realised that he actually wasn't changing the world and he should have been.

'Would you like to go back to work?' he asked.

Katy was torn. Part of her was desperate to. To go back to old Katy, in control Katy, competent Katy, respected Katy. What a breath of fresh air that would be. But was that the mum she wanted to be? The one who couldn't wait to shed her duties and leave the care of her baby to someone else. She could already feel her heartstrings being tugged.

'I'd love to go back to work, but—'

'We could do it,' Ben interrupted. 'Not straight away, of course. I reckon if I tell them now they'll let me leave at Christmas, so maybe you could go back straight after New Year. Millie will be four months old by then. That'll give you a bit longer with her, then I can take my turn.'

Katy was staring at Ben open-mouthed.

'What?' he asked. 'You think I want to do this so I don't have to work, don't you?'

'You think looking after Millie isn't work?'

'No . . . I wasn't saying that exactly, I was just saying that of course caring for Millie won't take up all my time during the day, but I won't be slacking around or anything, maybe just give myself an hour a day off, you know, for like, lunch.'

'An hour a day?'

'Yeah.'

'You're expecting an hour a day to yourself?'

'Sure.'

Katy laughed. The hysterical laughter of a woman who was sleep deprived and had had her world totally turned upside down and didn't know which way was up any more.

'What are you laughing at?' asked Ben.

Katy couldn't stop. Tears were now rolling down her face.

'I really don't see what's so funny,' said Ben.

'You have no idea, do you?' said Katy, using her tissue to wipe away her hysterical tears. 'You'll be lucky to have a minute to yourself, never mind a whole hour.' She began to get up. Ben had totally lost the plot, she was tired, and this discussion was keeping her from her sleep.

'Well, maybe if you were a bit calmer about it all then Millie might relax more and you'd find that she spends less time crying and needing your attention.'

Katy took a sharp intake of breath and sat herself back down again.

'What are you saying?' she hissed.

Ben shrugged. 'Just that I can tell you're all tense and hormonal and all that, and maybe if you just relaxed a bit you might find it easier.'

Katy couldn't speak. The anger and the hormones were building up inside her to an almighty blowout, but she couldn't quite formulate her fury into words.

Ben ploughed on. 'I mean, maybe there's a reason why Millie falls asleep the minute I'm home and we have a cuddle. I'm just more relaxed about the whole thing than you at the moment, which is perfectly understandable. Don't get me wrong, I totally sympathise with why you're all wound up all the time, but I'm just saying that chilling out a bit might help.'

Katy couldn't believe what she was hearing. Of course she was bloody well always wound up. Seven pounds four ounces of relentless demands had passed through her uterus. Demands that she constantly worried she was failing to meet, and here was Ben assuming that because he appeared to be akin to the baby whisperer for maybe one or two hours a day that he had it nailed. That she was making a big fuss about nothing.

'Okay then,' she said after she'd waited for the tide of anger to ebb slightly. She considered briefly trying to explain to him how hard it was, how relentless it was, how you lived with the constant terror that you were going to do something that would kill your child, and how exhausting that was in itself. How daily you were doing things and making decisions about stuff you had no clue about but were essential to the wellbeing of this tiny little bundle of life that relied on you for everything . . . absolutely everything.

'Okay then,' she said again. Swallowing hard to try and remain calm. 'You think you can do a better job, then let's try it. Let's swap. On a trial basis.'

'I didn't mean I thought I could do a better job,' Ben protested. 'I just thought it might be a better way for all of us.'

'No, you're absolutely right. You're way better with Millie than I am. You try it. You be mum for a while. I'll go back to work.'

'Are you sure?'

'Sure.' Katy nodded vigorously then got up, determined to actually make it to bed this time. 'You go for it. I'll call work in the morning.'

'Good,' said Ben. 'That's all sorted then.' He watched Katy leave the room, not feeling the relief he'd thought he might. Something in the look Katy had given him made him think that the swap wasn't going to solve as many problems as he'd thought.

CHAPTER SEVEN

'Matthew, Matthew,' cried Alison. 'Look, Rebecca's face!'

Matthew peered round at Rebecca's face to see what on earth was bothering Alison so much. A tiny bit of dribble was creeping its way down her chin and was about to drop onto her pristine sugar-pink dress with white ribbon trim. He was just about to shove a finger in its path when a tissue appeared out of nowhere and spirited it away. Matthew grinned at Alison, who was sitting next to him on a plush green velvet Chesterfield outside the studio of Leeds' best family portrait photographer. As she smiled back, he caught sight of someone he'd not seen in a very long time. Her face lit up, and suddenly he saw the beautiful, confident Alison he'd fallen in love with all those years ago before they began their difficult journey to having children. Before the disappointment of her failure to get pregnant followed by the relentless rounds of fertility treatment had turned her into a worn-out rag with a face as long as the wait they'd had for these two miracle babies. Today she shone. Groomed to the hilt and still showing a hint of baby weight, which totally suited her, the old Alison was back, and he couldn't help but let out a small sigh of relief.

'I'm so glad you wore a tie,' Alison told him. 'You look just perfect with Rebecca.'

'Well, if I can't dress up for my daughter, then quite frankly, who can I dress up for?' Matthew planted a kiss on Rebecca's head.

'I never thought this day would come,' he heard Alison say, suddenly emotional.

'I know,' he said, reaching over to take her hand.'

'We've been through so much,' she gulped.

'We have,' Matthew nodded. 'But we made it. You made it. You had it the worst. I want you to know I'm so proud of you, Alison.'

She looked at him, but then had to look away and swallow hard. She fanned her eyes with her hand to try and prevent tears from ruining her perfectly applied mascara.

'He'd better get a move on,' she commented, trying to distract herself.

'What time are we booked in for?' he asked, looking hopefully at the heavy oak doors that separated them from the inner sanctum of Calvin McDonald.

'Any minute now,' she replied, looking at her watch and stroking George's hair down simultaneously. 'We need to begin soon, or else they'll start to get hungry and crabby and not at their best.

'I'm sure he'll be out soon,' Matthew said soothingly. He knew she desperately wanted the perfect family photograph, and he wanted it to be perfect, for her sake.

'Although we are running slightly behind schedule ourselves. Did I tell you that Charlene called and asked me to cancel our antenatal gathering at the last minute and changed all our plans this morning?'

Matthew raised his eyebrows. His wife's continued contact with Charlene never ceased to amaze him, given their opposite personalities. You never would have put them together in a million years, if it wasn't for the fact that they'd met in antenatal classes and had been encouraged to support each other beyond giving birth. Although Matthew did secretly suspect that Alison enjoyed playing the role of baby expert to Charlene's apparently clueless efforts.

'You will not believe why she cancelled,' Alison continued. 'Honestly, I don't know why I bother with her sometimes.'

Neither do I, thought Matthew. Charlene scared him.

'She bumped into Katy at the registry office, apparently, and Katy asked her to go to a music class with her. Can you believe it? She cancels for Katy, of all people, who's never once bothered to come along to one of our meet-ups. Honestly, the cheek of it.'

Matthew froze. It had been a while since Katy's name had been mentioned between them. Alison had thankfully given up trying to entice her to come to their post-birth gatherings. He'd heaved a huge sigh of relief and assumed that Katy was now firmly back in the past where she belonged.

'She tried telling me that Katy was in a bad way, that she wasn't coping and needed someone to talk to,' Alison went on.

'Oh,' was all Matthew could think to say without giving away his inner turmoil.

'I can well imagine, actually. She never struck me as the most maternal of people. Never really looked like she was looking forward to being a mother.'

'Mmmmm.' Matthew nodded, pretending to study Rebecca's ribbon around her tubby little waist.

'She never really listened in the classes, either. Always looked totally preoccupied. As if she wished she were somewhere else entirely.'

She did, thought Matthew. As far away from him as possible.

'I told Charlene to give her my love, though,' Alison said. 'And that no-one will think badly of her if she wants to start joining in now. In fact, it would be really good to have her back. There is only so much celebrity gossip with Charlene that I can handle.'

Never going to happen, thought Matthew. Katy had more sense than to walk back into their lives.

'I'm sure Katy will do what she needs to do,' he said. 'She's probably fine. You know what Charlene's like. She's probably not seeing Katy at all – more likely to have found out there's a sale on at Primark or something and needed an excuse to get out of meeting up.'

'She better not have done. I'd made brownies and everything. Now what am I going to do with them?'

'I'll eat them,' he offered.

'You can't eat all of them.'

'Why not?'

'You'll start getting middle-aged spread like your dad.'

Matthew instinctively sucked his waist in.

'I'm nowhere near middle-aged yet,' he said.

'Well, you'll look it if you eat too many brownies. I'll put them in the freezer. We've rearranged for next week, so I'll save them for then, just in case Katy decides to come along too.'

'Don't' get your hopes up,' said Matthew. 'She's probably got her own group of mums to hang out with by now.'

'I bet she's still embarrassed because Ben knocked you out at Charlene's wedding.'

'He didn't knock me out,' said Matthew defensively.

'You were out cold for at least two minutes and you had a bruise the size of a grapefruit on your chin.'

'It was nothing, just a misunderstanding,' he muttered.

'I know,' said Alison. 'But I can understand if that's why Katy's been avoiding me. She's probably still mortified. Maybe I should call her, tell her that you've forgiven him. Or why don't you call her? It would be better coming from you. She'll have to believe you've forgiven him if you tell her. And you've got history.'

'What do you mean?' exclaimed Matthew, getting more alarmed by the second.

'Well, you went to school together, didn't you?' Alison said. 'So technically she knows you better than she knows me. I'm sure she'd appreciate a call from you.'

'No,' said Matthew sharply, causing Alison to raise her eyebrows. He couldn't believe they'd moved on this far and yet now they were somehow back skirting around the lies again. Alison had never discovered that he and Katy had actually been more than classmates and were involved in an all-consuming teenage romance until Matthew had broken Katy's heart. These were facts that needed to stay in the past, just like Katy did. Future harmony depended on there being no contact between the two couples whatsoever.

'Just let it drop,' he tried to say as calmly as possible. 'If Katy had wanted to be friends she would have been in touch by now. It's not down to you or me to call her. She should be the one doing the running.'

Alison didn't respond for a moment.

'You're right,' she agreed eventually. Matthew tried hard not to show his physical relief. 'It's her boyfriend who hit my husband. She knows where I am if she wants me. Neither me nor you should go crawling to her.'

'Absolutely,' said Matthew, squeezing her hand. 'You're worth more than that.'

'Thank you.' She smiled back at him gratefully, just as the large oak doors opened and out trotted a young couple with a bright red, screaming baby.

'Call my assistant and we'll try and fit you in next week to see if he's in a better mood then,' said a man dressed in tweed trousers and a waistcoat who'd poked his head around the door. He turned and addressed the group waiting patiently on the Chesterfield.

'The Chesterton family?' he asked.

'We most certainly are,' said Matthew, getting up quickly to leave behind the conversation they'd just had. He hoisted Rebecca onto his shoulder and offered his free hand to Alison so he could escort his wife into the studio to have their first official family portrait taken. 'All four of us,' he said to her with a relieved smile as he watched her eyes well up for the second time.

CHAPTER EIGHT

Katy was grateful that she could finally look at her reflection in the long mirror in the bedroom. She and Ben had agreed to get Christmas over with and then Millie would be shipped out of their room and into her own next door. It was a relief to be able to see herself in the mirror, her first morning back in a business suit, without the baby paraphernalia in the background reminding her of the significance of what she was about to do.

She looked okay, she decided. Admittedly, body-shaper tights had been roped in to create the illusion of a tummy unaffected by being blown up to three times it's size before being deflated to a saggy shadow of its former self. She turned to take a side-on view and was pleased to see that her ankles no longer looked like they'd been clad in bread dough, though they were already protesting at the indignity of being put back in high heels after so many weeks of the blessed relief of Uggs. As for her upper arms, they had never looked so good. Who knew that hours

spent parading the flat trying to bounce a baby to
sleep, lugging the dead weight of a car seat around
everywhere, and the constant collapsing and the
uncollapsing of a pushchair could have this effect?
It was probably the best thing that had ever happened to her triceps. She leaned forward and added
a last dab of lipstick, then automatically sniffed at
her jacket lapels to check for baby sick. Satisfied she
looked the part, she picked up her bag and went in
search of Ben and Millie to face her first goodbye as
the breadwinner off to work rather than the parent
left holding the baby.

As she walked down the corridor to the lounge
she couldn't quite believe the day had come. It was
over two months since Ben had got her out of bed
in the middle of the night and proposed the swap.
He'd left without a word the next morning and she
wondered whether he would return that night and
announce he'd made a huge mistake and regretted
everything he'd said. But just after lunch she received
a text from him telling her he'd had an informal chat
with the Head, and he'd said as long as they could
recruit a replacement he would be able to leave at
the end of the Christmas term if he wanted to. Did
she want him to? She'd stared at the text for a long
time. She put her mobile face down on the counter whilst she tidied up the kitchen then fed Millie.
She left her mobile at home whilst she went out and

walked around the park, hoping Millie would drop off to sleep and give her headspace to think this thing through. Eventually she settled and all was quiet, so Katy headed home, intending to compile a list of pros and cons for Ben's grand role-swap plan. She'd just got the pushchair through the door and was taking her coat off when she heard a snuffle. She knew what was coming and wanted to scream. She needed to think, but Millie was having none of it. She wanted out of the pushchair and she wanted input, whether in the form of a nappy change, or a bounce on a knee or a jiggle on a shoulder or a swing in the air, anything as long as she had the undivided attention of her mother. She valiantly battled her tiredness with toe-curling wails for over an hour, successfully preventing Katy from even going to the toilet. Eventually Katy snatched up her phone and texted *Do it* in reply to Ben's message before she could even stop herself. Of course Millie chose that exact moment to calm down and snuggle into Katy's chest, her eyelids slowly and gently closing.

Katy stared at her phone, a mixture of euphoria and dread swirling around in her head. As she sat there with her little angel sleeping contentedly in her arms, she mentally listed all the reasons why her going back to work didn't make her a bad mother –a list she would refer to every day in the weeks leading up to her eventual return to work.

She was a good mother and going back to work was a brilliant thing to be doing because:

— Millie and Ben could bond properly.
— She could earn more money in fewer hours than Ben, meaning that they could spend more time together as a family.
— They could save up for a house with a garden, then Millie wouldn't be the only child without a trampoline.
— She was setting a very modern example to her daughter that women's careers are just as important as men's, and there is no reason why a mother shouldn't work and a father be the main carer.
— She and Ben would start having sex again – surely?
— They could save up and have the wedding they both dreamed of.

This list was rotating around Katy's mind for the hundredth time when she entered the lounge to find Ben in his pyjamas, lying on the sofa with Millie sound asleep on his chest whilst he watched a recording of *Match of the Day*. He turned to smile at her, his mouth slightly obscured by the bright ginger beard he'd been cultivating over Christmas. She couldn't tell if it was an encouraging, *don't worry* smile, or a slightly smug, *look, this is a piece of cake* smile. She'd tried throughout the holidays to tell Ben anything she thought he might find useful once he was left alone for hours on end with Millie. She feared, however, that her lack of confidence in her own maternal skills made her a poor teacher, and he'd only half listened to her mutterings about the chaos of a normal day with a baby.

'So you all set, then?' she asked, resisting the urge to succumb to the lump in her throat.

'Sure, yeah,' he said, waving a hand over Millie's dozing head. 'We'll be absolutely fine. Don't you worry about a thing.'

'Are you sure you don't need me to—'

'I've got this,' Ben interrupted, suddenly looking stern. 'I can do this, okay? I may not be capable of a lot of things but I can look after my own daughter. Now go.'

'Right,' replied Katy, knowing she'd offended him. Not a good way to start in their new roles. 'Well, I'm off then.' She bent to kiss Millie's head. She pulled away sharply as the touch of soft baby hair brushing her lips made tears suddenly spring to her eyes.

'Bye,' said Ben, engrossed once more in the football. 'We're all good here.'

'I know,' she murmured, and fled before she changed her mind about everything and never walked out the door again.

An hour later Ben woke with a start to the sound of Millie bawling. He was confused for a moment. His recording of *Match of the Day* must have finished, as all that remained was a blank blue screen. He sat up quickly, launching Millie onto his shoulder, and rubbed his eyes. So what should he be doing now? He leaned forward to pick up the remote control to banish the blue then grabbed his phone to check on the time.

'Shit,' he gasped, dropping the phone back on the coffee table. He'd had a text from Charlene reminding him that she would save a piece of floor next to her at the Music, Mummy and Me session, which was due to begin in twenty minutes. Katy had said to him that he didn't have to go, but he wanted to show her that he was all-in with looking after Millie. Truth be told, he was looking forward to it. His first morning and he was going to a baby class with his daughter. It had *successful stay-at-home dad* written all over it. In any case, Charlene had been texting him daily to make sure he was going. He suspected she was overexcited about being the only one who knew the novelty parent in the class, so there was no way on earth she was letting him get out of it.

R U ON UR WAY ☺ came the next text as Ben leapt up, trying to work out where to put Millie whilst he got dressed. He rushed through to the bedroom and laid her on the bed, and she wailed. He spotted the bouncy chair in the corner and put her in there. She wailed. He sang her a football chant, which normally did the trick. She wailed. He began an exaggerated dance, flinging legs and arms in all manner of awkward directions. She watched, mesmerised, as Ben continued his body contortions whilst trying to put on his underpants. He fell over twice.

Clothes successfully on, he brushed his teeth, forcing him out of Millie's sight for a few moments. She wailed. He momentarily admired his bright ginger beard. What a bonus of being a stay-at-home dad . . . no shaving. It was like a dream come true not to have to spend precious minutes of every day scraping his cheeks with an electric torture instrument. Going back to sweep Millie out of her chair, he glanced at his watch. He had ten minutes to get to the Community Centre. Piece of cake.

Five minutes later and he was still battling to get the pushchair to stay up one-handed whilst he bounced a wailing Millie on his shoulder. What on earth was wrong with her? She was never normally this upset when she was with him. He was determined to get the stupid contraption up using one hand. He'd seen Katy do it, so it couldn't be that hard, surely. He'd left the bouncy chair in the bedroom and he couldn't put Millie on the floor, as it was a very hard Moroccan tile. *One more go*, he told himself.

'Fuck!' he screamed, as his violent shake of the contraption caused the pushchair to trap his hand. He stalked back to the bedroom to get the bouncy chair.

'Is this where I should be for Music, Mummy and Me?' Ben gasped as he barged through the double doors of the Community Centre.

All eyes turned to stare at the dishevelled-looking young man with a bright ginger beard marching towards the group of women sitting on the floor, clutching babies on their laps.

'Ben!' shrieked Charlene. 'Sit with me, sit with me right here,' she said, shuffling up to make room. 'This is Ben,' she said to the other mums, who were all agog. 'We were in antenatal classes together. His girlfriend, you know, Katy, earns tons more money than him, so she's gone back to work. He's a *stay-at-home dad*.' She completed her last sentence by raising her pencilled-on eyebrows to the top of her forehead, as if she'd just announced he was a male stripper.

'Thanks, Charlene,' said Ben, dumping himself down next to her with Millie.

'Hi, Ben,' said Abby, suddenly appearing from behind Charlene, fluttering her mascara-caked eyelashes whilst holding a phone up in front of her. 'Good to see you again.'

'Er,' Ben faltered, struggling to cross his muscular legs. 'Hi again.'

'I said you were coming, and she said she'd come along and give you moral support. She's also filming me and Rocco at baby music class to put up on my Teenage Mums Facebook group page,' said Charlene.

'And I don't go to college on a Monday,' added Abby.

'Oh,' said Ben. He held Millie's hand up to do a little wave at Abby then looked around, suddenly feeling awkward that everyone was staring at him.

'I'm Linda,' announced a woman wearing a poncho sitting in the middle of the group with a guitar rather than a baby on her lap. 'I'm thrilled to welcome a young man to our group,' she gushed. 'It's Ben, isn't it? Charlene has been telling us all about you for weeks. Now I don't want you to feel intimidated just because you're the only man. You are very welcome at Music, Mummy and Me.'

'Thank you,' Ben grinned back. 'You'll have to change the name to Music, Mummy, Daddy and Me now, though, won't you?' he joked.

'He's right, Linda,' exclaimed Charlene. 'You don't want to be done for bloody discrimination, do you?'

'Please,' said Linda. 'We *do* have children present.'

Ben couldn't suppress a smirk, which didn't go unnoticed by Abby or Linda.

'I'm sure everyone would prefer it if profanities were not used during the class, Charlene,' Linda added.

'Profanities?' Charlene queried. 'What are they? I don't think I've used one of them before.'

'You know what profanities are, you fuckwit,' said Abby, smirking back at Ben.

'Pleeeease,' shouted Linda. 'Shall we start again?' She coughed and shook her shoulders. 'So, as some of you are new to this class, maybe it would be an idea to quickly review the philosophy of Music, Mummy and Me before we make a start.'

'Fuck me,' Ben muttered under his breath. Abby stifled a giggle.

'Music, Mummy and Me was founded in 1992 by Mary Jane Becket in Cambridge, following a study which proved that babies who participate and interact with music with their parents, smile more, communicate better and show earlier and more sophisticated brain responses to music, including the recognition of rhythm *and* more amazingly a recognition of pitch.'

'Wow,' exclaimed Ben. 'That *is* amazing.'

Linda looked at him, unsure if her latest class member was naturally enthusiastic or merely sarcastic.

'Mary started her own group in Cambridge, and now there are over fifty classes being run in the UK every week where babies and their carers can come along and enjoy a structured programme of melodic play.'

Ben stared at Linda in stunned silence until she was forced to ask if he was okay.

'Melodic play?' he asked.

'Yes, that's right.'

Ben furrowed his brow.

'What exactly is melodic play?'

'It's play involving interaction with music and sounds,' she replied.

Ben thought for a moment.

'A bit like singing and dancing?' he asked.

'Well, yes. You could put it like that.'

'Except,' said Ben slowly. 'Babies can't sing or dance.'

Linda blinked rapidly.

'Well,' she said eventually, after a very long silence whilst Charlene and Abby sniggered and the rest of the mums looked uncomfortable. 'They can move and make sounds to the music, and that's what we are encouraging them to do during this class.' She gave him a false smile then leaned forward and flipped some laminated pages in a file in front of her.

'And *we* can sing and dance,' chirped one of the other mums.

'That's right, Caroline,' said Linda, beaming at her. 'The mums, sorry, *carers*, have a wonderful time singing and bopping along, don't you?'

Forced smiles all round. Ben gazed at them, dumbstruck.

'Are you serious?' he gasped. 'You're expecting us all to sing and dance at ten o'clock in the fucking, oops sorry, ten o'clock in the morning?' He turned to stare at Charlene in wonder. She'd never mentioned anything about *him* having to sing and dance . . . in the morning! What was she thinking?

'I can't do that,' he continued, turning back to Linda. 'We're talking at least four pints, some seriously loud banging tunes and a room dark enough that no-one can see where I am, never mind what I'm doing.'

There was silence around the room. Ben surveyed his co-carers, who were all looking anywhere but at him, clearly embarrassed by his outburst.

'Why don't we make a start,' said Linda, 'and then you can see actually what fun it is and you'll get right into it.'

'Okay,' said Ben slowly. 'Fine. Let's do it.'

'Good, good,' said Linda, moving her hands into position on the guitar and smiling around at her audience. 'Shall we start with the welcome song? After three. One, two, three.'

'Welcome, welcome, welcome, everyone
Welcome, welcome to a great new day
Welcome, welcome, welcome, everyone
Welcome, welcome, let's see who's come our way

Welcome, welcome, here is . . . Archie
Welcome, welcome to you today
Welcome, welcome, here is Archie
Welcome, welcome, let's see who else has come our way

Welcome, welcome, here is . . . Isobel
Welcome, welcome to you today
Welcome, welcome, here is Isobel
Welcome, welcome, let's see who else has come our way.

Welcome, welcome, here is . . .'

Ben stared back at Linda as if she had grown two heads when she paused in the song to allow Ben to insert Millie's name.

'Your baby's name?' urged Linda.

'Seriously!' exclaimed Ben, his eyes wide. 'It's ten o'clock in the morning and you expect me to sing this? Are you having a laugh? Are you winding me up because I'm new?'

Everyone stared back at him in stunned silence.

'You cannot honestly expect me to believe that anyone would pay to come and sit on the floor of some crusty old Community Centre, pretending to enjoy singing some pathetic, mindless tune to babies who are completely and utterly clueless as to what is going on around them.'

There were one or two gasps from the room as everyone waited for Linda to respond.

'Look,' she said, putting her guitar down. 'Perhaps you shouldn't be here if you do not think you can participate in the worthy goals and aims of this class. Although I do think if you were to consult Katy she would agree that she and Millie gained a huge amount by attending.'

'Katy came here and sang songs about welcome, welcome, drivel, drivel, drivel?' asked Ben incredulously. 'In public?' Katy, who didn't even dare tell anyone she preferred Radio 2 to Radio 1 these days.

'She did,' confirmed one of the mums. 'Along with the rest of us.'

Ben stared back at her.

'But why?'

No-one spoke; they all just looked at one another furtively.

'Shall I go through the Music, Mummy and Me philosophy one more time?' Linda offered.

'No,' said Ben, shaking his head vigorously.

'I come,' said Charlene, 'because it fills that gap after Jeremy Kyle finishes and before Toddlers, Tiaras and Tantrums start.'

'You come because you have nothing to watch on TV?'

'Yes,' Charlene nodded.

Ben looked round the rest of the room.

'I come because my husband takes the car on a Monday. I can walk here, and if I don't come I might not have an adult conversation all day,' 'fessed up another mum.

'I'm a child-minder,' said someone else. 'I'm paid to come.'

'Our heating's broken,' said another.

'So let me get this straight,' said Ben. 'This is actually what you do in this class, sit on the floor and sing stupid songs?'

'Yes,' said Charlene.

'But none of you actually comes for the music or the educational benefits to your child?'

'I really must ask you to leave now,' said Linda, standing up and pointing at the door.

'And do any of you actually enjoy it?' asked Ben.

There was a heavy silence as everyone looked at the floor.

'Right, that's enough,' said Linda, raising her voice. 'This is totally unacceptable. You are ruining my class.'

'Sounds to me like the only one ruining it is you,' said Ben.

'How dare you?' shouted Linda, finally losing her cool. 'I have been doing this for eight years and you swan in here like you know it all, trying to tell all these hard-working mums what they should be thinking. I have never in my entire professional career had a complaint. Not one. These classes are an extremely positive experience for all, and maybe it's just because you are a man that you can't see that. Maybe there is a very good reason why these classes are called Music, *Mummy* and Me.'

The entire class took a sharp intake of breath and turned to see Ben's response.

'Call yourself a professional?' he said, getting up. 'You're delusional.' He gathered Millie up in his arms. 'I don't need this, I don't need you. I'm going home to play the Arctic Monkeys VERY LOUD.'

CHAPTER NINE

'There's no answer,' Katy told Daniel as he waited patiently in her office to go with her for a late lunch. She held her phone to her ear as it continued to ring.

'He'll be at the pub or somewhere,' said Daniel. 'I don't know what you're worrying about.'

'But they should be home from music by now.' Katy put the receiver down and chewed her thumbnail. 'Where are they? He's not answering his mobile either.'

'Do you have any idea how boring you sound?' Daniel got up and straightened his jacket. 'Let's go, shall we?'

'One more try,' said Katy, picking up the receiver and pressing the number redial button.

'Boring, boring, boring,' said Daniel, sitting down and pretending to go to sleep.

'Do you think I should pop home and check everything's okay?' she said as she put the phone down again.

'No!' Daniel shrieked, getting up and striding around the back of her desk to forcibly lift her from her seat. 'You will get your arse down to this fabulous new wine bar I have found so we can have a proper gossip about who's shagged who in the office whilst you've been away.'

Katy gave Daniel an incredulous stare.

'I know,' he nodded. 'It's shocking. I would never have put those two together. In the lightbox room at the end of a very long night preparing for a pitch, apparently.'

'I cannot possibly go to a wine bar!' she exclaimed. 'I've not come back to work to enjoy myself.'

It was Daniel's turn to give Katy an incredulous stare.

'Then what's the fucking point?' he cried.

'The point, of course,' she replied, getting frustrated, 'is to provide for my family. Not to swan about gossiping with you like I used to.'

Daniel looked as though someone had slapped him in the face.

'And to think, I was so excited to have you back. God, I wish Freddie were still here instead of you. He'd have come to the wine bar all afternoon if I'd asked him to.'

'Of course he would,' retorted Katy. 'He'd have spread peanut butter on his stupid shiny bald head and let you lick it off, he was so far up your backside.'

Daniel creased his brow as if considering it as a serious option.

'That is a mental image I'm not wholly averse to,' he declared eventually.

'You're welcome,' spat Katy.

'That's the Katy I've missed,' Daniel said after a pause.

Katy nodded, feeling suddenly tearful. 'Me too.'

'Fucking bollocks, stupid fucker!' shouted Ben.

Millie was in the baby chair again on the kitchen floor, screaming her head off.

'It's coming, Millie, it's coming,' said Ben, raking his hands through his hair. 'If I can ever get this stupid bloody machine to do as it's told.'

He glared at the innocent-looking steriliser before jabbing wildly at the buttons for the millionth time in the vain hope it would do something . . . anything. He cast his mind back to Katy showing him what to do. It was so simple he'd told her not to worry about getting any bottles ready the night before, he'd sort it the following day. No problem. He could master a simple steriliser, absolutely no worries at all.

'You bastard!' he shouted when the machine failed to respond to any of his manhandling. 'You utter bastard. Which idiot designed this? All I need is a simple switch that just says ON. Not five switches with stupid symbols that mean bugger all to me.'

Millie continued to cry.

'Bugger, bugger, bugger, bugger,' Ben muttered, looking at the ceiling. He could sort this. He had to sort this. He couldn't ring Katy on his first day and admit he couldn't even work the steriliser. He suspected that Katy thought he wasn't up to the job, that he would fail and be forced to admit it was a lot harder than he'd realised. He was determined to be a success and he wasn't going to let a stupid blue and white machine trip him up on his very first day. He looked at the bottles lined up by Katy, ready to be sterilised. They looked clean enough to him. What if he used one without sterilising it? One couldn't hurt, surely? He picked one of the bottles up tentatively then collected a teat, pinching it between his thumb and forefinger.

'Fuck,' he exclaimed, dropping it on the floor. He'd touched it with his bare hands. Had he washed them properly last time he went to the toilet? It was entirely possible soap may not have participated in the ritual. He may have just done a cursory run of his hands under water, never guaranteed to do the job properly. He may have just covered his daughter's bottle teat in his own wee! Oh God, he was such a bad parent. He could have killed his own baby by making her drink his own wee. He should never have been allowed to be left home with her. His heart was racing now as the paranoia of being the sole responsible adult in charge of a helpless baby kicked in. He'd never felt like this before. He normally had back-up, he realised. There was always someone else nearby to take the responsibility. Now it was down to him. This baby would live or die because of him and *only* him. He needed back-up and he needed it fast. He reached for the only person he could think of who would be at home and available to help.

'Braindead,' he gasped into the phone, Millie balanced on his hip, still wailing.

'Yo,' his friend replied. 'What is that you're watching? *Nightmare on Elm Street* Three or Four?'

'Come here now! To the flat. It's an emergency!'

Fifteen minutes later Braindead was staring at the steriliser poised with a screwdriver.

'Do I have permission to go in?' he asked. 'It's clearly faulty. Let's open her up and take a look.'

'But it was working perfectly fine yesterday,' said Ben, bouncing Millie high in the air, which was distracting her for the moment.

'But it's not working now. You said so yourself. Come on, let's have a look. I'd love to see how one of these work.'

Ben gave a weary sigh and Millie resumed her distressed call.

'Alright,' he said. 'You take a look but make sure you can put it back together, okay? If Katy comes back and finds it in bits she'll go mental.'

'You have so little faith,' smiled Braindead as he turned the beast over and tackled his first screw.

Ben watched, feeling zero confidence that anything like an end was in sight. There was nothing for it but to try a Plan B, which he didn't hold much hope for either.

'Charlene?' he said when she picked up the phone.

'Hiya,' she replied. 'You were epic this morning. Half the class walked out after you did. Linda was broken.'

'Help me, Charlene, perleeease,' he breathed down the phone. 'I can't work the steriliser and Millie needs feeding, listen.' He held the phone next to her puce red face as she wailed down it.

'Abby's here,' said Charlene when he put the phone back to his ear. 'Can she have a word?'

'Noooo,' cried Ben. 'Just tell me what to do if I've got no sterilised bottles and I need to feed her.'

'Oh. Well, just pour boiling water over the bottle and teat. It'll be fine.'

'And that's okay, is it?'

'It's what I do sometimes, and Rocco doesn't seem to be suffering. He's a right little fatty.'

'Are you sure?'

'Yeah. My mum says there weren't these fancy sterilisers about when she had babies and it never did us any harm.'

'Right, right, okay,' said Ben. 'Brilliant, that's what I'll do. Thanks, Charlene. Look, gotta go feed Millie. Thanks again. Really. Bye.'

'Braindead – step away from the steriliser. Put the screwdriver down. Down, Braindead, down. Good, good boy. That's it. Now put the kettle on and let's get a bit of peace.'

Katy had intended to leave work bang on time at five p.m. Her coat was on and her computer was switched off but then her phone rang. She hesitated before picking it up. She couldn't be late home on her first day. She knew only too well what it felt like when Ben drifted home a mere ten minutes after he said he'd be back. She was prone to an apoplectic meltdown such was her desperation to be near another human being and no longer the sole carer for their bundle of help-lessness. However, the number flashing showed it was the Group Marketing Director for Family Cereals, who oversaw the Crispy Bix brand. She'd been trying to get hold of him all day to salvage the account they were teetering on the edge of losing due to Daniel and Freddie's digression into a literary rebranding. She picked up – she had to. Her boss had told her in no uncertain terms to do whatever it took to save the lucrative account.

There was no exchange of pleasantries. Richard Makeney's tone was stern, clearly indicating that the relationship between client and agency had turned very sour indeed. Before Richard could even begin to launch into a tirade of exactly what he currently thought of their level of service, Katy stepped in. She took him through a mentally rehearsed spiel on what action she had already implemented to steer the latest campaign back onto a sales-winning course. By the time she had taken him through the new brief she'd written, shared some of the initial idea's they'd brainstormed in a meeting that day and explained how she'd adjusted the timescales to make sure they still came in on time and on budget, Richard's tone was entirely different.

'I know that our Brand Manager is keen for us to revisit the Crispy Bix chipmunk, and I really like your idea for how we can do that in a new way. I think it could work.'

'Well, it so ties into your core brand values,' replied Katy, feeling the old jargon coming back to her as if she'd never been away. 'The Fifties were all about Mother being the centre of the family and caring for her children. We want mums to feel that by feeding their children Crispy Bix they're as good as any of those pinny-wearing homemakers around then. We do a Fifties retro campaign with the Crispy Bix Chipmunk at the centre of it – we get all those great home values in one.'

'And are the creative team on board?' asked Richard. 'They seemed to be the ones who were choosing to ignore the brand essence.'

'It was the Creative Director's idea,' she lied. She and Daniel had had a stand-up row during the brainstorming about the loss of the Shakespeare idea. A row not so much because they disagreed, more because they so loved shouting the odds at each other in front of the junior creatives, who cowered in the background. The retro slant had been her idea, knowing it would appeal to Daniel's desire to do something different. However, by the end of the meeting it was of course totally down to Daniel's genius that a solution had been found to suit all parties.

Katy smiled at herself as she put the phone down. The adrenaline rush of winning someone round, solving a problem, having a proper adult conversation, seemed at that moment like the best feeling in the world.

Then she saw the time. 'Shit!' she exclaimed, jumping out of her chair and grabbing her bag. It was already five-thirty. The witching hour in any household containing young children, when all hell could break loose and any sane rational thought would be thrown out the window. She had to get home fast.

'Leaving early?' the receptionist called to her as she ran out of the lift.

'Fuck off,' she muttered under her breath to the time-happy singleton.

'Hi,' said a tight-lipped Ben as she walked through the door.

'So sorry I'm late,' gasped Katy, taking Millie out of his arms immediately. 'Hello, baby, how are you?' she said, clutching onto her and showering her with kisses. 'Richard from Crispy Bix called and I'd been waiting to speak to him all day because they were about to ditch the agency. I'm so sorry. So how have you been? Everything okay?'

'Fine,' said Ben, nodding his head with a slightly glazed look on his face. 'Great, no problems at all. Seriously. Look, Braindead popped in just now for a chat and he's gone down the pub for a quick one. Mind if I join him? You don't mind, do you? Good, I'll see you in about an hour then. Bye.'

Katy stared after Ben open-mouthed, clutching Millie very tightly as she gurgled happily.

She walked into the kitchen to go and put the kettle on. However, she couldn't actually see the kettle, such was the chaos that met her. The dishwasher hadn't been unloaded, so there were dirty pots everywhere on the side. The pushchair and baby seat cluttered the floor and the steriliser seemed to have disappeared to be replaced by a screwdriver. Eventually she located the kettle on the breakfast bar next to a bowl of water. What on earth had gone on that day? She scrutinised Millie for signs of discomfort, distress or harm. She appeared to be fine. She gently laid her down in her baby seat and handed her a rattle to wave around and spit all over before she began the process of restoring some order into the totally trashed kitchen.

CHAPTER TEN

Ben, Braindead and Rick sat in the corner of the Nelson sipping on pints as they contemplated the white and pale blue steriliser sitting on the table in front of them.

Ben wasn't really taking anything in. His first day as a stay-at-home dad had hit him like a steam train. His ability for conversation was limited and his appearance – well, his appearance was dishevelled, to say the least. His usual post-work uniform of tracksuit bottoms and a hoodie had given him an active, lively air in the past, whereas today his shock of ginger beard, unbrushed hair, T-shirt he had slept in and stained tracksuit bottoms indicated boy on benefits at best, tramp at worst.

Braindead had plugged the steriliser into a socket he'd spotted on the wall and was peering at the buttons on the control panel.

'Is anyone going to tell me what that is?' asked Rick, nodding at the plastic contraption on the table.

Silence.

'Braindead?' asked Rick, when it was clear that Ben was not capable of speech just yet.

'Still not exactly sure,' replied Braindead. 'Cleans stuff for Millie, I think. Ben called in a state, so I dropped everything. Well, luckily I'd seen the episode of *Location, Location, Location* I was watching. I went round and offered to open it up, take a look inside for him, but he stopped me before I could get stuck in.'

'It sterilises the baby bottles,' said Ben wearily.

'Right,' Rick nodded.

'Katy showed me how to use it and it looked so easy that I told her not to bother writing it down,' sighed Ben. 'But then I couldn't remember and tried to poison my own child.'

'Wow!' shrieked Braindead. 'You didn't mention that. How did you manage that?'

'I touched the teat,' said Ben, shaking his head. 'Always use the tweezers. I do remember Katy saying that. Not your fingers. Then I couldn't remember if I'd washed my hands.' He put his pint down on the table and buried his head in his hands.

Braindead and Rick stared at the broken man.

'Katy makes you use tweezers to touch her tits?' exclaimed Braindead. 'That's weird.'

'Not *her* tits,' moaned Ben, not raising his head.

'You are allowed to touch other women's tits as long as you use tweezers?' Braindead continued. 'Having a baby has seriously screwed with Katy's head, man. This is not right.'

Ben looked up.

'Not tits, *teats*,' he said. 'You know, the things that go on the top of babies' bottles. What the baby drinks through.'

'Is that like French for tits or something, then?' asked Braindead.

Ben stared at him for a moment before managing a sarcastic, 'Yes.'

'Jesus, that is fucked up!' exclaimed Braindead.

Ben didn't reply.

'So *La Teet* thingies all go in here, do they, to get clean?' asked Braindead.

Ben nodded.

'To protect Millie from germs?'

Ben nodded again.

'So?' said Braindead, looking confused.

No-one answered him.

'So,' Braindead continued. 'When Katy was breast-feeding, did she have to stick her tits in here too?'

Ben blinked at Braindead and chose not to answer, taking several large gulps of his beer instead.

'Of course she didn't,' he finally said.

'You have no idea, though, where those tits might have been,' Braindead protested. 'Why do you have to go to all that palaver over fake tits when you don't bother with the real thing?'

Ben sensed there was something entirely logical and rational in what Braindead was saying. Sadly, he realised he was no longer capable of being logical and rational. He was a dad now.

'You just do,' he shrugged.

'But why?' pressed Braindead. 'I don't get it. Who knows where Katy might have had her tits before she feeds Millie?'

'I don't know why,' answered Ben, hoping Braindead would drop it. 'You just do.'

'But that's stupid,' Braindead retorted. 'Why do something when you don't really know why you're doing it?'

'Because,' Ben said wearily, 'I've been told to do it in such a way that there's a slim chance something terrible might happen to my daughter if I get it wrong, and then I would be a baby killer and rot in jail.'

Braindead and Rick stared at Ben, open-mouthed.

'I know it sounds stupid,' he continued, 'but having a baby makes you do stuff you would never normally do because of the fear you might become a baby killer. That's just how it is.'

'So if we don't manage to make this thing work,' said Braindead, nodding back at the steriliser, 'then we could become baby killers too?'

'Precisely,' Ben responded grimly.

'Fuck me,' said Braindead, shaking his head. 'I'm not going to prison for the sake of some stupid white machine.'

'Why don't you just ask Katy to show you again?' asked Rick.

'Are you insane?' gasped Ben. 'Admit to Katy on my very first day that I wasn't up to it? I told her I could do this, no problem, piece of cake. How will it make me look if I admit I couldn't do something as easy as work a stupid steriliser?'

'Daft question, I know, but did you keep the instructions?' asked Rick.

'Keep instructions for this?' said Ben. 'Really? They were filed in the bin.'

'Well, is there anyone else you know with a baby who can show you what to do?' Rick persevered.

'Yes,' muttered Ben. 'I suppose asking her is better than the embarrassment of asking Katy again. I'll call her tomorrow.' He stood up to get another pint.

Katy watched as Ben flicked on the kettle when he got back from the pub. It had taken her an hour to put the kitchen back together into some sort of order, but Ben didn't seem to notice. The fact the kettle was magically back where it should be, rather than upended on the kitchen table, didn't seem to register at all.

'Braindead okay, then?' she asked, when Ben wasn't overly forthcoming with conversation.

'Yeah, yeah,' he replied, getting a mug out of an overhead cupboard. 'You know, usual Braindead.'

'I really am sorry I was late home,' she said, putting her hand on his shoulder.

'It's fine, really,' he said, turning and giving her a smile at last. 'Tell me how your day went.'

'Well,' she said, moving to perch herself on one of the high stools at the breakfast bar. 'It was a bit odd to start with, I really did feel like I was the new girl all over again, but then I went to the Monday morning directors' meeting and it was like I'd never left. Honestly, they were having exactly the same conversations as the ones they were having before I went on maternity leave. Ridiculous.'

'I can imagine,' said Ben over his shoulder as he put coffee in his mug.

'But Andrew was really clear with me when I caught up with him after the meeting. He said the only thing I needed to focus on was saving the Crispy Bix account. Apparently he'd had an irate phone call from the MD before Christmas saying they were on the brink of ditching the agency.'

'Blimey,' said Ben, turning to face her.

'Andrew said he'd told him he was dragging his top account director back from maternity leave to sort it out.'

'Wow,' said Ben. 'You must have been chuffed he called you his top thingy?'

'Well, yes,' Katy admitted, 'but talk about being under pressure on your first day back. Anyway, I got stuck into the creative team and we came up with a plan of action, so that by the time I spoke to the MD at Crispy Bix we'd solved all his concerns. I could tell when I picked up the phone he was ready to lay into me, but he seemed more than happy by the time we'd finished talking.'

'So mission accomplished then?'

'Yes.' Katy nodded, a highly satisfied smile on her face.

'So it was a good day?' he asked.

'It was. I thought, you know, that I might have lost it a bit having been away, but after today I think I can still do it.'

'I'm really pleased for you,' said Ben. 'Glad that today's been such a success.'

'Well, I wouldn't be there without you, would I?' replied Katy. 'So tell me how your day has been. You've breezed it, right? I bet she's loved having her daddy all to herself all day.'

'Yeah, piece of cake,' Ben shrugged. 'No problems at all.'

'Great. And how did you find Music, Mummy and Me?'

'Fine,' said Ben.

'I wasn't sure how you'd take to it, to be honest. Thought you'd find it a bit odd, you know, all that sitting around, singing stupid songs.'

Ben shrugged.

'It was alright.'

'Good,' she said. 'I'm glad.'

'Sure,' he said, turning away and pouring hot water into his mug.

'When you first suggested us swapping roles I thought you were mad,' she said to his back. 'To be honest, I didn't know how you'd cope being a stay-at-home dad.'

'Why?' Ben turned back to face her, frowning.

'It's just that it's not as easy as it looks, is it?'

'We have been absolutely fine,' said Ben, looking slightly irritated. 'You can go off to work and solve the nation's advertising woes and rest assured that I am capable of taking care of our child.'

'I'm sorry. I didn't mean to upset you.'

'You haven't,' said Ben. 'But if you stop me from getting in front of that telly to find out how Leeds have done tonight then I'm likely to get very, very upset.'

Katy stepped aside to let him go past her into the living room. She reached up to kiss his cheek but he wasn't looking and she was left pouting into thin air. She stared after him. This wasn't how she'd envisaged the end of her day. It was with a sense of excitement that she'd driven home to be back in the bosom of her family. She realised it was the longest period she'd ever spent away from Millie and she'd been longing to see her. A total contrast to the constant dull desire to have just five minutes to herself when she'd been at Millie's beck and call. She felt renewed, refreshed and ready to focus on some family time, and had expected both Ben and Millie to feel the same. However, Millie appeared to be indifferent to her mother's absence and was happily ignoring her under the baby gym, and Ben was doing everything to avoid talking to her. She could tell he'd had a difficult day. She knew Ben. He always went into himself when he was stressed, and his usually happy-go-lucky nature seemed muted.

She was also certain that he would have hated his first music class and he was lying when he said he'd enjoyed it. And what on earth had he done with the steriliser?

CHAPTER ELEVEN

One week later Ben sat in the doctor's waiting room dreaming hazily of the day when his greatest problem in life had been how to make a damn steriliser work. A phone call to Charlene the following day had provided him with the answer to all his problems . . . or so he thought.

'No idea,' Charlene had replied when he'd enquired if she had experience with the type of steriliser they had. 'Have you looked on YouTube?'

'You are a genius,' he'd declared then slammed the phone down and fired up the laptop.

'Come on . . . come on . . . come on,' he'd muttered over and over again as he waited for the lethargic machine to spring into action. His fingers tripped over themselves as he delved headlong into the YouTube search engine until he found his saviour in Melanie of Minnesota. She rambled through the inner workings of his model of steriliser in a cluttered, dark kitchen somewhere in deepest Midwest America. Her video would win no prizes for production values, editing or scripting, but after five separate viewings it had got its point across and Ben sat with a great sigh of relief in front of a fully functioning steriliser.

At that moment he felt he was back in control. That everything was going to be all right. That his plan to swap roles was actually going to work. But he had merely been on day two and it was a rookie error to think he'd nailed it. He was yet to experience that day three would be exactly the same as day two and yet entirely different. That he would ping round like a silver ball in a pinball machine, propelled from pillar to post in the desperate effort to meet the demands of an eighteen-week-old baby. Constantly trying to stay one step ahead of Millie's ever changing timetable as she slept and woke and ate and spewed and pissed and pooed on a whim and without warning as he ran round like a jackass trying to keep all the plates in the air without the slightest clue what he was doing.

He felt he probably could have coped with the total randomness of Millie's actions and his inability to be prepared for the right one at the right time had it not been for the utter exhaustion he was feeling, having taken over the night shift too. In a moment of madness, he had insisted that since Katy had borne the brunt of the worst of the initial sleepless nights during the breastfeeding phase, now that she was back at work, he should be the one to get up for Millie in the night. What he hadn't accounted for was that his options for catching up on all this lost sleep were precisely nil. A nap during the day? No chance! If Millie did deign to take a nap he was too busy clearing up whatever devastation they'd caused beforehand. He realised he could go to bed early, of course. But if he went to bed early, when exactly would he have a life? This issue perplexed him greatly. When exactly would he get to do what he wanted to do, not what a small baby dictated he should do? When would he get to watch the footie on the telly exactly? Football at this point came ahead of the need for sleep; however, at this precise moment, as his head began to droop at ten-thirty in the morning while he sat in the crowded waiting room, he began to think that he would have to let go of the last vestige of his manliness and start going to bed before the watershed.

'Ow!' he exclaimed as he felt a sharp pain in his ribs.

'You were snoring, dear,' said the elderly lady sitting next to him, who must have incredibly sharp elbows.

He glanced around him as he wiped drool from his mouth to be met with a sea of geriatrics smirking at him.

'Sorry,' he muttered, giving himself a shake. 'She had me up for two hours last night.'

'Cancer, was it?' his neighbour asked.

'What?' he said, giving the lady a look of alarm. 'I was going to ask the nurse if maybe she was teething or something.'

'Not the baby, your wife.'

'I'm not married.'

'She died before you got married? I'm so sorry.'

'Who died?'

'Your baby's mother.'

'She's not dead.' Ben looked up to check he was really having this conversation. By the looks of the captivated faces around him, he was not only talking about a non-existent dead wife, he was also enthralling the entire waiting room.

'So where is she then?'

'I believe she said she was going to a meeting about retro-chipmunk animation.'

'Oh, I see,' the lady nodded. 'So you've taken the day off to bring this little one to the doctor's, then.'

'You could say that,' replied Ben. 'Taken every day off, actually. I look after Millie. Katy, my fiancée, has gone back to work full-time.'

The elderly lady was now openly staring at him.

'And they call that progress,' she finally said through pursed lips.

Ben could feel his eyelids drooping again.

'Ray never even changed a nappy, never mind be left alone with my three. He was too busy out doing the real work.'

Ben jerked his head back quickly in an effort to stay awake.

'This is the hardest I have *ever* worked,' he muttered.

The woman turned to stare at him again.

'How many children do you have?'

'Just one.'

'One?' The woman laughed to herself. 'You just wait, young man. You wait until she's properly teething and you literally have no sleep, then weaning when you spend your entire life trying to get soggy food off the floor, then walking as you spend all day trying to stop them killing themselves, and then the devil that is potty training, by which time you've made the mistake of having another one, so you're right back where you started, only double the trouble. Believe me, if you find this hard you have a serious problem. Men are just not cut out for this kind of work.'

'Amelia King,' the receptionist shouted.

Ben leapt up, eager to escape the elderly know-all who was predicting his future as the most terrible nightmare imaginable. He rubbed his eyes and picked up Millie in her car seat, then set off down the corridor.

Five minutes later and he was finally sitting in front of a neat-looking woman whose name badge identified her as Pippa Harper, health visitor. In his haste to escape he'd failed to take note of who he was seeing or through which door they would appear, forcing him into an embarrassing return to reception to ask for directions in front of the evil woman.

'So how is Amelia doing?' Pippa asked.

Ben sighed. He hadn't been looking forward to his first trip to see a professional with Millie. He feared he would be under scrutiny to check he knew what he was doing, and he was sure it was abundantly clear to anyone that he didn't have a clue.

'We call her Millie, actually,' he mumbled. He knew this would happen. Having a different name on her birth certificate was already causing problems, just like he'd told Katy it would.

'Okay,' Pippa nodded enthusiastically. 'Of course, that's absolutely fine. So how is Millie?'

'Fine,' he replied cautiously. He had no idea if it was the right answer and was gripped with terror that Pippa was now going to find something hideously wrong with Millie and he would go to jail for neglect. 'She seems fine. She was fine when she woke up this morning,' he rambled.

'Good, that's great. Shall we get her weighed, then?'

'Okay.'

'So if you bring her over to the scales and take off her clothes and nappy just for a moment, that would be great.'

Ben took Millie over to a changing pad and started to take off her clothes. He was all fingers and thumbs as he could feel Pippa watching him whilst pretending to set up the weighing machine.

'Oh shit,' slipped out of his mouth before he could stop it. The smell was undeniable. Millie had filled her nappy. Pippa looked up, alarmed at his expletive, and Ben felt the blood rush to his cheeks.

'Erm, bit of a nappy situation,' he said. He looked around frantically before realising he'd left the nappy bag in the waiting room. Now what? It was out there now, the dirty nappy, Pippa had clocked it. Should he do the nappy back up again so Millie's bottom was enclosed in her poo whilst he fetched the bag, leaving her with Pippa, or did he remove the offending item without being able to wipe Millie clean and thus risk poo and probably fresh wee all over the changing mat? He stared motionless at the scene, his weariness unable to process the right answer under the scrutiny of perfect Pippa.

'I've left the nappy bag in the waiting room,' he announced eventually. 'I've never left it behind before. I'm normally really good with the bag. It's honestly the first time I've left it unattended.'

'It's okay.' Pippa reached behind her to get a packet of wipes. 'You go and get the bag and I'll get rid of this one.'

Ben was so happy he could cry. He bolted for the door and ran down the corridor. Fortunately, Evil Old Lady had gone, and he snatched the bag from beside the chair he'd been sitting in and headed back to Pippa.

'You can get her dressed again now,' she said. 'I've already weighed her. 'Do you have her medical record in that bag so I can mark down her weight?'

'Yes, yes, absolutely, yes,' Ben confirmed, delirious that he could answer a question in the affirmative. Katy had warned him that under no circumstances should he ever take Millie to a medical establishment without the red book that documented her progress. 'Basically, in the eyes of the NHS, Millie does not exist if you don't have that book with you,' she'd told him. Now he busied himself dressing Millie whilst Pippa flicked through her record and marked her weight chart.

'So Millie has gone from the fiftieth percentile to the thirtieth percentile on the growth chart,' Pippa announced.

Ben swallowed. What was she saying? He had no idea. Was it good or bad?

'Great,' he said whilst shaking his head, hoping he was covering all bases.

'Has she been taking her food okay?' Pippa asked.

'Oh, she's guzzling it down,' he replied. 'Can't drink it fast enough.'

'And how's she sleeping?'

Can you not tell by the massive bags under my eyes? he wanted to scream.

'Not great, actually,' he said. 'She was up three times last night.'

'Mmmm,' Pippa nodded. 'Do you think she might be teething early?'

Ben's eyes widened. What was she asking him for? Wasn't she supposed to be the expert here?

'She bit me yesterday,' he confessed. 'And it really hurt.'

'Right,' Pippa said.

'So, er, what does all that mean, then?'

'Well, often at this age if they start waking more frequently in the night and they're not growing as fast as they were, then it's likely they're just hungry. She needs more food to fuel her growth.'

'Oh, right, actually that makes sense, I get it.' He was relieved that he finally got something, and just maybe this was a solution to Millie's sleeping problems. 'So what do I feed her, then?'

'Oh, just carry on with the milk.'

'Just milk?'

'That's right.'

'But . . . but you said she was hungry. I can feel teeth. Shouldn't we be giving her more than milk?'

'No. The guidelines are that you wait until six months old.'

'The guidelines?'

'That's right.'

'Should I know these guidelines? Where do the guidelines come from?' he asked, starting to panic.

'It's information gathered by the NHS from leading health experts.'

'Oh.' Ben was confused again. Why did he seem to spend most of his life confused? He bit his lip for a moment but then couldn't help himself.

'And the guidelines say she shouldn't have solid food yet?'

'That's right.'

'But she has teeth,' he continued. 'And she is chewing . . . everything.'

'The experts say that a baby's digestive system is not ready for solids until around six months old.'

'And how do they know that?'

'Through a lot of studies.'

'Studies? So do they cut babies' stomachs open at four months and go, nope, not ready for puréed carrot yet?'

Pippa said nothing. He had a vague sense that he was asking the kind of questions Braindead might ask and that Pippa was looking at him as if he was brain-dead.

'Did they ask to see all the stomachs of dead babies so they could decide exactly when parents should be buying a blender?' he continued.

'I'm sure that however they have come to this conclusion it was through very thorough and moral means,' said Pippa, turning to get something off her desk in order to mark the conversation as finished.

'But Millie has teeth,' pressed Ben. 'Teeth! Which means she can chew. Teeth are in the human body so we can eat solid food. It's part of our evolution over the past thousands of years. When did these so-called health experts decide that six months was the right age to start chewing food?'

'In 2003,' replied Pippa.

'Really?'

'Yes.'

'And what did they think before 2003?'

'Prior to then they were recommending between four to six months.'

'Millie's age now.'

'Yes.'

'And what changed their minds?'

'Research findings.'

'Are those the same research findings that tells us one minute not to eat sugar, then not to eat fat, then not to eat carbs, then actually good fats are alright as long as you combine them with good sugars and only on Tuesdays?'

'Are you making fun of me?'

'No!' exclaimed Ben. 'No, seriously, I'm not. It's just that I'm new to all this. I'm a baby virgin . . . no, bad choice of words.' He noticed Pippa's cheeks redden slightly. 'Look, I'm sorry, it's just, none of any of this baby stuff makes sense to me, and I'm so tired. I really am incredibly tired.'

'We are here to help you,' said Pippa softly.

Ben nodded dejectedly.

'So I should just increase Millie's milk,' he said, feeling his shoulders slump in defeat.

'That's the best advice I can give you at this point.'

'But I shouldn't give her proper food, even though she has teeth.'

'That's right.'

'Will that make her sleep more?' he asked, desperate for something good to come out of this meeting.

'Probably not.'

'So what will make her sleep through the night? What do the experts say about that?'

'Well, that's a very difficult question. Every baby is different. You just have to be patient.'

Ben couldn't stop himself from letting his mouth fall open in amazement.

'So the experts are more than willing to spend their precious time on the notion of when babies are allowed to eat, which seems plainly obvious to me, but the truly useful answer to making a baby sleep through the night is not a subject that the NHS is willing to investigate. Do you realise how much money could be saved if we cracked that? How many fewer murders would be committed if parents could just get a decent bloody night's sleep?'

Pippa didn't answer – just sat looking startled.

'I'm sorry,' said Ben, shaking his weary head. 'It's not your fault.'

'Perhaps your partner could take over tonight,' said Pippa gently. 'You look like you need a break.'

'No,' said Ben quickly. 'It's fine. She works full-time. Millie is my responsibility.'

'But if you told her you were struggling . . .'

'I'm not struggling,' said Ben firmly, opening his eyes wide to stave off yet another wave of tiredness. 'I'm only doing what thousands of women do every single day. It cannot be that hard. I can do this. I know I can.'

CHAPTER TWELVE

'Where have you been?' demanded Braindead as Ben sat down on a worn leather sofa opposite him the following week. 'And what on earth possessed you to suggest meeting here? This place is weird. I've spent more money in here in the space of ten minutes than I spend in an entire night down the Red Lion and I have bugger all to show for it.'

'Believe me,' said Ben flopping backwards, 'given the day I've had, I'd love to be meeting you down the pub, but I'm not sure that drinking beer at four o'clock in the afternoon with a baby in tow is to be recommended.'

'Look at this,' demanded Braindead, holding up an oversized cup and saucer. 'I could have bought a decent pint for less money than this cup of hot water with a dash of caffeine cost me. And who really wants to drink this much coffee? I mean really? I didn't wake up this morning thinking I can't wait to be off my tits on copious amounts of coffee today.'

Ben didn't reply. Perhaps they should have met at the flat. Who knew a visit to a coffee shop could make Braindead this mad?

'She asked me what size I wanted,' Braindead continued, nodding dismissively over to a girl standing behind a coughing and sputtering brewing machine. 'Then she reeled off a load of words that bore no relation to size whatsoever. She may as well have said we only sell enormous so that we can extract an enormous amount of cash from your wallet.'

'Look, I'll pay for your coffee,' Ben sighed.

'And the cake?' asked Braindead.

'You bought cake, in here? Are you insane?'

'Oh yes, and I've spent the last ten minutes trying to find the gold leaf they must have put in it in order to feel the need to charge me what they did. Why do people come here exactly?'

Ben had got Millie out of the pushchair and was bouncing her up and down on his knee. He looked around at the fake homely interior jammed with mismatched wooden furniture and worn leather sofa's gathered around low tables. People of all ages were clustered together for a chinwag, hugging drinks and nibbling on overpriced food.

'It's like it thinks it's a pub,' Braindead pointed out. 'It charges as much as a pub, but there's no beer. 'It's a big fat con. I don't get it.'

'Probably everyone here is just too embarrassed to go to the pub this early,' offered Ben.

Braindead shook his head in disbelief and took a sip out of his enormous cup, eyeing Ben over the brim.

'So what's up then?' he asked. 'You sounded like you had another baby machine malfunction situation going on when you rang.'

'I don't think I can do this,' said Ben.

'Do what?'

'Be a stay-at-home dad.'

'I thought you'd sussed it. Got that weirdo machine to work.'

'If only the only problem I had was machine related.' Ben didn't continue, just shook his head with a look of defeat.

'So what is it then?' asked Braindead.

'Well, besides the utter exhaustion, it's the conversation,' said Ben, getting a milk bottle out of his bag.

'The conversation?' Braindead echoed.

'Yeah.' Ben looked around distractedly. 'Can you just hold Millie whilst I get this warmed up?'

He plopped Millie down on Braindead's lap before he could protest and wandered off to the counter to see if they would warm a bottle for him. Millie blinked up at Braindead and he blinked back. If he didn't move an inch it would be alright, he told himself. He was just reciting football scores in his head when he noticed a woman sitting on her own by the window was smiling at him. That never happened. He smiled back. She didn't stop smiling. That certainly never happened. Ben reappeared, obstructing his view.

'Do you want to feed her?' he said, offering the bottle.

'Shit, no,' said Braindead with a start, and thrust Millie back into his arms. Ben sat back down and Braindead peered round him to see if the woman was still smiling at him. She wasn't.

'I think I've pulled,' said Braindead.

'What, here?' said Ben.

'Yeah, maybe this place isn't so bad after all. Don't look now, but the woman sitting behind you was smiling at me before you came back.'

'Oh, that happens all the time.'

'What does?'

'If you're on your own with a baby then women seem to find it attractive. Must be because it shows your caring side or something.'

'Why didn't you tell me that before? Hand her back over here. I'll feed her.'

'Noo,' cried Ben. 'You cannot drag Millie into your desperate efforts to get a woman.'

'Aw, come on. There has to be some upside to you doing this stay-at-home gig, doesn't there? If it gets me a girlfriend, it will all have been worthwhile, won't it?'

'I'm not sure any more,' said Ben. 'I had the weirdest experience possibly of my entire life this morning. I'm really not sure I'm cut out for this. I don't think I can ever go back there.'

'Back where?'

'Playgroup.'

Braindead contemplated Ben for a moment.

'You're a grown man,' he declared. 'You shouldn't be anywhere near a playgroup.'

'I know,' said Ben. 'But Katy used to go, so I thought I should.'

'Attracted by the thought of a room full of women, maybe?' asked Braindead. 'Hey, I should take Millie,' he said, glancing over to the woman who'd smiled at him.

'You wouldn't last five minutes.'

'Why not?'

'Braindead, it's like . . .' Ben was lost for words. 'It's the single most boring thing you could ever do with your time. I mean, it's literally mind-numbing. It's like a form of torture. If they'd locked Saddam Hussein in a playgroup for an hour he'd have been squealing like a baby to get out.'

'It can't be that bad, surely?'

'Oh, it is. You arrive, right? Bit nervous because you don't know anyone, but you tell yourself it's only a playgroup so nothing to be scared of. So you go in, get Millie settled on a blanket, get told off for not putting a pound in the tin and then guess what happens?'

'What?'

'Absolutely nothing. Everyone ignores you. No-one comes over to say hello. It's like you're a leper. Now I don't know if it's because I'm a bloke, but seriously, I have never been so successfully ignored in my life. And then it gets worse.'

'What? I'm on the edge of my seat, mate. This is the best story you've ever told.'

'Then everyone disappears. They go off into this room, but you've no idea why and no-one has told you to go, so you don't know if it's a girl only thing, but anyway, I'm so bored I pick Millie up and wander in. They're only all sitting down having coffee and biscuits. They all look at me but no one speaks, so I just sit down and grab myself a coffee. It's the most disgusting coffee you have ever tasted – like the sort you used to get when coffee was just cheap stuff, like tea.'

'Those were the days,' replied Braindead, picking up his enormous cup of oversized, over-expensive coffee.

'Anyway, I try not to spit it out, and then lo and behold, someone speaks to me. I've been there over an hour and someone finally says, 'Would you like a digestive biscuit?'

'Chocolate?' asked Braindead.

'No. Plain.'

'Digestives aren't a biscuit,' cried Braindead. 'They're . . . they're a commodity, an ingredient, only to be eaten supporting a mass of cheesecake. You can't just eat a digestive as a biscuit. Hobnob, yes, Bourbon, yes, maybe even a party ring, but to offer a digestive . . . who are these people? Are they living in the Dark Ages?'

'I know, but that wasn't the worst of it,' Ben continued. 'Little did I realise that actually being ignored would be a far better situation than being part of the conversation. Once I'd been offered a biscuit it opened the floodgates. Everyone wanted to talk to me.'

'Brilliant. That's great. You fitted in. Well done.'

'Oh no,' said Ben, shaking his head again. 'Believe me, you do not want to fit in with this conversation. It was horrific. I have never been so ashamed of myself in my entire life.'

'What did you do?'

'Braindead, we discussed baby poo, baby sick, nappy rash, diarrhoea, the direction babies piss in – you name it, we covered it, and Braindead, I couldn't help it, I joined in. What is happening to me?'

'It's alright, lad.' Braindead leaned forward to pat him on the shoulder. 'There must be rehab available for this.'

'It's like I had nothing else to talk about. Like anything interesting I had to say had been zapped out of my head to be replaced with the bodily functions of babies. It's like I've become some kind of baby zombie. What am I going to do?'

'You must have talked about something else at some point, surely?'

'Well, we did digress for a moment, but I had nothing to offer to the brief reality TV show discussion. I came away thinking I have no choice but to watch crap telly, because otherwise I'm stuck on baby poo for the next God knows how many months. And they were all very nice, intelligent women, but it's like they're possessed by some brain-altering movement and all they've got left is babies and reality TV. This is what I'm going to become, isn't it? What am I going to do?'

'You need a lads' night out,' declared Braindead. 'Oestrogen is seeping into you at a shocking rate. Look at us. We're in some poncey coffee shop! We wouldn't have been seen dead in one of these before you gave up your job to look after Millie. I've got just the place. You and me down that new microbrewery. I'll have you back up to speed with scintillating conversation in no time.'

'Microbrewery,' sighed Ben. 'I suppose so.'

'What!' gasped Braindead. 'What is wrong with you? Normally you'd jump through flaming hoops to get to a microbrewery. Are you ill or something?'

'No, yes, I don't know,' said Ben. 'I have never felt so tired in my entire life. I ache all over – what's that all about? I run around like a headless chicken every day and I'm stressed, Braindead. Stressed, me? I never get stressed, but the effort of trying not to screw this up is doing my head in. I think I am actually going mad, seriously.'

'This is serious shit, man,' said Braindead, looking worried for the first time. 'You really need to talk to Katy if it's making you feel like this.'

'I know,' replied Ben. 'But I so wanted to make this work, you know. Make her proud of me. I can't bear the thought of telling her I can't cope.'

Braindead leaned forward to grab Ben's arm. 'I'm here for you, mate.'

'Thanks, Braindead. What do you think I should do?'

'Fuck knows,' Braindead shrugged. 'But one thing I do know is that you're not going to find the answer in here. The answer will most definitely be found in a microbrewery. Friday?'

'Beeeeeeen,' came a high-pitched wail just as Ben and Braindead were packing up baby paraphernalia to leave the coffee shop.

Ben turned to see Charlene and Abby fast approaching. He swivelled back to Braindead to urge him to prepare for a swift exit, but his friend's eyes were already out on stalks at the sight of Abby's generous assets making their way towards them.

'Hi, Charlene,' said Ben. 'Fancy meeting you here.'

'We come here every Wednesday afternoon for a treat as I have Rocco on my own all day on a Wednesday.'

'And I don't go to college on a Wednesday,' added Abby.

'Not on a Wednesday either, Abby?' Ben queried. 'What are you studying, exactly?'

'Media Studies,' she replied.

'Makes sense now,' said Ben. 'Look, you can have our table, we're just leaving.' He heard a cough behind him. 'Oh, sorry. This is Braindead. Braindead, this is Charlene and Abby. Charlene's baby is the same age as Millie.'

'The name's actually Bryan,' announced Braindead. 'But, you know, Braindead is a better name than Bryan.'

Charlene and Abby barely acknowledged Braindead. Charlene was distracted by her phone whilst Abby was nudging her.

'You going to show him?' she said, nodding at Ben.

'Show me what?' asked Ben.

'You are the next big thing, Ben. Just give me one second,' said Charlene, still deeply absorbed in her phone. 'There. Got it. Take a look at this.' She turned to show Ben the screen. To his surprise, his face filled it. He was looking upset with something but it wasn't clear what until the picture panned out and he could see he was watching a recording of him at that damned music class. His heart sank. Why was Charlene showing him this? A painful reminder of yet another horrendous encounter as a stay-at-home dad.

'Why is this on your phone?' he demanded.

'Remember I was filming Charlene and Rocco for Charlene's Facebook page? Well, you were much more interesting,' said Abby coyly.

'I can't believe that was the week that Abby came along to film,' cried Charlene in excitement. 'To think if she hadn't have been there you would never have got famous on the internet!'

'What!' exclaimed Ben, nearly dropping Millie's car seat.

'I'm going home to listen to the Arctic Monkeys very loud!' boomed out of the speakers on the phone.

'Get you,' said Braindead, slapping Ben on the back. 'You totally socked it to that psycho music bitch.'

'You did!' said Charlene, looking really pleased with herself. 'And lots of other people think so too. I put it up on my Teenage Mums Facebook group page, and so far you have over four hundred shares. And look at some of these comments.' She grabbed the phone out of his hand.

'My hero,' she read aloud. *'Wish I'd have said that weeks ago in the music group I go to. I'm never ever going again.* And listen to this one. *I'll have whatever he's having. He is sooooo right.* And what about this one? *I want him to run a music class. Music, Mummy & the Arctic Monkeys. Finally a baby class worth going to.* Ben, you should totally start your own music class. It would be so brilliant. We'd help, wouldn't we, Abby? We could sit around and play brilliant music like the Arctic Monkeys and the Kaiser Chiefs and One Direction and have plastic tambourines and maracas for the kids and serve cocktails and stuff like that. Do it, Ben, please, go on! Say you'll do Music, Mummy and the Arctic Monkeys?'

'Hang on a minute,' cried Ben. 'Just slow down, will you? I think I need to start by asking what on earth possessed you to put me on your Facebook page without asking?'

'You're not bothered, are you?' said Charlene. 'It's just Facebook,' she shrugged.

'It's not just Facebook,' said Ben. 'It's the world-wide web, and I'm out there now and you never even asked me?

'But,' replied Charlene with a look of utter confusion on her face. 'You're famous.'

'Not really, am I, Charlene? And I don't want to be famous anyway.'

'What?' But why not?'

'Because I don't. Especially not for having some poxy video on Facebook. I don't deserve to be famous for that.'

'But you have deserved it,' said Charlene, still looking confused.

'Who says?'

'All these people.' She stabbed at her phone. 'They're freaking over the moon to have someone dare say that baby music classes are pants and you shouldn't go if you're not enjoying them.'

'You shouldn't have done it without asking,' Ben huffed.

'Okay,' said Abby, stepping in. 'You're right. We should have asked, but you really should read the comments. They all think you're amazing. Seriously.'

Ben stared at Abby like she had just landed from the moon.

'They have no idea what they're talking about,' he said. 'I'm not amazing at all. I can't even hack it in a poxy music class.'

'You are amazing,' declared Charlene. 'You are like the best stay-at-home dad ever.'

'No, I'm not,' said Ben, shaking his head. 'I'm rubbish at it. In fact I'm starting to think dads were just not meant to be mums. I'm going to have to tell Katy she was right after all. Swapping was a stupid idea, because I didn't have a clue how hard it was to look after a baby. I am a failure.'

'Hey, fella,' said Braindead, putting a hand on his shoulder. 'There is no shame in being a failure.'

'You are not a failure,' said Charlene firmly.

'Most definitely not,' added Abby.

'But I don't know what I'm doing,' Ben cried. 'I'm not doing it properly and no-one can tell me what I should be doing. Everyone is telling me different things. None of it makes any sense.'

'Listen to me,' said Charlene, grabbing his shoulders to make him look at her. You can do this and I know exactly the person who can help you.'

'Do you?' asked Ben, wide-eyed at Charlene's commanding tone.

'Are you at home tomorrow?'

'Of course. Where else would I be?'

'Right,' said Charlene. 'I'll bring her round. She is seriously brilliant at babies. She knows absolutely everything.'

'Who is she?' asked Ben.

'You'll see. You won't regret it, I promise. She'll make you into dad of the year in no time.'

'Okay,' Ben sighed. 'I suppose it's worth a try.'

'Cool,' said Charlene, clapping her hands in excitement. 'Tomorrow at yours it is then.'

'Can I come?' added Abby.

CHAPTER THIRTEEN

'OMG,' gasped Charlene the following morning when Ben opened the door to her. 'I have been waiting all my life to have a look inside one of these riverside flats, seriously! No wonder you let Katy go back to work if her job gets you all this!'

She pushed past him down the hallway, and he became aware of a commotion in her wake.

'Look, if you let me park the double buggy here then there will be more than enough room for the other pushchair. Trust me, I can fit this pushchair into the most awkward corners. It comes with the job.'

Ben could not believe his ears or eyes. He'd been waiting with nervous anticipation for Charlene's arrival, even though he suspected it was unlikely that she was actually going to provide the answer to his parenting problems. He'd made a special effort for Charlene's baby guru, whoever she was, and dressed Millie in the dreaded pink as well as actually tidied up a bit. It was all very well for him to live in a pig-sty all day but he really didn't think visitors should be subjected to his poor domestic habits. However, when he peered around the door and could see what was coming, he wished he'd made no effort whatsoever; in fact, he wished he'd fled the country.

'Hello,' said Abby, her cleavage arriving before her head. 'Hope you don't mind me coming along for the ride.'

'Er, yeah,' said Ben, looking petrified. He started to cough as Abby leaned into his personal space, nearly knocking him out with the reek of celebrity perfume.

'Can you get a move on?' said the woman standing behind her in the hall. 'I am carrying twins, you know.' Abby stroked Ben's arm as she slowly pushed past him, following Charlene into the lounge.

'Alison?' said Ben when there was no longer the barrier of another person between them. 'Is that you?' He barely recognised her. She was much slimmer, of course, since the last time he'd seen her, at Charlene's wedding. Alison had been enormous then, as she was on the verge of giving birth to twins, and beside herself with anger at Ben for punching Matthew. He'd never wanted or expected to see her again.

'Here, can you just hold George for one second?' she said, thrusting a baby into his arms whilst she adjusted another one into a sling tied over her shoulder.

This could not be happening, thought Ben. Charlene was supposed to be solving his problems, not bringing into his house the unknowing wife of the man who'd shagged his girlfriend.

'That's better,' Alison said, once she'd got baby number two into position. 'Now, there's no need to worry.' She placed a hand on Ben's flinching shoulder. 'When Charlene said you were in a state and needed my expertise, how could I refuse? But I know what you're thinking . . .'

I very much doubt it, thought Ben.

'I am the last person who should be rushing to your side, given what happened at Charlene's wedding.'

'Look—' Ben started.

'No, listen,' Alison interrupted. 'Matthew explained everything. And I totally forgive you.'

'Really?' Ben couldn't help but exclaim.

'Of course,' said Alison. 'It was just a bit of jealousy, that's all. I understand.'

'You do?' Ben couldn't believe what he was hearing. Could Alison really understand Ben's jealousy of her husband sleeping with his girlfriend? He'd always thought that Alison was slightly weird, but there was weird and there was utterly bonkers.

'I know we are very fortunate with our lovely big house and brand-new car and all that. It's easy to see how you could let a little bit of envy get the better of you, especially when you were drunk.'

Ben was speechless.

'And I know that Matthew has totally forgiven you, so if he can forgive you for leaving him lying in the middle of that dance floor, unconscious, when his wife could have gone into labour at any minute, then so can I.'

'Well, thank you,' said Ben slowly.

'You're welcome,' said Alison. 'Besides, when Charlene told me that Katy had demanded to go back to work leaving you holding the baby, well, what could I do? It is my duty to support my fellow stay-at-home mums-slash-dads.' She plucked George from Ben's arms and strode past him into the lounge.

Ben closed the door behind her, taking in the traumatising sight of three pushchairs outside his front door, including some monstrous contraption made for two babies. How had this happened? Today was supposed to be about regaining control and he already felt like he was fast spinning out of it. He walked into the lounge in a daze.

'She's so got your eyes,' said Abby, gathering Millie from the baby gym in the middle of the floor and clutching her close to her chest. Millie started to cough. *Good grief,* Ben thought, *she's going to stink of cheap perfume.* How would he explain that to Katy? Millie screwed her face up, a telltale sign that she was about to wail. Sure enough, she opened her mouth, her face turned red and she let out a piercing scream.

'Oh, it's okay, baby,' said Abby, bouncing her furiously up and down, much to Millie's distress. 'It's okay now, I'm here.' Millie clearly didn't agree and wailed even louder. Ben stepped forward to take the child from her.

'No,' shouted Abby above the din. 'It's okay, I'll take care of her. You sit down, Ben.'

It was clear that the perfume fog surrounding Abby and Millie was going to do nothing to soothe her, so Ben reached out just as Charlene stepped between the two of them, sweeping Millie out of Abby's arms.

'You don't do it like that, you idiot,' said Charlene. 'Put her on your shoulder like this. Are you watching, Ben? This is how you do it. They like being on shoulders, you see. Means they can see stuff.'

There were no signs that being able to see stuff was having a calming influence on Millie.

'Let me have a go, Charlene,' Ben urged. 'It's not working, is it?'

'No,' said Charlene. 'Like Abby said, we are here to help. This is what you do, put the baby on your shoulder. She'll calm down in a minute, honestly.'

'Charlene,' came a stern voice from behind Ben. 'Give Millie to me now.'

Ben turned to look at Alison. She was holding her arms out with an empty sling across her waist. George and Rebecca were laid out on a neatly folded blanket next to her, clutching teething toys, cooing and dribbling gently. Alison lifted Millie off Charlene's shoulder and laid her in the sling, and as if someone had sprinkled her with contentment dust, she went quiet immediately. Alison reached over to her bag, pulled out a teething ring and handed it to her.

'Don't worry,' she said to Ben. 'Freshly sterilised this morning. Speaking of which, Charlene said you were struggling with your machine. Do you want to show me where it is? Charlene and Abby can be in charge in here, but I will be leaving the door open to keep an eye on you,' she said, as though issuing a warning. 'Kitchen?' she demanded, turning to Ben.

He stood with his mouth open before allowing Alison to steer him around and lead him out the door. Before he knew it, he was standing in front of the steriliser with her whilst Millie contentedly nestled in the sling. He could hear the dulcet tones of Jeremy Kyle drifting out of the living room as Charlene and Abby made themselves at home.

'So,' said Alison, pulling the machine towards her. 'Let's take a look, shall we?'

'No, it's okay,' said Ben, still in a daze. 'I worked it out. I found a video on YouTube.' He couldn't take his eyes off her. Alison was in his kitchen. The real Alison. Matthew's wife. Matthew and Alison, whom he and Katy had vowed never to see again.

'YouTube?' Alison said, turning to him in amazement.

'Yes,' he nodded. 'Melissa from Minnesota was extremely helpful.'

'I very much doubt it,' laughed Alison, shaking her head. 'YouTube is hardly where you should be seeking childcare advice.'

'I know, but I was desperate,' he said.

'But didn't Katy show you how to do all this stuff before she went back to work? I mean, it's all very well wanting to go back to your career and have it all, but not telling you what to do, what her routines are?'

'Routines?' asked Ben

'You know, how she schedules. When does she feed Millie, what time does she go to sleep, what time do you wake her up?'

'Wake her up?'

'Yes.'

'Why on earth would we ever wake her up?'

'If she sleeps too long.'

Ben blew his cheeks out. Alison was even weirder than he remembered. Ben and Katy seemed to spend most of their lives praying that Millie would sleep too long. It never happened.

'But babies can't sleep too long. It's impossible.'

Alison shook her head sadly at him.

'Oh dear,' was all she said.

'What's that supposed to mean?'

'You haven't got Millie into any kind of routine, have you?'

'She's a baby! Babies don't do routines.'

'What's the longest length of time that Millie sleeps?'

'I don't know,' Ben gulped, starting to panic again. 'Depends on what time she goes down at night. If we manage to get her to sleep by half past eight—'

'Half past eight!' gasped Alison.

'What?' asked Ben. 'What does that mean? Is that too early? Too late? See what I mean? Every time I say something about Millie someone looks at me like that. Like I'm an idiot who should not be in charge of a baby. Which of course I am.'

'George and Rebecca are in their cots at seven sharp and sleep right through until six a.m.,' Alison announced. 'Though to be fair, they are quite advanced for their age.'

Never had a piece of information disturbed him so much.

'They sleep through the night? Are you drugging them?'

She gave a self-satisfied smile.

'Routine, routine, routine,' she said, slamming her hand down on the counter top each time she said it. 'Perhaps it's my nature or perhaps it's having twins, but George and Rebecca have been put into a routine since the day they were born. Scheduled sleep times, scheduled play times, scheduled food times, scheduled individual massages, scheduled social time. Their lives are run like clockwork. It's the only way.'

'But how?' muttered Ben in total awe.

'You just have to be disciplined. I know when I leave here at eleven fifteen that we will get home, have lunch, have some scheduled kicking time, then bed for two hours' sleep when I can put my feet up and relax unless I have washing scheduled.'

'Two hours?'

'Yes.'

'Every day?'

'Yes. Did Katy not do any of this?'

'I'm pretty sure she didn't. I think she just winged it,' Ben replied.

'No wonder she wanted to go back to work,' said Alison. 'Left you to pick up the pieces.'

'No,' said Ben firmly. 'It wasn't like that, really. I asked to do it. I wanted to contribute to the family. I thought I could do it. But it's just a lot harder than I realised.' He looked away in shame. He couldn't believe looking after a baby had left him a broken man.

'Come over to our house tomorrow and I'll tell you what to do. Set you up with a schedule. It'll take a while, but once you've got into it, it will make your life so much easier, I promise.'

Ben snapped his head up.

'No,' he said quickly. 'I can't do that.'

Alison reached out and put a very soft and smooth hand over his.

'I know it will be really hard walking into our beautiful home again, but there really is no need to be intimidated.'

'No, no, it's not that,' protested Ben, thinking fast.

'I can help you,' said Alison.

But you don't know what I know screamed through his head. He and Katy had somehow got to a good place regarding her indiscretion with Matthew. It was in the past and they'd moved on.

'I really don't see what choice you have, actually,' said Alison matter-of-factly. 'Charlene said you were on the brink of giving up and telling Katy you couldn't cope. Do you really want to have to do that?'

Ben looked at her. He knew she was right. He'd dug himself a right hole telling Katy he was capable, when he clearly wasn't. But having Alison help him? He couldn't explain that one to Katy.

'You don't have to tell Katy if you don't want to,' said Alison, as though reading his mind. 'If you're too embarrassed to admit you need support.'

He looked down at Millie, who had fallen asleep in Alison's sling. The flat was the calmest it had been in a long time despite the fact there were four babies in residence. Perhaps if he just went over once. Gleaned everything he could from Alison. Matthew would be at work and Katy would be none the wiser. It might make all the difference. Katy would be so impressed.

'If you come at nine-thirty,' said Alison, 'Rebecca and George will be asleep and I can take you through what I do properly. Then Millie can socialise with them for half an hour after they wake up. It will be good for her.'

'And you won't tell Matthew?' he said eventually.

'I don't keep secrets from my husband,' replied Alison firmly.

He certainly keeps them from you, he thought, trying hard not to pull a face.

'If it bothers you that much, I won't tell him it's you,' she conceded. 'I'll tell him I'm helping a stay-at-home dad but won't give him your name.'

Bloody hell, thought Ben. He'd only been back in Alison's company for less than an hour and already the lies were building up.

'Here,' she said, carefully lifting the sling over her head and hooking it over Ben's shoulder without waking Millie. 'You can give it back when you come over tomorrow. I've got to go now so we can get home before George and Rebecca get tired and fall asleep in the car. You remember where we live, don't you?'

Of course I remember, he thought, not daring to move, as Millie looked so content. That was where he'd unearthed the first lie Katy had told him about Matthew.

CHAPTER FOURTEEN

'The M1 was hell,' said Matthew as he strode into the kitchen, dumping a carrier bag on the spotless granite work surface with a loud clanking sound.

'Bugger,' he uttered, opening it up quickly to check he hadn't broken the contents. He pulled out a bottle of red wine then strode over to the sink to hide the unbranded carrier in amongst the rest of the crinkly plastic neatly jammed into a bag collector in the cupboard below. Heaven forbid he'd have to admit to Alison he'd bought wine from a *corner shop*!

There were no lights on in the kitchen apart from the neon strips hidden under the overhead cupboards and the spotlights that shone onto carefully staged artifacts which looked like they belonged in a museum rather than a functioning kitchen. Matthew flicked some switches, instantly shifting the atmosphere away from subtle and moody to brain surgery performance level. Having found a glass, he poured himself a generous slug before standing under a blaze of electric light and taking a huge gulp – which was how Alison found him when she bustled into the kitchen.

'Oh Matthew,' she sighed.

'What?' he shrugged, mentally going through a list of what could have caused such a reception. Too many lights on, drinking alone, drinking mid-week, tabloid newspaper strewn on the counter, standing up, not sitting down, female intuition that could tell the dodgy provenance of his wine, five minutes past the time he said he'd be back, even though he'd rung ahead to say he was going to be late . . . the list could in fact be endless. He held his breath, waiting to see which she would pick.

'What is the point of Auntie Brenda buying us those everyday *red* wine glasses for Christmas if you insist on using the everyday *white* wine glasses? Here, give it to me,' she said, holding her hand out and taking the glass from him. She turned and located a slightly different shaped glass and poured Matthew's wine into it.

'It's such a waste if you don't use them,' she said, handing it back to him before putting the wrong glass into the top of the dishwasher.

Matthew took another large gulp before slumping down on a dining chair behind him and loosening his tie.

'It's been a hell of a day,' he said.

'I know,' replied Alison. 'I have no idea where the time went.'

'Simon dumped a presentation on me forty minutes before a potential new client was due to arrive. Forty minutes!'

'George woke up in a bit of an odd mood. He didn't latch on like he usually does. I do wonder if he might be coming down with something.'

'And do you know why *he* didn't do it? Afterwards he had the gall to tell me that I was much better suited to present, given my experience. I tell you, I nearly lost it with him.'

'Anyway, so I gave him some Calpol and he seemed to be okay, but I've been checking his temperature every four hours just to be sure.'

'I mean, honestly. He knows I wasn't happy when he was brought in above me. He's only been with the company five minutes and then he wants me to do his job for him. Unbelievable.'

'And then Rebecca had a funny poo before she went to bed. You know those ones she used to have when she was tiny. The really pale ones.'

'The ones that oozed out of her nappy. They really were disgusting,' Matthew commented. 'Anyway, I told Ian that I'm going to go to Jim and tell him I'm doing this new guy's job for him. It's just not fair. Then Ian told me how much money he's on. God knows how he found out. Apparently it's twenty grand more than what the job was advertised for internally. It's so fucking typical. The idiots on the board bring in a chap from outside, pay him more and then he expects everyone else to do his work for him. I'm so angry.' He reached for the wine bottle and poured himself another large glass.

'I'm wondering if I should cancel tomorrow now,' Alison said to herself. 'Don't want any more germs coming into the house. We could always leave it a couple of days. See how they both are.'

'Might be wise,' said Matthew. 'But you know what will happen now, don't you? We'll only go and win the frigging business and who will get all the glory? Blooming golden balls, new boy Simon, that's who. Well, over my dead body. I'm telling everyone that he had bugger all to do with that pitch.'

'I'll see if either of them has a temperature in the morning. And if they do I'll tell him not to come round. Better safe than sorry.'

'Is that the new gardener coming to give you a quote?' asked Matthew, picking up the newspaper and spreading it out on the table. 'He can stay outside, can't he? No need for him to come in.'

'Er, no,' said Alison, turning her back on him to get the offending wine glass out of the dishwasher and wash it by hand in the sink. 'No, actually, it's someone I said I'd lend a hand to.'

'Oh,' said Matthew, turning to the sports pages. 'Who's that, then?'

'Oh, just some friend of Charlene's.'

Matthew didn't reply immediately, as he got absorbed in the post-match write-up for the previous evening's game.

'One of Charlene's friends, you say?' he said eventually, still staring at his paper. 'Not one of the ones who did that hideous dance with her at her wedding party?'

'Actually, it's a man,' stated Alison. 'He's a stay-at-home dad.'

'A stay-at-home dad?' said Matthew, looking up.

'Yes,' said Alison, now polishing the wine glass with a clean tea towel, holding his gaze. 'Have you got a clean shirt for tomorrow?'

'I've no idea,' he said, studying his wife closely. 'So have you met this stay-at-home dad person?'

'Of course I have,' she replied, now wiping down the sink with the clean tea towel.

'And?'

'And what?'

'Well, what's he like?'

'He's just a man, Matthew. And he needs help. His partner clearly had no clue so I offered to help him, that's all.'

'Right,' said Matthew, leaning back in his chair and looking slightly perplexed. 'And he's a friend of Charlene's?'

'Yes, that's what I said.'

'And he's coming here?'

'Yes.'

'And you're sure he's okay?'

'Of course.'

'But you don't know him. *I* don't know him.'

'He's fine, honestly. Do you seriously think I would do anything to put me or George and Rebecca in danger? He just needs some help with his baby.'

'Well, I think that's admirable, I really do, Alison, but you're bringing a stranger into our home, and I know he's a friend of Charlene's, but really, that's nothing to go by, is it? You may never get rid of him. He might be some kind of weird stalker. He could be on our doorstep every day wanting more and more help. And what happens if he asks for money? What then? Is that the kind of help he's after? Can you really be sure you know what he wants? He could walk in here, see the stereo, and it could be gone next week. Really, Alison, this isn't like you. You're normally so protective of our home. A stranger, really?'

'Matthew,' she said calmly, 'I really do take umbrage at the fact you don't trust my judgment in this matter.'

'I'm sorry,' said Matthew. 'But you barely know him. Tell you what. Why don't you invite him round at the weekend instead, then at least I'll be in the house as well.'

'I can't do that,' said Alison.

'Why not?'

She gave a big sigh. 'Because he doesn't want his partner to know that he's getting help.'

'He wants to keep it a secret?'

'Yes.'

'So he's going to be here in our house and he's not telling anyone he's coming?' 'Yes.'

'The more you tell me about this bloke, the more dodgy it sounds. I'm not sure I'm very comfortable with this.'

'Oh, for goodness' sake,' said Alison, throwing the tea towel in the sink. 'Look, he made me promise I wouldn't tell you, so if I tell you now, you have to promise not to tell anyone else, okay?'

'What?' cried Matthew. 'What do you mean?'

'Just promise me you won't tell anyone.'

'Okay. If I must.'

'It's Ben,' she stated, putting her hands on her hips. 'You know, as in Ben and Katy.'

Matthew did well not to drop his wine glass or pass out.

'Katy's decided to go back to work and left Ben holding the baby, quite literally if you ask me,' Alison continued. 'Didn't I tell you she wasn't maternal? Anyway, Charlene called and said Ben was struggling – desperate, actually – and needed some help. Would I go round with her and get him on the right path? Well, what could I say? I could hardly leave him in the lurch, could I? So we went round there this morning, and, well, it was pitiful really. He had no idea what he was doing. That poor child must have been dragged up so far. Of course I offered to share my expertise. But Ben doesn't want Katy to know, for some reason, and he made me promise not to tell you. I think he probably thinks you haven't forgiven him for punching you, but I tried to tell him you are a better man than that and you totally understand his motivation and, well, it's all water under the bridge now, isn't it?'

Matthew stared at his wife, his mouth open.

'Isn't it?' she demanded.

'Isn't what?' was all Matthew could muster.

'Water under the bridge.'

'What's water under the bridge?' he asked slowly.

'Ben punching you – you've forgiven him, haven't you? Honestly, Matthew, if you could see him now. I felt sorry for him, I really did. 'I don't know how Katy sleeps at night knowing she's left him to fend for himself when he's no idea what he's doing.'

'Katy's gone back to work?' Matthew asked.

'Yes, that's what I've been saying. Aren't you listening? Ben needs us, Matthew. That's why he's coming round here tomorrow, so I can teach him the basics.'

'Ben is coming here!' stated Matthew, not so much to Alison but to the world in general. Someone must realise what a ludicrous thing this was to be happening.

'Yes, as long as George and Rebecca aren't running a temperature.'

Matthew found himself praying for one of his children to have a temperature before he stopped himself. There must be other ways of preventing this potentially cataclysmic meeting. And what was Ben thinking, accepting help from Alison? It didn't make any sense. He'd have thought that Ben wouldn't want to be within a hundred miles of Matthew, let alone come to his house with . . . oh my God. Matthew fought hard to keep his face in a normal pose when all he felt like doing was allowing it to crumple into a million pieces. He'd be bringing the baby. Katy's baby. The baby that had nearly turned all of their worlds upside down.

'I'll just go and kiss George and Rebecca good-night,' he squeaked, not trusting his reactions any longer.

'Just check how hot they are, will you?' Alison shouted after him. 'Put your hand on their forehead and see if it feels too hot.'

Matthew wasn't listening. He was already half-way up the stairs and heading for the master bed-room. Once inside he went into the en-suite, which reminded him of a prison cell due to its matching wall and floor tiles and its absence of any personality whatsoever. He sat on the pointless bidet and put his head in his hands. This couldn't be happening again.

CHAPTER FIFTEEN

'How anyone can work dressed like that, I have no idea,' Daniel muttered to Katy as he watched two women walk across the reception of Wholesome Cereals wearing white overalls and hairnets. 'Hairnets? One of the great unanswered questions of our time.'

'Hygiene,' Katy muttered back distractedly.

'In what way could that ever be hygienic? Hygienic would be a rubber swimming hat. Nothing gets through those babies, believe me. I kept my cash under mine at Jimmy and Chris's wedding pool party in Vegas last year. Dry as a bone. Now that wouldn't have happened if I'd been wearing a hairnet, would it?'

Katy said nothing. She wasn't really listening.

Daniel picked a thread off his Armani trousers.

'And as for this reception, it has to be the most depressing place on earth – seriously. How many shades of biscuit can you get in one room? I can feel every drop of joie de vivre literally seeping out of my shoes the minute I step onto the hideous carpet. Why, Katy, why?'

Katy gave a massive sigh. She really didn't give a damn, to be honest. Leaving Millie that morning had somehow proved to be the hardest ever. All the euphoria of her spectacularly successful initial return to work had melted away and now she was back to feeling incredibly guilty that she wasn't the one staying at home to look after her daughter. Besides which, Ben was barely speaking to her. He just grunted and told her not to worry about anything. A statement that was guaranteed to make her worry. Daniel jabbed her in the ribs to point out the shiny black blob of chewing gum curved over the armrest of the sagging settee they were sitting on and she realised he would not rest until she engaged in conversation with him about the state of their current location.

'I guess the factory and this building were built a long time before they knew they needed a swanky reception to impress the likes of some shallow person who draws pretty pictures like you,' she shrugged.

'Really, you can go back on maternity leave now. Your insults have been a novelty so far, but today they're just insults.'

'Maybe I would go back on maternity leave, if I could,' Katy muttered.

'What?' exclaimed Daniel. 'And miss coming to glamorous outposts like this?' He swept his arm round in a grand gesture. 'Isn't this what you were dreaming of when you were scraping baby poo off the floor?'

'Actually, no,' Katy admitted, slumping her chin down on her hand, 'but I just didn't expect to feel like this.'

'Please don't make me do it, Katy, I beg you.'

'Make you do what?'

'Ask you how you are coping without having a pooing, weeing, burping, yakking machine attached to your thigh? If Lynn comes into a meeting once more and gives you that *"we working mums are in this together and isn't it soooo hard without our babies attached to us and no-one else understands"* look, I might have to throttle the pair of you. And if she tells me once more she has to leave at four fifty-five p.m. precisely because it costs her a trillion pounds a nanosecond if she is late picking up at nursery, I will throw her out of the window.' Daniel took a breath then jabbed his finger at Katy. 'It's your choice, my girl. Please don't allow it to affect my working life. And I know about difficult choices. Being gay isn't a choice, but choosing to be out and proud is. It's the lifestyle decision I have made but I don't expect the rest of the world to let me go home early because of it.' He leaned back in his chair and folded his arms resolutely.

'Bloody hell,' said Katy, 'where did that come from?'

'It's just that all too often people make choices and expect the rest of the world to make allowances. I don't think that's fair.'

'Mmmm,' she said, settling her chin on her hand again.

'So why the face that looks like you woke up on Christmas morning and discovered Santa has left you a knitting pattern?' Daniel asked eventually when Katy showed no interest in making polite chitchat.

'I have no idea what is going on,' she said, turning to look at him with a look of bewilderment.

'No change there then,' he replied.

'Seriously,' said Katy. 'It's like there is some whole parallel universe going on whilst I'm at work and Ben refuses to tell me anything. He just says "fine" when I ask him how his day's been, nothing else. And . . . and weird things keep happening.'

'Like what?'

'Well, first it was the steriliser going missing.'

'The steriliser?'

'Yes. I got home on my first day back at work and it wasn't there. It had totally vanished. And it's not as though it's a small thing that can be easily mislaid. It stands out a mile.'

'Don't they do coordinated baby equipment to blend in with the sage and taupe colour scheme in your kitchen? asked Daniel.

'No, they don't. It's blue and white.'

'Hideous,' Daniel shuddered. 'So did you ask Ben where it was?'

'Well, he went to the pub as soon as I got home and then when I saw him later he was so defensive about his day I didn't dare ask him in case he thought I was accusing him of something. But when I got up the next morning, there it was. Back in its place as if it had been there all the time.'

'Mmmm, the case of the missing steriliser. I can see why that has turned your world upside down. I have no idea how you are sleeping at night if you have random domestic appliances vanishing and reappearing apparently of their own volition.'

'But it's not just that,' said Katy. 'I got home last night, and . . .' She paused and blew her cheeks out.

'And what?' demanded Daniel. 'Had your hairbrush been moved? Oh my God, it's a crisis.'

'Daniel, I could smell perfume when I walked in.'

'Which brand?'

'I don't know. Why's that relevant?'

'Gives us scale, of course. Cheap stuff and I think you can relax, we can deal with that. Expensive designer brand and you may not be able to compete.'

'Why do I ever share my problems with you, tell me again?'

'You love my clinical honesty.'

'So you agree then that Ben has already installed another woman?'

'I didn't say that. Answer the question. Cheap or expensive perfume?'

'Cheap, definitely cheap.'

'Was the flat tidy?'

'Well, funny you should say that. I did notice that it was definitely tidier than normal.'

'Well, isn't it obvious then?'

'No.'

'He's employed a cleaner.'

'We can't afford a cleaner. Besides, there was something even more worrying. When I turned on the telly it was on ITV. How weird is that?'

'You turned the telly on and it was on one of the most watched channels in the UK. Average thirty percent market share at any given time, rising to forty percent in daytime. Do you never listen to the boring presentations the media guys do?'

'But this is Ben. He's not average. If he is in control of the TV he watches sports channels, period. Daytime ITV? Never in a month of Sundays.'

'Perhaps he put something on for Millie.'

'*This Morning, Loose Women*? I don't think so. It's just not him is it?'

'So let's examine the evidence,' said Daniel. 'A vanishing steriliser, an unreliable level of tidiness, cheap perfume and ITV.'

'What does it mean?' Katy demanded.

'Haven't a clue,' replied Daniel. 'Just ask him. Put yourself out of this misery. I can't bear to work with someone with a face like that.'

'I asked him if he'd had any visitors and he said no, which is clearly a lie, and he was very vague about what he did all day.'

'Well, if you're convinced he's lying then that is a whole different ball game.'

'But why would he, and who is it?'

'Do you have any cheap-looking neighbours?'

'Not really. They're all career couples or dull, single auditors.'

'Auditors are always single,' stated Daniel.

'Goes with the job,' Katy agreed.

'Anyone shown an unlikely interest in him recently? It's bound to be someone you know.'

Katy started to shake her head then slowly turned to face Daniel.

'Abby!' she exclaimed.

'Abby?' Daniel echoed. 'What kind of woman is an Abby? You cannot go down to an *Abby*.'

'She's a friend of Charlene's. We met her at the registry office. The cheeky cow invited him on a night out under my nose. I couldn't believe it.'

'Well, if we're only dealing with an Abby, I reckon you've got it licked. You could beat an Abby in a showdown any day.'

'Hang on a minute, I'm not sure it is her yet, and I'm not even sure what *it* is. I can hardly go steaming in with wild accusations based on a whiff of perfume and a TV channel.'

'True', it sounds a bit thin. Supporting evidence is what you need. How are things between you and Ben generally? Have you noticed any changes in behaviour?'

'We've just had a baby, Daniel. Everything has changed.'

'I know, I know, and obviously the lead-up to the birth was fairly traumatic, what with the whole sex-with-Matthew thing.'

'Thanks for bringing that up.'

'You're welcome. Do you think that's it? Is he getting his own back for the whole sex-with-Matthew thing?'

'Please do not say sex and Matthew again. That's all behind us now.'

'Is it really? You all back to normal now?'

'As I said. As normal as we can be given that we have a baby.'

'And sex?'

'Oh, don't you bloody start.'

'I'm sorry, but I have to ask if we are trying to establish the likelihood of your fiancé having an affair.'

'No, the sex is not back to normal, but I would like to reiterate, I have just had a baby!'

'Alright, I can tell it's a touchy subject. So would you say you were having sex slightly less than normal, less than normal, much less than normal, or are the cobwebs forming?'

Katy looked away.

'Last time?'

'A few months ago.'

'*Months!* Shit, Katy.'

'We've been busy, okay? Stuff's happened. There's never been the right time.'

'There has never been the right time to have sex with your boyfriend to stop him having sex with Abby?' Daniel shrieked.

'Shhhhhhhhh,' she muttered as a crowd of men in boiler suits walked through reception, their ears pricking up at the man in the posh suit shrieking the word 'sex' every five minutes.

'He's not having sex with Abby,' said Katy firmly under her breath.

'But what about the missing steriliser?'

'What's that got to do with it?'

'I've no idea, but you haven't stopped harping on about it since we got here.'

'I wish I'd never mentioned it now.'

'You and me both,' huffed Daniel.

They fell into silence. Daniel got up and strode across the reception so he could go and turn his nose up at the framed photos of employee of the month.

'So what happened in November and December, do you think?' he whispered when he sat back down.

'What are you talking about now?'

'There's no employee of the month for November and December. Why's that?'

'I don't know and I don't really care,' she replied.

'You can't just *forget* to do employee of the month, can you? You have to do it monthly or else it makes a mockery of the entire thing.'

'Guess so.'

'I mean, the message it sends is that you are pre-pared to share with everyone who walks through here that not one of your employees was deemed worthy of employee of the month for two whole months. Either that or the management just could not be bothered to award it. Either way it looks bad. Wouldn't you say it looks bad?'

'If you say so.'

'They shouldn't introduce these things if they can't keep them up.'

'You're right, I suppose.'

'You know what you need?' said Daniel, putting an arm round her drooping shoulders.

'What?' Katy sniffed.

'A night out at Cocktail Emporium with Ben. A couple of Dang Dang Whisky Slider Bombs, and to be honest I could literally shag anything.'

'Are you suggesting that I have to get Ben drunk for him to have sex with me?'

'Er, yep.'

'Daniel!'

'Any better ideas?' he asked. 'Look, you've been through a lot, the pair of you, and you just need to break the seal. Get it over with and you'll be fine. Get out there as Katy and Ben, not the personality drained baby monitors you've become.'

'But it's not that straightforward,' she protested.

'Why isn't it?'

'Well, we need a babysitter for a start.'

'I'll babysit.'

'You?'

'Yes, me.'

'You hate babies.'

'I do not,' protested Daniel. 'I just couldn't abide one of my own.'

'You wouldn't know what to do.'

'You can leave me instructions, can't you? It can't be that hard. Dealing with brand manager cretins every day is hard. Spending time with someone who is not blinkered by social norms and conventions sounds like a dream come true to me.'

'Are you sure?'

'Yes. Now stop looking at me like that. Tell me a night and I'll book you a table with Carlos.'

'Carlos?'

'Owner of the Cocktail Emporium. Goodness me, how long have you been out of the loop if you don't know who Carlos is?'

'Too long.'

'Clearly. Dang Dang Whisky Slider Bombs,' he reminded her, patting her knee as the Brand Manager for Crispy Bix emerged out of the lift at the far end of the reception. 'Known to cure all ills. Physical, mental and sexual. We'll have you back in the saddle in no time. Louise!' he said, leaping up and embracing the mousy-haired twenty-something in a bear hug. 'You are like the kiss from a rainbow in this world of mediocrity. A bowl of cereal with lukewarm milk awaits us in the boardroom, no doubt? Shall we?' He swivelled to offer Louise his arm, which she took, throwing a petrified look at Katy. It was going to be a difficult meeting, thought Katy.

CHAPTER SIXTEEN

'Gents' toilets. Now!' demanded Matthew as he strode up to Ian's desk. He turned on his heel and walked off before Ian had the chance to respond in any way. It was still only eight-thirty and the office was virtually empty, apart from the people who were keen to get ahead on emails before the day started, those escaping the morning hell of getting children off to school, or those surprised by an unusually quick drive into work, leaving them wondering what to do with the extra twenty minutes added to their day. Ian was in the latter category and had been sending crude texts to Becki before Matthew claimed Ian's bonus time for his own.

He finally caught up with Matthew on the second-floor landing of the five-storey building they worked in.

'Fifth floor,' said Matthew grimly, striding past the toilets right next to them and making for the stairs.

Bloody hell, thought Ian. Whatever it was that Matthew needed to talk to him about, it was serious. The fifth floor was occupied by the senior partners and board members. The gents up there were rarely used, as it was considered that once you got that senior, having to pee next to another human being was below you, and thus many of the offices had en-suites. Your very own toilet was a massive status symbol at Hearst & Wycombe, generally more sought after than a corner office. It did, however, mean that the toilets on this floor were one of the few places you could achieve privacy in the building. Useful for clandestine meetings, or if you were Ian, somewhere to have a quick kip if you'd been up all night experiencing the wonders of Becki.

'To what do we owe the pleasure of a trip to the fifth-floor toilets this morning?' he enquired, watching Matthew go straight to the sinks, lean both hands on the surface and take several deep breaths.

'I am so fucked,' he breathed eventually.

'I thought we had this out the other day,' Ian said. 'You're not fucked. That's the whole problem. Seriously, I'm buying you a waterbed for your birthday.'

Matthew turned and faced him.

'You don't understand,' he said. 'It's happening all over again.'

'You look pale, mate. What's happening again?"

'Katy.'

'*Katy?* You are kidding me, right?'

'No,' said Matthew, shaking his head as if he couldn't believe it himself. 'I'm not.'

'So? What? You've seen her again? She's dumping the baby on you? What?'

'Worse than that. It's Alison.'

'Alison! Fuck me, she knows, doesn't she? She found out. You are screwed for a shag now, mate, I'm telling you.'

'No, she doesn't know. But she's seeing Ben. Remember Ben? Katy's boyfriend.'

'Seeing Ben?' repeated Ian. 'Are you sure? How do you know?'

'She told me.'

'What kind of seeing?'

'Just seeing. Well, I think it's just seeing. Katy's gone back to work, so Ben's staying home to look after the baby, apparently. Alison caught up with him somehow through the antenatal class and he's only gone and asked her to help him.'

'Help him do what?'

'Look after the baby!'

'Whose baby?'

'His baby, of course.'

Ian faltered then decided to plough in.

'Alison's helping Ben look after the baby that could be your baby?'

Matthew raised his eyes from the floor where he had been mindlessly gazing at the grey grouting. The two men stared at each other. The door behind Ian swung open and a cleaner popped her head around the door.

'How long will you be?' she barked. 'I need to get this floor done by nine.'

'Could be a while,' said Ian, not taking his eyes off Matthew. 'I'd skip 'em' today, if I were you. We won't tell anyone.'

'Right you are,' she replied. 'I'll leave the Cleaning in Progress sign outside for a bit whilst I go out for a fag. Just don't fall over it when you come out.'

'No worries.' Ian threw her a casual wave. He and Matthew continued to stare at each other in silence until they heard the door swing shut.

'I mean what on earth is Ben thinking, asking Alison of all people to help him,' said Matthew raking his hands through his hair. 'How could he be so stupid?'

'So hang on a minute,' said Ian. 'I have to say, I've lost track a bit, this is so complicated. Let me get this right. Ben knows you shagged Katy?'

'Yes,' confirmed Matthew.

'So the only person who doesn't know is Alison?'

'Yes. That's why none of this makes any sense. Ben hates me. The last time I saw him he punched me. Why would he willingly walk back into our lives?'

'Revenge?'

'Seriously!' exclaimed Matthew. 'Come on. We're grown-ups. People don't do stuff like that. Do they?'

'Well, I've never met Ben. Do you think he'd seduce Alison just to get his own back on you?'

'No!' said Matthew, shaking his head violently. 'He may be a lot of things, but I can't see him doing that.'

'Mmm,' said Ian, deep in thought. 'So what kind of guy is he, then?'

'Well, he's young. A lot younger than Katy. Maybe late twenties. He was working as a PE teacher at Castle Hill but clearly he's jacked that in. He was just your typical, sport-obsessed kind of guy. Not a lot more to him, really.'

'So young, fit . . . good-looking?'

'Shit . . . how should I know? He's a bloke.'

'Muscly?'

'I've no idea. I never spent much time looking at his body.'

'And how did he get on with Alison?'

'Enough, Ian. We are not going down this road. Alison and Ben together is ridiculous. Total opposites. You know Alison. She likes the finer things in life and she likes things just so. Ben's happy as a pig in shit with a tinny in front of *Match of the Day*.'

'So he'd be Alison's bit of rough on the side, then?'

'No,' said Matthew. 'If you'd met Ben you'd understand. Can we just drop this angle, please?'

'Okay. Up to you.' Ian blew his cheeks out. 'So what exactly are they doing together?'

Matthew shrugged.

'He's going round there today, apparently. She's going to do him a schedule so he can work out how to look after the baby.'

'Shouldn't Katy be doing that?'

'You'd think, wouldn't you?'

'Do you think she knows?'

'No way,' said Matthew. 'She wouldn't let Ben within a million miles of us, I'm sure. He's doing this behind her back.'

'But why?'

'I don't know!' cried Matthew, turning round and kicking the sink cabinet. 'I've been up half the night trying to work it out and none of it makes sense.'

Ian blew his cheeks out again.

'Amazing how everything comes back to sex, isn't it?' he muttered.

'How do you work that one out?'

'Well, what I mean is that you had sex with Katy, she got pregnant, and it looks like that random shag will haunt you for the rest of your life. You had sex with Alison, she didn't get pregnant and now you're not having sex at all. However, you now have sexy toy boy entering the fray, which either might reignite the juices, or worse still, allow the whole random shag thing to come out, meaning no-one will be having sex *ever* again! I return to your initial statement: that lot would seem to indicate that indeed you are 'fucked'. But actually not, if you see what I mean.'

'What the hell do I do?' begged Matthew. 'You have to help me.'

'Well, I would have thought that was obvious, isn't it?'

'No!' cried Matthew. 'That's the whole point, *nothing* is obvious.'

'As I've been telling you constantly for the past few weeks, you need to have sex with Alison. Simple as that.'

Matthew's mouth dropped open.

'But . . .'

'But nothing. Woo her, seduce her, pull out the big guns, spend money, whatever switches her on, do whatever it takes, but you need to get back in that bedroom together, pronto. She needs distracting from that hunk of male testosterone, then telling that she hasn't got time to be helping every waif and stray that walks through the door. If she's got time to help out a father in need, then that's you, not Ben. Yeah?'

Matthew stared back at Ian for some time before he started to nod.

'Yeah,' he said slowly. 'I see what you're saying. What's she doing wasting our precious time on him?'

'That's it,' said Ian. 'Get back in charge of that family, kick Ben into touch and it's happy families all the way, I'm telling you.'

'I think you might be right,' Matthew said.

'I'm always right. Why is that you always come to Uncle Ian when you land yourself in it like this?'

'Honestly, I have absolutely no idea. It must be something to do with the fact you have made such a success of your own marriage, I guess.'

'All I can wish for is that you learn from my mistakes, my friend.'

'Why is that not reassuring in the slightest?' Matthew tugged down his jacket and strode purpose-fully out of the gents' toilets. Next moment there was a crash as he fell over the *Cleaning in Progress* sign.

CHAPTER SEVENTEEN

Ben winced as he heard the scrunch of gravel under the car tyres. Nothing heralded your arrival at a house brimming with wealth and success more than the sound of a deep gravel drive. He pulled up outside the glossy black door guarded by pillars and topiary and switched the engine off. It felt like a lifetime ago when he'd last sat there following his hasty exit from the dinner party, having spotted that Matthew had an identical tattoo to Katy. It had been a stormy night and he remembered watching two hanging baskets sway precariously on wrought-iron hooks as he waited for Katy to make her excuses and join him to explain herself. She'd admitted they'd been a couple, as teenagers, as they sat there with the wind howling around them. She'd explained that Matthew didn't want Alison to know, as she was prone to jealousy. He'd accepted the explanation and moved on, right up until the hurt had exploded inside him on discovering they'd slept together just a few months previously. He'd never felt like that before. He was traumatised at how much pain her indiscretion had caused him. Finding out she'd slept with Matthew had woken something up inside his twenty-something laid-back self. Made him understand he had to grow up, admit he had feelings and deal with them. It had shocked him into realising that he was in love with her. A situation he'd never had to address before.

Millie was gurgling in her car seat in the back, oblivious to the history that was playing through his mind as he revisited the place where he'd sat nearly six months ago at the moment when his life had started to unravel. They'd got through it, though, hadn't they? They'd kept it together, and here he was now, engaged to Katy and the father of a beautiful baby girl. So what was he doing here taking this risk of blowing it all up again? This was wrong. This was a massive mistake. He scratched a non-existent itch on his head, trying to work out how on earth he had got himself into this position. He unclipped his seat belt and leapt out of the car, leaving Millie safe inside. Time to put a stop to this before it got out of control.

He knocked firmly then took a step back from the door. He cleared his throat, glancing back at Millie to make sure she was okay. Half a minute and he would be back in the car and on his way back home, having thanked Alison for her kind offer of support but he'd decided it wasn't fair on her.

He heard the clicking of several locks and then there stood Alison, a screaming baby in one arm whilst wails could be heard coming from somewhere behind her.

'You're late,' she said, thrusting wailing baby number one into his arms. 'You'll have to wait whilst I feed them now. Just hold on to Rebecca whilst I get George. If you go in the kitchen there's a rug with some toys on it.'

Ben stared down at Rebecca in his arms. *Why me?* he mouthed. He turned to get Millie out of the back seat, which involved an interesting balancing manoeuvre with Rebecca, then he hustled the two babies inside, slamming the door behind him.

He thought the kitchen must be at the back, since that was the only room he hadn't been in when they'd been there for dinner. They'd eaten some minute excuses for starters in the twenty-five-foot lounge listening to Matthew's amazing stereo system. The main course had been served in a highly civilised manner in the dining room until Matthew had chucked boiling coffee down his shirt, forcing him to remove it rapidly and reveal the incriminating tattoo.

He peered behind the half-open door to find an immaculate kitchen which displayed none of the chaos he'd left their own kitchen in earlier. Surfaces were clutter-free and domestic appliances appeared coordinated, rather than like they'd landed from Mars and no-one knew quite what to do with them. Even the laptop that sat open on the large island in the middle of the kitchen looked like a styled accessory rather than a functional but untidy necessity. No messy wires spewed out of its backside. Alison clearly liked her machines charged and free from entrails. The only randomness that appeared to exist in this kitchen was a chopping board laid out with a carrot, a peeler and a small vegetable knife, along with an ice cube tray. Perhaps Alison was following a recipe on the internet, although what could involve a carrot and an ice-cube tray he dreaded to think. Something concocted by that Heston Blumenthal, no doubt, who annoyed Ben intensely with his unnecessary desire to mess about with perfectly good food.

A charming seating area had been created next to the large bay window. A rose-covered sofa with coordinated scatter cushions (although clearly never scattered) stood on a large, furry rug complete with pastel-coloured baby gym and several toys. Ben put Millie's car seat down on the floor and carefully laid Rebecca under the baby gym. Her arm leapt out and bashed a plastic ring dangling above her and all was quiet. He heaved a sigh of relief. Someone else's baby successfully undamaged whilst in his care. Now it was time to make a getaway.

'I thought you were coming for nine-thirty.' Alison had arrived back in the kitchen with George on her shoulder.

'Well, er, it took me a while to find clean clothes for Millie and then I couldn't remember where I'd left the baby wipes.'

'Rule one. Always pack the nappy bag the night before for the following day,' said Alison. 'You can do it after they've gone to bed so you're not trying to look after them and find all the necessary equipment you might need at the same time.'

'Right,' said Ben. 'Yes, good idea. Look, Alison, I don't think I should be taking up your time like this, really.' He glanced over to her then hurriedly looked away as he realised that she had settled herself on the sofa and was busy breastfeeding George. 'Oh God, sorry. Look, I'll go, this really isn't a good idea,' he gasped, picking Millie's car seat up.

'Put that car seat down,' Alison commanded.

Ben put it down. How could you not follow the demands of a mother mid-breastfeed?

'Go and look at that laptop,' she said, pointing to the computer on the kitchen island.

He didn't know what to do. He couldn't look at her again to plead his escape: he might see her breast. He trudged over to the laptop, trying to plan his next move.

'I've done you a simplified spreadsheet of our timetable,' she said as he looked down at the immaculate grid on the screen. 'It's colour-coded. Green for feeding time, red for playing time, yellow for sleeping time, purple for activities outside the home and blue for Daddy time.' Ben let his mouth drop open just slightly. 'That gives you something basic to aim at so that you can feel in control of everything. Makes life so much easier. Then I thought for today, because you mentioned that Millie might be teething and you're terrified of the whole weaning thing, that I'd just show you how to purée basic vegetables and then freeze them so that you have them readily available when the time is right.'

Ben couldn't help but look up at Alison in awe, breastfeeding no longer the most amazing thing she was currently achieving.

'You are a machine,' he declared in admiration.

'What do you mean?' she blinked back whilst unhitching George and tossing him over her shoulder to burp.

'How do you do all this?' he continued, looking at her as though she was some alien from another planet. 'How do you *know* how to do all this?'

'You just have to be organised, that's all,' she replied, rubbing George's back gently. 'Bring the laptop over here and I'll talk you through it. You can get Millie out and put her down next to Rebecca.'

It was all too seductive. It was peaceful, it was quiet, and it was calm. Alison must be some kind of baby whisperer, since her kids seemed to do exactly what they were supposed to when they were supposed to. That's what he wanted. That's what he needed. Before he could stop himself, he unclipped Millie and laid her down next to a gurgling Rebecca then lifted the laptop from the kitchen counter and sat down at a respectable distance from Alison's feeding breast and allowed her to talk him through the ins and outs of her colour-coded baby chart.

'. . . and so if you do it that way, you see, it means that on most days you should get at least one hour to yourself, which of course is of enormous benefit to you. Means that when you're dealing with those difficult times, when they cry for no reason whatsoever, you are so much more relaxed and able to deal with it. Now I want you to tell me if you can remember the three most important things you need to do in that forty-five-minute morning nap time?' asked Alison a little while later, when she had finished going through the chart and Rebecca had also had her feed.

Ben smiled to himself. Alison may not be a teacher but her background in human resources and training had taught her all the necessary tools on how to drill knowledge into other people. Repeating instructions back to him was a standard technique he used in his PE classes to get even the densest of students to listen.

'Sterilising, shower, change of clothes prepared,' replied Ben.

'Excellent,' said Alison. 'And what do you do after Millie has had her forty-five-minute nap in the morning?'

'Wake her up. If she sleeps longer she won't sleep at lunchtime and I won't get to play online poker.'

'If that's what you choose to do with your Daddy time, so be it. I've been using my Mummy time printing photographs and putting them in an album of their first year.'

'Good for you,' said Ben, entirely confident he wouldn't be following suit. 'But what happens if she doesn't sleep at all in the morning?' he asked, feeling slightly sceptical that Millie would be the type of magic baby Alison appeared to have cultivated.

'Well, to be perfectly honest, because Millie hasn't been following a routine since day one, it will be a bit of a struggle to start with. You just have to be firm and stick to it, no matter what, and eventually it will fall into place.

'But what if it doesn't?'

'Ben, *you* are in control. Remember that. *You* can make this happen. Take it day by day and set yourself some small objectives first.'

'I know, but this is not a rational human being we are talking about. This is a baby who wouldn't understand a small objective if it came down in a baby bouncer twirling dummies around its head.'

'Well,' said Alison, getting up and carefully folding a muslin before putting it back in the nappy bag. 'If you think there is a better way, then you do it that way.'

Ben tapped his fingers furiously on his knee. He had no other way and she knew it.

She bent to pick up George and put him in a baby swing to the side of the sofa. 'You ready for a bit of action, Georgie?' she cooed, flicking a switch on the top, causing the swing to sway gently backwards and forwards whilst emitting an irritating tune. 'So,' she said, standing up with her hands on her hips. 'Shall we proceed to weaning? Let's purée, shall we?'

Millie was happily chewing on some sort of ring and smiled up at him. Three babies, all contented. Unbelievable. He almost daren't move in case he set one off. He'd watch the carrot-cooking thing then he'd go. He'd learned enough to set himself up. Even having not put any of it into practice, he already felt more in control than he ever had. Perhaps there was something to be said for Alison's way.

'So you sit on that stool there in front of me,' said Alison, as he approached the island where she had gathered her essential items for the cookery demonstration. 'Then Millie can see you and you can see her.' Alison was busy washing her hands in the shiniest sink Ben had ever seen. Not just rinsing, really washing, including attacking her nails with a scrubbing brush. After this ritual was completed she reached for an apron out of a tall cupboard and wrapped the pretty floral number, which matched the sofa, around her. She cleared her throat and placed her hands on the bench, assuming a serious expression. Ben giggled.

'What's so funny?' she demanded.

'You,' he replied. 'You're taking it so seriously.'

'Do you want me to help you or not?' she threw back.

'Yes, of course I do,' he said, feeling instantly bad. 'But . . . but we can have a bit of a laugh, can't we?'

'Not sure what there is to laugh about when it comes to the nutrition of your child, Ben.'

'Of course, you're right, Alison. From now on I will have my serious face on.' He frowned back at her. 'And I will not mention that the carrot you have selected for this demonstration is unusually deformed in a manner that makes it appear to be growing a penis.'

'It's organic,' said Alison, without missing a beat or smiling.

'An organic penis. I see,' replied Ben. 'So no supplements have been added in order promote growth?' he enquired.

'Do you have to be so juvenile?' asked Alison.

'Do you have to be so serious about *everything*?' asked Ben. 'Who can take a carrot growing a penis seriously?'

'I can,' said Alison, picking up the carrot and slicing off the orange protrusion in one fell swoop. 'Do I have your attention now?'

Ben sat with his legs pressed tightly together, screwing his face up.

'I think so,' he said in a very high-pitched voice.

'So, first things first, do you have the necessary equipment?' asked Alison.

'I thought I had until you started waving that dangerous weapon about.'

Alison gave a big sigh and raised her eyes to the ceiling.

'I will not continue until you take this seriously,' she announced.

'Sorry, sorry, I am now in the zone, I promise,' said Ben. 'Hit me with it.'

'Good. So let's start again with equipment. You will obviously need a knife and peeler, but do you have a vegetable steamer?'

'A what?'

'A steamer. One of these,' she said, reaching behind her to take from the stove top what looked like a very tall saucepan.'

'I have never seen one of those before in my life,' he declared proudly.

'Well, I suggest you buy one. Order one online this afternoon.'

'Right, okay,' he nodded.

'Do you think you should write this down?' she enquired.

Ben looked at her in panic. Clearly the whole carrot cooking thing was not going to be as easy as he'd envisaged. He'd need to remember stuff, domestic stuff, which had never been his forte. He stared at the steamer, trying to commit it to memory, then he came up with a brilliant idea.

'Can I film all this on my phone? That way I won't forget what to buy and how to use it.' He was already reaching into his pocket to pull out his phone.

'Er, well,' said Alison, her hands instantaneously flying up to her hair. 'You can, but I'll need to just check my hair and face first.' She was already untying her apron and dashing towards the door.

'Really?' exclaimed Ben. 'No-one's going to see it. Just me.'

Alison paused in the doorway, clearly in a quandary.

'No, I can't go on film looking like this,' she decided. 'Watch the babies,' she yelled over her shoulder before she disappeared.

A few short minutes and Alison was back in the room complete with an embroidered clip in her hair and a dab of lipstick. She had the grace to blush slightly at her vanity as she resumed her spot behind the counter and retied her pinny, not looking at Ben until everything was in place. Ben had no idea what was going on but decided to just go with it. If she needed to be wearing lipstick whilst being filmed cooking carrots, then so be it.

'You may begin,' she said, giving him a slight nod.

Luckily Ben realised she meant filming and he picked up his phone from the counter, flicked the screen a couple of times and then held it up and shouted, 'Action.'

'Good morning,' said Alison with a slight nod and a smile. 'I am about to demonstrate the most efficient way to steam and purée carrots for your newborn once you start to wean them.'

Ben fought very hard to prevent himself from cracking up. Alison was doing an unbelievably professional job; it just seemed ridiculously over the top.

'The equipment you will need for this is a peeler, a knife, a chopping board, a steamer like the one we have here, a food processor or hand-held blender if you have one, and finally an ice-cube tray.'

'Carrots?' shouted out Ben.

'I'm sorry?' said a flustered Alison.

'Carrots,' said Ben. 'Don't you need carrots?'

Alison smiled sweetly, directly into the phone.

'Very funny, Ben,' she said sarcastically. 'So, I have chosen only to feed my children organic vegetables, as these are not grown using any harmful pesticides or fertilisers.'

'And they grow their own penises, which improves any vegetable, in my eyes.'

'Now, as you can see, I have chopped the penis off this particular carrot in order to be able to use the vegetable peeler and to prove a point that penises are always easily removed. Once you have peeled two or three large carrots then you can slice them so they steam quicker.'

'Do you cut circles, Alison, or sticks when you are slicing carrots?' Ben asked.

'Batons, Ben,' replied Alison, and she swiftly dealt with the carrots. 'They are called batons. No-one cuts circles any more.'

'But does it matter?' asked Ben. 'You're going to bash them to a pulp any minute, aren't you?'

'Standards, Ben,' Alison replied. 'So, once you have sliced all your carrots you half-fill the bottom pan of the steamer with water, place the carrots in the top section then put a lid on and bring to the boil. You can then leave the pan for approximately fifteen minutes to make sure the carrots are totally soft. I recommend you use a timer so that if you get distracted by another task you don't forget your carrots and allow the pan to boil dry. This, of course, would cause a potential hazard in the home as well as ruining your steamer. Are you with me so far?'

'Totally.' Ben turned the camera off and put it down. 'I'll start filming again when they've finished steaming.'

'Good, good,' Alison said. 'I think I got all the essential points in. If I'd known you were going to be filming it I would have been better prepared.'

'Alison,' said Ben. 'You are the most well-prepared person I have ever met. How could you be more prepared?'

'I would have laid the equipment out differently,' she replied, furrowing her brow and casting her eyes down towards the surface. 'So it was all visible.'

'Alison, that was perfect. Seriously. You explain stuff really well, like any idiot could do it. That's a real gift. I know, I'm a teacher.'

'Thank you,' said Alison, flashing him a grateful smile. She glanced up at the clock on the wall. 'We've just got time for a bit of a play with the babies before we purée,' she announced. She strode over to Rebecca and scooped her up then sat down on the sofa bouncing her up and down on her knee.

'Er, can I get you a drink or something?' asked Ben as he copied her and picked Millie up to have a gander over his shoulder.

'Sorry?' said Alison, looking up.

'Coffee? If you tell me where everything is I'll make you one.'

'Oh,' she said, looking taken aback. 'Yes, thank you. Erm, I'll have an orange juice. There's some in the door of the fridge and the glasses are in the cupboard over the sink.'

Ben heaved open the enormous American-style fridge and pulled out a carton of fresh juice. He poured a glass for Alison and one for himself before returning the carton to the fridge, taking unusual care not to spill anything inside the door of the gleaming fridge.

'There you go,' he said, taking it over to Alison and sitting himself down next to her after he'd grabbed his.

'Thank you.'

'Not a problem,' he replied, taking a long gulp. 'Not after all this help you're giving me.' He felt overcome with shame. Alison in her own, very anal way was being incredibly generous to him, and he had the audacity to accept that generosity despite knowing a secret that could devastate her.

'Matthew's a very lucky man,' he finally said. For all her faults, Alison was without doubt an amazing mother, and Matthew was lucky not to have lost her as part of the one-night stand fallout.

Alison ignored him, making gurgling sounds at Rebecca.

'You must make his life so easy, having total control over all this stuff,' he continued, sweeping his arm around the picture-perfect scene of domesticity. 'It must be great for him to know that he doesn't have to worry about the kids or anything.'

'You'd think, wouldn't you?' she replied, raising her eyebrows.

'I'm sure he's delighted he can toddle off to that tax office place and not give a second thought to what's happening here.'

'If only,' sighed Alison, laying Rebecca down and picking George up.

She began blowing raspberries on his tummy. Ben didn't like to probe any further.

'He comes home and . . . and . . . well, he just does everything wrong,' she said finally when she came up for air the third time. 'I spend all of my time working out exactly what the best thing is for my babies then he breezes in at the end of the day and throws everything out, messes with the routine, or worse, suggests what he thinks would be a better way of doing something.'

'He's probably just trying to help,' offered Ben, having been on the receiving end of Katy flying off the handle when he dared suggest something he thought might make life easier for everyone.

'But how can he know?' Alison turned to glare at Ben. 'I spend every waking hour with them. I've read everything, watched everything, and done everything I possibly can do to make sure I'm doing what's best for them.'

'Perhaps he just wants to be involved,' said Ben. 'They are his kids too.'

'But he doesn't know what's best for them,' said Alison, shaking her head. 'How can he? You have no idea what I put my body through for five years to get here, to get to hold my very own babies in my arms. Does he honestly think that I would put myself through all that and then not be taking the absolute best care of them?'

She pulled George into her chest and held him tight.

'I would never let anything happen to them,' she said quietly. 'I'm their *mother*. If anything ever happened to them . . .' She bit her lip and Ben could see that there were possible tears on the horizon. She was scared. No wonder she looked after her children like a military operation. It was the only way she could deal with the terrifying thought of not being the perfect mother she'd set out to be. He did the only thing he could in the face of Robo-Mum shedding tears and put a rather awkward arm around her as he tried to summon up words of empathy.

'For fuck's sake, Alison, don't you realise you're bloody brilliant at this?' He gave her a squeeze. 'Look at you. I mean really. You have twins, for Christ's sake, and you still not only have time to cut carrots in the right shape but also to show a fuckwit like me how to get my shit together. Seriously, Alison, you're like some crazy mother guru type person.'

Alison had taken a handkerchief out of her pocket and was dabbing her eyes as she clutched George to her chest. She shrugged.

Ben thrust his hand in his pocket and pulled out his phone, then reached his arm around Millie so Alison could view her carrot puréeing skills for herself.

'Look at you,' he urged. 'You are the perfect mother. You know how to do all this stuff. You *care* about it.'

Alison stared at the screen, sniffing gently.

'I told you I should have laid the equipment out so you can see it at the beginning,' she said eventually.

'Are you kidding?' cried Ben. 'This is brilliant. You do it so an idiot can understand. You should do more of this. We stay-at-home dads could really do with someone like you in our lives.'

Alison blinked up at him.

'I'm serious,' said Ben, seizing on the fact that she'd stopped crying. 'You're way better than that other bird on YouTube demonstrating the steriliser.'

'Melissa from Minnesota?' said Alison with half a smile.

'She was a dog,' Ben declared. 'Look at you in your lipstick and your pinny. Bit of eye candy for the dads wouldn't go amiss either.'

'Ben! Do you have to be so . . . so . . .'

'Right,' offered Ben.

'So . . . juvenile,' Alison concluded.

Ben raised his eyebrows.

'It was you who insisted on lipstick once you knew you were going on camera.'

'Well, as I said earlier, it's all about standards,' Alison said quickly.

'Anyway, I'm just saying that you're good at this, and I bet there are other dads out there who would appreciate your help . . . and your lipstick,' he said with a wink and another squeeze of her shoulders.

Alison looked away, and if Ben wasn't mistaken she was blushing slightly, but she still looked sad.

'We're all terrified of doing it wrong,' he told her. 'You're not alone.'

She turned and gave him a weak smile.

'Thank you,' she whispered. She sniffed. 'I don't know how Katy does it.'

'Does what?'

'Walk out the door and leave her baby.'

It was Ben's turn to fall silent, then he shrugged.

'She doesn't have a choice, does she?'

'Maybe not, but it must be so hard for her.'

'She would have a choice, of course, if she'd got together with someone who could afford to let her stay at home, but she didn't, did she?'' She lumbered herself with me, a poxy PE teacher, and the best I can do is tell her to go back to work and earn the big bucks whilst I make a hash of staying at home and trying to be Mum. And I can't even do that right.'

'A lot of men wouldn't even contemplate what you're doing. She's lucky to have you.'

'Lucky!' he exclaimed with a laugh. 'I don't think she would describe our situation as lucky. Having a partner who can support you whilst you care for the family, that's lucky. Even having a partner who when he offers to take care of the baby can do that without screwing it up . . . that's lucky. If Katy knew I was here, that I couldn't even take care of my own daughter for five minutes without needing help . . . well, she'd think I was such a loser.'

'We'll soon get you up to speed,' said Alison. 'Just see how Millie gets on with the routine I've set out on the spreadsheet. Hopefully you'll soon start to see a difference. Then perhaps we should just do a bit more on weaning next time, then you're good to go. Katy need never know.'

'Mmmm,' said Ben. This situation wasn't ideal, but boy did he need it just to get him on the right track.

'You didn't tell Matthew, did you?' he asked.

'Of course not,' she lied.

'Thank you,' he said with a sign. 'It's just, well—'

'No need to explain,' she interrupted. 'I under-stand perfectly.'

'Good,' Ben nodded, thinking he might just get away with this. Make Katy think he was handling the baby caring thing brilliantly, make her proud, even. He'd just get himself to the point where he knew what he was doing then extract himself from the situation. What could possibly go wrong?

CHAPTER EIGHTEEN

'Hiya,' shouted Matthew as he entered the house that evening, trying to sound as breezy as possible. As he'd driven home through the dark, rain-soaked streets of Leeds he could sense himself feeling more and more on edge as his windscreen wipers thumped the sides of his windscreen. Usually it was the hideous amount of traffic that irritated the hell out of him at this time of night, but for once the endless lines of moving headlights were way down his list of immediate concerns. All he could think about was whether Alison and Ben had got together that morning and what might be the fallout from the high-stakes encounter. He'd been attempting some kind of amateur analysis of Ben's character: his motivation for implementing such a stupid meeting, how he would handle it, how Alison would handle it. Would he walk through the door to a state of carnage in his marriage because Ben had used the opportunity to wreak his revenge on Matthew for sleeping with his girlfriend?

He took his shoes off in the hall, half expecting to see a line of suitcases heralding the departure of his family from his life. The hallway was as spotless as always, his slippers waiting for him exactly where he'd put them that morning, as regularly instructed by Alison.

There had been no answer when he'd shouted his greeting. Perhaps she was already gone, a *Dear Matthew (you bastard),* letter waiting for him on the mantelpiece. He peered round the door of the living room. No stiff white envelope obscured the newborn baby photographs of Rebecca and George displayed above the fireplace.

He heard movement in the kitchen, a chair scraping. He took a deep breath and pushed the door open tentatively, then stepped in.

'Oh, I'm glad it's you,' boomed a strange voice followed by a cackle. 'I was all poised here ready with the iron in case you were a burglar.' Matthew stared at the total stranger standing behind an ironing board in his kitchen accusing him of attempted burglary. Alison seemed to be hosting all manner of strange people in the house whilst he was at work. The woman cackled again then disappeared as she grappled with an enormous duvet cover, her waistline billowing almost as much as the mass of material. 'My Jack came up behind me once when I was ironing,' she continued when she reappeared. 'Frightened the living daylights out of me. I spun round and clocked him right on the side of his head. Took weeks for the iron mark to disappear. He never spooked me whilst I was ironing again,' she said, shaking with laughter.

'You're home early,' declared Alison, bustling in behind him and putting a large wash basket of ironing on the kitchen table. 'Ivy, this is my husband Matthew.'

'I know,' she said. 'Good job I recognised him. He was about to meet the hotplate, weren't you, Matthew?'

'Er, yes,' said Matthew, 'although I'm very sorry, but who are you exactly?'

'Oh Matthew,' huffed Alison. 'Ivy does our ironing every Wednesday. You know she does.'

Matthew felt slightly ashamed to realise that every day he took a clean, beautifully ironed work shirt out of the built-in wardrobe and never really gave a second thought to how it had got there.

'Of course,' he muttered. 'Pleased to meet you, Ivy.'

'Pleasure's all mine,' said Ivy. 'Your photographs don't do you justice,' she added with a wink.

Alison and Matthew exchanged looks. Alison gave a barely perceptible shake of the head then left the room without further comment, clearly on a tight schedule.

He looked over at Ivy, who was momentarily hidden behind a tablecloth. He needed to follow Alison but somehow it didn't feel right, just walking out of the room on someone you'd just met. That would be rude, whether it was the hired help or not. He at least had to make some sort of conversation. Acknowledge that he didn't just see her as someone they paid to do their dirty work. She had intimate knowledge of his work shirts. She knew that he was prone to sweating, which turned the underarms a bit yellow. This lady had to iron over his sweaty armpits. He felt terrible. She knew all that about him and he couldn't even be bothered to make polite conversation. No, he had to exchange pleasantries and then he would go and ask Alison about her day.

'So,' said Matthew, rapidly wondering what you talked about to the person who ironed your sweaty armpits. 'You been ironing a long time, have you, Ivy?'

She glanced up at the kitchen clock.

'Only about three quarters of an hour, love. Another good hour piled up here.'

'Right. Actually, I meant have you ironed for a long time as, you know, part of your career?'

Ivy threw her head back and roared.

'Oh my days,' she said, wiping her eyes. 'You are brilliant,' she continued, waving a finger at him. 'I'll have you know I've never done anything as part of a career. Nothing. And if I had, it certainly wouldn't have been ironing.'

'Yeah, I see what you're saying,' said Matthew. 'But you enjoy it, yeah, the ironing?'

Ivy had stopped laughing now and was staring at him with a look of amazement.

'No,' she said flatly and bent her head to concentrate on ironing a decorative frill on the tablecloth.

The ironing lady had dismissed him in his own home. She would prefer him to leave the kitchen and let her do the ironing rather than attempt any more of his ridiculous small talk.

'So nice to meet you,' he said, stepping backwards and knocking into a chair. 'Must go and er . . . speak to Alison about something.' He was out the door and back in the hallway again, breathing heavily. He could hear the whimsical chime of baby toy music floating from above his head and deduced that his family must be upstairs. He took another deep breath and went up, pushing open the door to the twins' bedroom very carefully, just in case they were sleeping.

They were both lying on changing mats, nappies off and vests akimbo, having a right good kick as though they were in training for the next World Cup. Meanwhile Alison marched between a basket and a chest of drawers, carefully laying colour-coordinated and beautifully ironed Babygros and vests to rest. Matthew sank to his knees and stroked both their bellies, marvelling for the umpteenth time at how soft and smooth their skin was.

'George's temperature was fine when he woke up this morning,' Alison announced, not breaking her stride.

'Good, that's a relief.' Matthew glanced up and tried to read her face. It looked the same as it always did, quietly determined, with an air of *don't mess with me, I'm concentrating on caring for my children.*

'So you had a normal day then?' he ventured.

'Pretty much,' she replied, holding up a white Babygro that still held a faint stain at the nappy end.

She did an about-turn and strode into the en-suite at the other side of the room, re-emerging seconds later without the rejected Babygro.

'See anyone?' he asked with what he hoped was a nonchalant shrug.

'Well, half the class didn't turn up to baby massage this afternoon. I mean, who are these people? How are they ever going to get the benefit of these classes if they don't bother attending?'

'Mmmm,' said Matthew. Perhaps Ben hadn't come round, he thought. She'd have mentioned it by now, surely. He wanted to ask, but the thought made his throat clench up.

'Oh, and Ben came round this morning,' she said, putting sugary pink cardigans on mini coat hangers. 'Remember, I told you last night he was coming round to pick my brains.'

'Oh yeah,' Matthew said nonchalantly. Remember! He'd thought of nothing else since. 'So how was he?'

Alison paused mid-stride to the basket, appearing to consider his question deeply. Matthew stopped breathing.

'Good,' she nodded eventually and carried on. 'It was actually really nice to see him.' She didn't elaborate, just continued her march across the room in front of his eyes, making him feel slightly queasy.

He had so many questions. *Are you seeing him again? What does the baby look like? Did he say how Katy was? Did he tell you that I used to be her boyfriend? Did he tell you that I slept with her at the school reunion? Did you ask him what on earth he's doing coming to our house knowing all that?* But she'd said it was nice to see him. That was a good sign. He should hold on to that. It couldn't possibly be nice to see anyone who came with tidings that your husband had been unfaithful.

'So he's well, is he?' he pressed.

'Yeah.' Alison stopped again to think about it. 'He was really sweet, actually. Very grateful and appreciative. I honestly have no idea how Katy could have just walked out like that.'

'She hasn't walked out completely, has she?' Matthew gasped.

'Well, no,' said Alison. 'But from what I understand, she's gone back to work leaving Ben to figure it all out for himself.'

'Oh, I doubt she's been as harsh as that,' said Matthew. 'Doesn't sound like Katy. She probably has told him what to do but he didn't take it in. You know what he's like. He's such a joker he probably didn't even listen to her.'

Alison halted in mid-stride yet again and turned to look at Matthew.

'I honestly don't think Katy had a clue how to look after a baby from what I can see. Millie has no routine whatsoever. Ben told me that most nights they don't get her settled until eight-thirty. Can you imagine? Between you and me, I think Katy was glad to go back to work.'

'I doubt that's true,' Matthew protested.

Alison shrugged.

'She always struck me as being a bit in denial about being pregnant. She never really listened at the antenatal classes, did she? In fact, I always assumed that she didn't plan to get pregnant, that it was a mistake, especially as they aren't married and there's such an age gap.' Alison stopped as though she expected Matthew to respond. He looked away, staring down at George's foot.

'Who knows?' he shrugged, not looking at her.

'I just know that if it were me there is no way I could leave that gorgeous baby and go to work,' Alison went on.

'The baby's okay, is she?' Matthew found himself asking. 'I mean, she looks okay and everything?'

'Oh yes,' said Alison, smirking. 'She looks just like Ben, actually.'

'What?' said Matthew, jerking his head up. 'How?'

'Bright ginger hair, bless her. There must be some very strong ginger genes running through Ben's family.'

Matthew had to look away from Alison for fear he was openly gaping. Millie was ginger! A surprise fact that couldn't be ignored. Surely this proved that Ben was indeed the father – his own family were bestowed with boring mousy brown hair, without a hint of fiery red anywhere. He wanted to go and lie down in a darkened room and absorb this piece of information, which could finally allow him to close the book on his ill-fated reunion with Katy. The last chapter had been missing, the one that revealed who the father of Katy's child was. Now he had evidence, which proved surely beyond reasonable doubt that it wasn't him. A weight was released. He literally felt like he was floating and had no idea what Alison had just said to him.

'Sorry? What did you say?' he asked.

'Just that ginger can be very striking on girls as they get older,' said Alison. 'If she's lucky it'll go that beautiful deep red and then she'll be thanking her dad for her hair colour.'

'Mmmm.' Matthew needed to get out of the room and gather himself. He grinned down at George and Rebecca and hauled himself up. He felt light-headed – not a feeling he'd expected to come home to today. 'Mind if I take a shower?' he said. 'Then tell me what I can do to help with these two.'

'Nothing,' said Alison instantly. 'I'm about to feed them.'

'Right. Are you sure? You could put your feet up for a bit and let me take over after that.'

'Of course I'm sure,' huffed Alison. 'I do know what I'm doing, you know.'

'I was only asking,' said Matthew defensively. 'I'll just go for a shower then.'

'No problem,' Alison replied tersely. 'Take your time.'

They sat opposite each other at half past seven as they did every night, chewing on jacket potatoes and whatever Alison had put in the slow cooker that morning.

'I think this is the best lamb you've ever done,' Matthew remarked.

'It's leftovers from last week out of the freezer,' Alison answered, without looking up.

'Well, freezing must bring out more of the flavour, perhaps.'

Alison didn't reply, just stared back at him and raised her eyebrows.

Matthew coughed. He felt nervous, which was ridiculous. It was as if he was about to ask her out on a first date again. Perhaps he was scared, because at the moment he didn't trust his mouth to come up with anything sensible. It seemed as though every single suggestion he'd made to Alison about anything in the last few weeks was likely to end in out-and-out warfare. Inviting her out for dinner could spark a cold front until at least next year.

'I rang my mum earlier,' he announced.

'Oh,' said Alison.

'And guess what?'

'She won five pounds at the bingo?'

'No. Actually the bingo is closed for refurbishment.'

'Oh dear. What on earth is she finding to do with her time?'

'Well, funny you should say that,' he continued. 'She's offered to babysit for us on Friday night. Isn't that brilliant? And I've managed to get us a table at Grants. They'd literally just had a cancellation. I couldn't believe it. I was all ready to beg the maître d', tell him it's your favourite restaurant and it's our first night out since our twins were born, but luckily I didn't have to. I did ask him if he'd sit us on the upper level, though. I know how you hate being near the toilets downstairs. And I checked that they still have calamari on the menu because I know that's your favourite dish. Also, I thought we might go on to the wine bar if you're not too tired. It'll be fun, won't it, to go out just the two of us and . . .'

He trailed off. He was aware that he was waffling, attempting to cram in as many reasons as possible for Alison to be unable to refuse an evening out with him. But he was forced to stop as she slowly and deliberately raised her hand to indicate he should halt.

'If you think I'm leaving Rebecca and George in the care of your mother you must be insane.'

Matthew slumped. He'd suspected it was his mother who might be the weak link in his plan. Alison's and his mother's parenting styles were as far apart as they could be. Brenda had brought Smarties for the twins last time she'd visited, despite the fact they weren't on solids yet.

'They'll keep, love,' she said when Alison pointed out how inappropriate it was for babies to eat chocolate. 'Little Matthew loved Smarties, didn't you?' she added, squeezing his cheek.

'I think Alison is very keen to encourage healthy eating when they do start having proper food,' Matthew replied. His mum stared back at him as though she didn't recognise her own son.

'Smarties never did you any harm, lad,' his dad said, roaring with laughter, knowing exactly how to wind Alison up.

'Only because he's on a well-balanced diet now,' Alison replied before putting the Smarties in the cupboard kept for unwanted gifts that could be offered as raffle prizes.

Alison had resumed eating, confident in the knowledge that the argument for a night out was closed.

He needed to win this one. He needed a relationship with his wife. He needed to sit and talk to her on neutral territory, not here in the home, which was now the domain of her and the babies. Sometimes he felt like some kind of lodger who rented a room to help pay the mortgage. Maybe that's what he was now to this family. The guy who stayed with them and paid the mortgage. It wasn't fair. He was going to win this one, whether Alison liked it or not. He must play her at her own game.

'The restaurant is booked for eight, meaning Mum can arrive at seven-thirty, after the twins are in bed asleep. The meal will take approximately ninety minutes, during which time the babies will be asleep, but in the unlikely event they wake we can walk from the restaurant to here in ten minutes. I timed it. I will brief my mother to call the instant either child wakes up, threatening her with an exclusion order should she fail to do this. If there have been no calls by nine-thirty when we leave the restaurant, we can call home to check all is well, then move to the wine bar on the corner for an after-dinner drink. We can be home by ten-thirty if you wish and Rebecca and George will be none the wiser.'

Alison had stopped eating, her knife hovering over the crest of her potato. Matthew stared back at her in what he hoped was a confident manner. He had thought of everything, he was totally in control. He'd sewn it up tighter than one of his client's tax relief spreadsheets. There was nothing Alison could say to argue that they couldn't go out.

'But I've got nothing to wear,' she protested.

Matthew felt his shoulders slump with relief. Permission to go out with his wife on Friday night successfully acquired.

CHAPTER NINETEEN

Katy had been desperate to get home early that Friday night. *I must leave work at five on the dot,* she kept telling herself all day. If she left at five she could be home by five-thirty, leaving her plenty of time to spring her surprise 'date night' on Ben. Under Daniel's advice she'd kept her plan a secret, but she wasn't convinced this was the right strategy for Ben. She'd expressed her concern during a lunchtime dash to the chemist's with Daniel to buy all the necessary equipment for a transformation from working mother to something that Ben might just want to rub up to.

'You have to show him you can be spontaneous,' Daniel had encouraged, 'that you can go out on a Friday night just like you used to. As grown-ups, untethered by a poo- and sick-making machine. He'll love it.'

'But what if he wants to stay in? What if he doesn't fancy a cocktail bar? What if he wants to do something different?'

'I would like to refer back to our conversation earlier this week. The facts that you laid before me were as follows. Ben has been acting strangely and, even more worrying – secretly. You believe it is possible that there is another woman involved. And finally, and the most damning evidence of all, is the fact that you and Ben have not had sex in a very long time.'

'Condoms!' she shrieked suddenly, making the woman steering a pushchair down the aisle in front of them look behind her in alarm. Katy looked away, feeling her cheeks go hot. 'I *need* to buy condoms,' she whispered to Daniel. 'I didn't bother going back on the pill after I had Millie because . . . because . . . well, you can guess.'

'There's no point going on the pill if you're not actually having sex,' said Daniel loudly enough to make the woman with the pushchair blush too.

'Come with me,' urged Katy.

'What for?' Daniel exclaimed.

'Pleeeease,' Katy begged. 'I haven't bought any for ages and there's so much choice these days I'll buy the wrong ones, I know I will. I'll get home and discover I've bought the ones labelled *petite* or something. Can you imagine?'

'No,' said Daniel firmly.

'I could ruin it before we've even started. You have to help me choose.'

'Are you for real?' said Daniel in a high-pitched voice. 'You want me to help you buy condoms for Ben?'

The lady with the pushchair scuttled off.

'Come on,' said Katy, grabbing his hand. 'They're just down this aisle.'

They approached the display and both went silent for a moment, considering the options.

'They really need to reconsider their branding,' said Daniel, shaking his head.

'Just what I was thinking,' Katy agreed.

'Thin feel,' said Daniel, 'is not a term that should ever be in the vicinity of a product associated with penises.'

'And have you seen the colours they've used on that range?' added Katy. 'Exactly the same as for Calpol. You really don't want to be confusing condoms with baby medicine, now do you?'

'Mmmmm,' Daniel nodded. 'It's just shockingly poor design work if you ask me.'

'Shall I just get the bog standard ones?' Katy said, after they'd both fallen into silence again for a few seconds.

'Probably safest,' sighed Daniel. 'You're right. It's really hard to make sense of all that lot.'

'The Essentials range?' she asked. 'Are they just the normal ones, do you think?'

'Or does that mean the cheap range?' asked Daniel.

'Oh,' said Katy, putting the box back on the shelf. 'I don't want cheap ones. I want quality, not cheap.'

'Well, I think you're going to have to choose between Excite Me or Tickle Me, then.'

'But what about Ben? It's not just for my benefit. I want him to enjoy it too.'

'I think you're meant to assume that's a given. He is a man, after all.'

'Right,' shrugged Katy. 'So Excite Me, then, do you think?'

'How should I know? It's you doing it. Do you want to be excited or tickled?'

'I don't care. I just want to have *sex*,' hissed Katy, so that two men in suits in the next aisle turned to look at them.

'Oh, for goodness' sake,' said Daniel, putting two boxes into her basket. 'Let's be optimistic, shall we, and have one of each.'

'I can't walk around the shop with two boxes of condoms in my basket,' she protested. 'Everyone will think I'm a slapper.'

'Well, you'll be the first slapper not to have had sex in months, then, won't you? Now go and pay. You're giving me a headache.'

Katy's afternoon went dramatically downhill when she returned to the office after lunch. What should have been a routine planning meeting went totally tits up when she uncovered that Freddie, her stand-in, hadn't filled out the timesheets correctly. She'd had to retrace his steps on all the projects he'd handled to try and work out how much they should be billing their clients.

To top it all the rain had come to dampen the spirits as well as bring Leeds to a virtual standstill. It wasn't until six-thirty that Katy stood at her front door painting on a forced smile and preparing to apologise for her lateness yet again. She only hoped that the surprise night out would be enough to secure Ben's forgiveness and by some miracle they would get Millie to sleep by eight-thirty before Daniel arrived to babysit.

'Hiya,' she shouted as she heaved the door open, carefully hiding the unsexy bag of shaving implements and contraception underneath her coat in the hall, to be retrieved later. There was no response. *Strange*, she thought. The pushchair was there so they must be in. She listened. Normally there would be the TV on or at the very least the radio, but all was quiet and an unusual sense of calm prevailed. She walked down the hall, aiming at the living room, but was run off course by a noise coming from the bathroom.

'Hello?' she shouted again.

'We're having a bath,' came Ben's response. *Unusually early*, thought Katy. She carried on, kicking her shoes off, and pushed the door to the bathroom open. The room was gloomy as only the light above the mirror was on. Ben was leaning over the bath supporting Millie in the water.

'Has the bulb gone again?' asked Katy.

'No,' replied Ben, not looking up. 'I'm just trying something. Keeping it dark so she might be ready to go to bed earlier.'

'Oh,' said Katy. 'Right.' She didn't know what to say. She hadn't expected to come home to Ben dreaming up new childcare methods.

'Worth a try, I suppose,' she said in what she hoped was an encouraging manner. 'Sorry I'm late again. Do you want me to take over?' She leaned over his shoulder to smile at Millie.

'Er, if you don't mind I'll do it,' he said, looking a bit awkward.

'Oh,' she said, taken aback. She really wanted to put Millie to bed so she could make sure she was asleep by eight-thirty.

'Yeah,' he continued. 'I'm, er, trying to get her into a new routine. I woke her up early this afternoon so she could have her food early, and then I've been keeping her awake so she's tired now, see. She's got a bit of milk left to have in her room, then I want to get her to bed by seven.'

Katy's mouth was hanging open. It was all she could do to stop herself bursting out laughing. Had she entered a parallel universe? Ben was talking about routines and Millie in bed by seven. She'd heard of babies that did that but she was convinced that Millie wasn't one of them. Still, she couldn't blame Ben for trying.

'Okay,' she said, nodding. 'Of course, if that's what you think, that's brilliant, because guess what?'

'Shhhh,' he said as Katy's excitement at the prospect of a night out spilled into an increase in volume. 'We're trying to be calm and quiet.'

'Okay,' whispered Katy, suddenly wanting to giggle at the seriousness of his face. 'I was just going to tell you that we have a babysitter and I have planned us a brilliant night out.' She gave him a massive grin.

'Tonight?' he asked, a look of concern crossing his face.

'Yes,' she hissed, nodding vigorously.

His face fell and he looked disappointed. Not the reaction that Katy was expecting.

'I've said I'm going to the pub with Braindead. He's coming round at eight.'

'But you never said,' said Katy, feeling utterly crushed.

'You didn't say either,' he replied.

'But . . . I've got a babysitter,' she continued.

'Can't they come another night?'

Oh my God, thought Katy. *Ben would rather have a night out with Braindead than with me.*

'No,' she said. 'I've got it all planned. I thought . . . I thought we needed to spend some time together, you know, as a couple.'

'Why didn't you tell me?' said Ben. 'Braindead's all excited about it. We're going to a microbrewery. He says the beer is to die for. That's it!' he said, suddenly looking back up at Katy. 'That's what we'll do. Why don't you come with me and Braindead to the pub? It'll be just like old times. Braindead won't mind. He was only saying the other night that he misses you coming to the pub with us.'

Katy felt like crying. She didn't want to be in a pub with Braindead on her first night out in months with Ben. It wasn't like old times when she didn't mind spending time with Ben's mates because her possibilities for nights out were infinite. Nights out were like gold now, and couldn't be treated casually. She wanted – no, she needed a night out with Ben on her own, where they could be themselves again. Act like teenagers, get a bit tipsy, snog in public without caring, and then consummate the evening somewhere – preferably in the comfort of their own bed.

'Normally,' she said carefully, 'I would love to spend the night with Braindead, but we haven't been out together in months. Couldn't you go out with him another night and just the two of us go out tonight?' She paused. 'Please,' she added as he turned to look at her. He appeared to think for a moment then he nodded, giving her a small smile.

'Okay,' he said. 'You're right. But you need to call Braindead and let him down. He won't swear as much at you as he would at me.'

'Okay,' she said. 'Of course. I'll blame it all on me.'

He lifted Millie out of the bath in all her shimmery glory and laid her on a towel on the floor.

'Say, night-night to Mummy,' he said. 'And promise to go to sleep quick so Mummy and Daddy can go out and pretend they're normal human beings who go out on Friday night and talk crap. And I mean crap of the ridiculous variety, not crap of the shitty nappy variety.'

Over an hour later and Katy still hadn't got hold of Braindead. He wasn't answering his mobile. She'd texted him explaining the situation, asking him to confirm he'd received the message, but there was no response. Her efforts to contact him had been interspersed with attempts to turn herself into the fabulous person she used to be when stepping out for the night with her boyfriend. The legs were now smooth since she'd slathered them in moisturiser after shaving, but she was kicking herself for not having done a bikini wax the night before. She daren't risk it now – the sight of her lying there prostrate with goo round her bits wouldn't exactly get Ben in the mood for some love later.

Her outfit selection was also proving to be a shocker. She'd been planning to wear her old faithful LBD, which she could always rely on to show off her assets brilliantly, but her boobs seemed to have metamorphosed into an entirely different shape. They were bulging out all over the place, and if she wore the bra that could keep them under control then it was visible over the low neckline. At a loss, she started rifling through all her old going-out outfits until there was a pile on the bed, none of which her amended body shape was entirely happy with. She wanted to feel good tonight – feminine, sexy and glamorous – but it was rapidly looking like she would be shrouding herself with clothes she normally reserved for her zero body confidence days. Clothes that didn't display her assets but hid her lumps and bumps in copious amounts of fabric.

In the meantime Ben had shrugged on a shirt and jeans. She was desperate to ask him to shave but didn't like to come across as the hen- pecking wife. He was now lying on the bed reading the paper whilst Katy fretted over clothing and Millie wailed via the monitor.

'I'll go, shall I?' Katy said when Ben made no move to go and soothe her. She was eager to take her fair share of trying to get Millie to go to sleep by babysitter arrival time.

Ben shook his head and glanced up at her.

'Not yet,' he said. 'She needs to learn that we won't appear by magic, just because she cries.'

'Oh,' said Katy, unable to hide the confused look on her face.

'Just something I read,' he said hastily. 'You have to teach them to stop themselves crying.'

'Right,' said Katy, nodding. Ben reading some- thing that was not sport related? Too weird.

'So you just let them wail?' she asked, as Millie's shouts got louder. She wanted to go to her, but she had no right, she realised. With a pang it hit her that it was Ben's right now, to call the shots on Millie.

'For a bit to start with. Then you go to them so they know you're there, but you don't pick them up. You are calm and reassuring and then you walk out again. They get it eventually, apparently,' he shrugged.

'So where did you read all about this then?'

Ben looked quickly up at her.

'Can't remember,' he said. 'Must have been in one of the Sunday supplements.'

Ben didn't read Sunday supplements. In fact, he often said they were a waste of the earth's resources and should be banned. He thought no-one in their right minds should want to be preached at on a Sunday by self-righteous journalists telling them how to improve their lives. He didn't know who gave a toss any more about the TV listings, and why should he be bothered about the latest art show or theatre production in London when he lived on the other side of the country? And he could not care less about the intimate details of the stupid, inane lives of ridiculous reality TV personalities.

'Anything wrong?' he asked.

Katy was suddenly aware that she was staring at him. He was lying. He didn't go near the Sunday supplements. *Why* was he lying?

'Nothing,' she said, looking away and picking up her phone to see if Braindead had responded. 'Nothing at all. If you're okay with Millie I'll just go and try Braindead again.'

She left the bedroom and walked down the corridor and into the living room, closing the door behind her so she couldn't hear Millie's cries. She tried Braindead again but he still wasn't answering.

She glanced up and spotted the pile of newspapers beside the sofa. Looking furtively at the door, she bent to rifle through them. Sure enough, the supplements from the weekend were still safely in their plastic. It was clear that Ben hadn't touched them.

She sat back on the sofa, thinking. Ben was behaving so weirdly. It was then that she spotted his mobile sitting on the coffee table. She caught her breath. She couldn't . . . could she? Yes, she could, she decided, and reached to pick up the phone. She knew his entry code. It was the date his football team won the FA cup final. She was in. She looked up at the door again to reassure herself that it was shut and so she would have warning if Ben decided to come in. She clicked on his text messages, glancing up and down the screen. Braindead, Rick and her own name came up over and over again but then she stopped as something unusual appeared.

He had texted someone called 'A'. Just 'A', nothing else. She opened the text, holding her breath.

Thank u 4 yesterday – Ben

She didn't have time to process it before the doorbell rang. She leapt up, surprised by the alien sound. She put the phone back down and hurried out the room to the door.

For what? she kept thinking. What was he thanking A for? Who was A? She was still racking her brains when she thrust open the front door, to be confronted by Braindead standing there in a jumper and jeans and absolutely soaked through to the skin.

'Can I get into your tumble dryer?' he asked, pushing past her to stand shivering next to the radiator in the hallway.

'Didn't you get my message?' she said, feeling instantly terrible that Braindead had come all this way in the rain for nothing.

'What message?'

'I texted and rang several times to tell you we've managed to get a babysitter.'

'Really?' said Braindead, looking uplifted from his sodden mess. 'So you can come out too? Wow,' he said, leaping forward as if to hug her. She caught his wrists just in time to stop him soaking her through.

'Oh Katy,' he exclaimed. 'It'll be just like old times. You, me and Ben. Let's ring Rick, see if he's around. We could even go to the Red Lion in Otley. See if we can steal a friend for Gloria.' He was grinning in excitement. 'It was the best day of my life when you managed to sneak that stuffed puffin out of there. Seriously. Let's go there again and see what else we can get.'

Katy raised her eyes to the ceiling. This didn't bode well. How was she meant to explain she'd scuppered his entire evening?

'To be honest, that's why I was calling you,' she began.

'To tell me we were going to get a mate for Gloria?' asked Braindead.

'No,' said Katy, now regretting having stolen the said stuffed puffin just to prove to Ben and his mates

217

that she was as young and daring as them, despite her being eight years older and pregnant. She took hold of Braindead's wrists again in an effort to get him to focus on what she was saying. 'I was ringing to tell you that I'd no idea that Ben had planned to go out with you tonight and I'd planned a surprise night out for the two of us instead.'

'Aw Katy, what a lovely thought. I know we haven't seen much of each other lately, what with you being busy with work and the baby and what have you. Actually, I do have lots of questions to ask you about Cheryl at work. She's taken a dislike to me and I have no idea why, or what to do.'

Katy let go of Braindead's wrists. This really wasn't going to be easy.

'I meant me and Ben, not me and you,' she said.

Braindead didn't respond for a moment, clearly considering the situation.

'But you see Ben all the time,' he said eventually. 'Why do you need to go out with him?'

How could the evening already be turning into more hassle than it was worth? she thought. And they hadn't even gone anywhere yet.

'Because we haven't been out together since before Millie was born.'

'But you've been together all that time. Katy, I know maths isn't your strong point, but if you counted up how many hours you'd spent with Ben in the last few months you'd realise that you were in no way deficient of spending time together. Ben and me, however, are sadly lacking, and me and you, well, virtually zero. I think if we all just sat down and thought about this and ran up a quick chart, we would certainly conclude that the people most requiring a night out together are in fact me and you, Katy. So let's go now and get ourselves to that microbrewery before Ben even notices. You can explain the numbers to him when we get back.'

Katy counted to five before she responded.

'Flattered as I am that you would like to spend the night with me . . .'

'Drinking, nothing else, mind. No offence, Katy, but I just don't see you that way.'

'I'm so pleased to hear that, Braindead,' Katy sighed. 'So like I say, nice as it would be to have a night out with you, I really need to spend some time with Ben. I'm really sorry you've had a wasted journey, but Ben can't come out to play with you tonight. Maybe one night next week, eh?' What about Sunday night? Is the microbrewery open then?'

'What have we here?' came a voice floating from the stairwell.

'Hi Daniel,' Katy called.

'Danny boy,' exclaimed Braindead. 'Long time no see. Must be, what, the day Millie was born? What are you doing here?' He turned back to Katy. 'Are you and Ben going out with him? How come he gets to go out and I don't?'

Katy put her head in her hands. This could not be happening. She looked up at Daniel pleadingly.

'Ben had already arranged to go out with Braindead,' she said, as calmly as she could. 'I'm just trying to explain to him that me and Ben are going out and unfortunately Ben needs to postpone his night out with Braindead to another time.'

Daniel coughed, put a large vintage suitcase down on the floor and unwrapped the scarf from around his neck before he responded.

'Leave it with me,' he said, putting a reassuring hand on her shoulder. 'Go and put something on that at the very least makes you look pear-shaped rather than potato-shaped and I'll sort this out.'

'Thank you,' gasped Katy, scuttling away. She'd accept the insult if Daniel could get rid of Brain-dead.

Daniel watched her disappear then turned to face Braindead.

'I'm here on extremely important work,' he hissed. 'We are staging an intervention and your presence could blow it all.'

'Staging what?' asked Braindead.

'An intervention.'

'Never heard of it,' shrugged Braindead. 'Is this some new type of play or something?'

Daniel blinked at Braindead several times before he could recompose himself.

'No,' he said. 'An intervention is when you can see that someone has a problem and you step in to try and sort it out for them.'

'Right,' said Braindead, nodding slowly. 'So what's the problem then?'

'Well,' said Daniel, glancing down the hallway. 'It's a bit delicate, actually. I'm not sure if I should be telling you.'

'I can do delicate,' replied Braindead. 'What makes you think I can't, Danny Boy?'

'Please don't call me Danny Boy.'

'If I don't call you Danny Boy, will you tell me what's delicate?'

'If I tell you, will you leave?'

Braindead thought for a moment.

'Okay then,' he shrugged.

'Well,' said Daniel, lowering his voice, 'Ben and Katy actually haven't had sex in—'

'A fucking long time,' interrupted Braindead. 'Yeah, I know, and so?'

Daniel looked taken aback.

'You know?'

'Yeah, Ben must have mentioned it sometime.'

'Right, okay,' said Daniel, slightly thrown. 'Well, that's the problem that we are staging the intervention for. Katy is taking Ben out for the night for a few drinks to loosen everyone up a bit. I'm babysitting, and while they're out I've brought the necessary equipment in this case here to prepare their bedroom for Luuuuurve.'

Braindead looked down at the battered brown case.

'What's in it then?' he asked.

'Just a few tricks up my sleeve. I will transform that room into the sexiest thing you have ever seen whilst they're gone. If they don't end up having sex, well, then I'm a Dutch cap.'

Braindead glanced between the case and Daniel several times.

'Can I help?' he said eventually.

'No,' replied Daniel instantly.

'But I need to know how to prepare a bedroom for luurve. It's clearly what I've been missing all this time. I need to know your tricks, Daniel. You show me how to set up this room of love thing and I will be your best mate ever, seriously. You could change my life – well, my sex life at least. Please, Danny Boy, please.'

'Don't call me Danny Boy.'

'Sorry. Look, I can help you look after Millie too. If she wakes up I'll hold her. She likes me, seriously. You show me the love bedroom and I'll look after Millie.'

It didn't take Daniel long to accept. He'd been mildly concerned about what he was going to do if Millie woke up, not that he'd told Katy that.

'You're on,' he said. 'But there will be no inflating of condoms or playing with matches,' he added firmly.

'Understood,' replied Braindead, giving him a swift salute. 'This is epic,' he continued. 'There was me dreaming of a pint of Old Peculiar all day. Little did I know I was going to turn my sex life around. Just shows that you never know how a Friday night can turn out.'

CHAPTER TWENTY

It wasn't a microbrewery, thought Ben as they approached their venue for the evening. There was too much sparkle and reflection and weird lighting fixtures for it to be a microbrewery. And was that a doorman? Definitely not a microbrewery. He could feel his heart sinking. He should be excited about a night out with Katy, he knew he should. And she was absolutely right, they needed some quality time together, but he'd spent all day gearing himself up for the microbrewery with Braindead. It was the same as when he used to plan with Katy on a Friday morning that they were going to have a Chinese that night and then he'd get home and Katy would have changed her mind. She fancied a curry instead. It wasn't that there was anything wrong with curry – Ben could pine for a good curry any day of the week – but when you'd spent all day planning exactly what you were having from the Happy House Chinese Takeaway, then having a curry came as a crushing disappointment. He also realised as they sidled past the black-suited doorman that he'd come out dressed to go to a microbrewery. He'd unearthed a slightly cleaner pair of jeans than the ones he'd been wearing all day, then thrown an England rugby shirt on. Katy had made a real effort, he realised guiltily. She looked every bit like she fitted into this well-dressed crowd. He, however, stood out for all the wrong reasons.

'Don't panic,' said Katy, as they got squashed together in a large group hovering just inside the door. 'Daniel's reserved us a table because he knows the owner. Blimey, can't believe how popular this place is.'

Neither can I, thought Ben, taking in more of his surroundings. Bars that served overpriced drinks that took you nanoseconds to consume didn't strike him as very appealing at all.

'So nice to try somewhere new, isn't it?' she shouted into his ear over the too-loud music as they did their best to surge through the crowd to the bar area.

'Yeah,' he shouted back. 'Brilliant.'

'Why don't you wait here and I'll try and find our table,' she shouted back again.

'Okay,' he said, shoving his hands in his jeans pockets and standing still.

He swayed to and fro, getting jostled by his fellow carousers. He'd never been one for people-watching in bars. He never really understood what pleasure there was in watching someone else have a good time, or worse, a bad one. But just now he had no choice. Stranded alone, his only entertainment was the people around him.

First date, he concluded, as a couple sitting at a high table caught his eye. Both eager. Both attentive. Overkill of giggling and make-up on her side with much touching of hair. As for him, he could see that he was thoroughly enjoying the fact that he could talk non-stop about himself without being interrupted. Women only listened really on a first date, he decided. After that you usually couldn't get a word in edgeways.

A crowd of about half a dozen men then erupted through the door, full of banter and excitement. They bounced off each other like they were in a pinball machine, constantly nudging and poking. They strode up to the bar and ordered bottled lager and then one by one turned to survey the potential of the room. The nudging and poking recommenced as they spotted the slew of short-skirted, tower-heeled girls, and soon one of them was dispatched to spearhead the campaign to get to know them better.

They were a similar age to him, he guessed – probably mostly in their late twenties – but he felt a world apart from them. They looked happy to be in this kind of bar, hoping the high-priced lager meant a higher standard of women. They cared what they looked like, dressed in variations of a checked 'going out' shirt, unlike Ben, who was wearing something he often wore intermittently for weeks on end without washing it. Seeing them made him so relieved he didn't have to go out trailing the bars, week in, week out, all dressed up. In fact he considered it one of the major benefits of finding your life partner that standing in a bar like this was no longer necessary.

'It's a good job Daniel sorted a table for us, isn't it?' Katy said, as she sat down on a high stool somewhere near the back of the bar.

'Yeah,' he muttered as he hauled himself onto another stool opposite Katy so they would both have to lean forward constantly and shout to get themselves heard. He wondered if he should suggest now that they bail and find somewhere less fashionable where they had a fighting chance of having a good time.

'The design of the bar is crazy,' she shouted, pointing over to the glowing neon altar of booze. 'Daniel said it's a direct rip-off of a bar he went to in Vegas.'

'Right,' Ben nodded. 'It's hideous. Hope the drink tastes better than the bar looks.'

'Carlos is bringing us over two Dang Dang Whisky Slider Bombs on the house. Courtesy of Daniel.'

'Right,' Ben nodded again. Hopefully they could down these and then he could suggest they try somewhere else without upsetting Katy's carefully laid plans.

'So,' she shouted at him. 'Tell me what you've been up to with Millie. How's it all going?'

'Fine,' he shrugged back. She raised her eyebrows. 'Well, it's taking a bit of getting used to,' he added. 'And to be totally honest, I was a bit all over the place to start with, but I'm getting there. I think

I've turned a corner. How's it going with you?' He was keen to get her off the subject of childcare and avoid the guilty knot in his stomach.

'Oh,' replied Katy, clearly surprised that he'd asked. 'Well . . .' She hesitated, looking somewhat awkward, 'It's great, actually,' she finally said with a sigh. 'I feel terrible,' she continued. 'I've missed Millie, of course I have, but I have loved being back in the thick of it. I must be a terrible mother.'

'No, you're not!' exclaimed Ben. 'Being good at your job and enjoying it doesn't make you a bad mother.'

'But I feel so bad that I'm out there and you're stuck at home.'

Ben looked at her, trying desperately to stop himself thinking how the pint at the microbrewery would be tasting now. He'd been so looking forward to real ale and light-hearted banter with someone who thought talking about what he'd had for breakfast that morning was deep. He really didn't want to spend the night eradicating Katy's guilt and steering round awkward questions about what he'd been up to. He needed to cut this line of conversation short.

'Look, Katy,' he said. 'It was my idea, wasn't it? You haven't forced me into anything, I offered. And touch wood,' he said, planting his hand firmly down on the empty table, 'our daughter has not been killed or maimed as part of the process, so let's just say so far, so good, shall we, and move on.'

Thankfully two tall glasses arrived at the table at that point and Ben couldn't help but raise his eyebrows at Katy over the paraphernalia that was poking out of the top.

'That, my friends,' said Carlos, slapping them both on the back, 'will have you warmed up in no time. Have a good one,' he said, winking at Ben. 'But don't drink too many, or else it might hamper your performance – if you know what I mean.' He winked again and scurried off smirking.

'What was that all about?' said Ben, turning to Katy. She had turned bright red. She took a large slug of her cocktail.

'Katy?' he said again. He didn't think he'd ever seen her turn bright red before.

'Daniel thought . . .' she started. 'Daniel thought that if we had a night out and loosened up a bit, you know, well then, we would perhaps manage to go home and, well, you know . . .'

'Know what?'

'Have sex,' mouthed Katy.

It was Ben's turn to take a slug of the cocktail.

'Are you telling me that this is a whole seduction thing cooked up by you and . . . Daniel?'

'No!' Katy exclaimed. 'No, I'm just very conscious that we haven't, you know, done it . . . you know, in a while, and . . . well . . .'

'And you've spoken to Daniel about this?'

'Well yes, I needed to talk to someone. I was worried that you might have gone off me or something.'

Bloody hell, thought Ben. He wished with all his heart he was in a microbrewery right now with Braindead.

'Of course I haven't gone off you. I just, well . . . when on earth are we supposed to do it now? I don't know, do you?'

'That's exactly what I said to the doctor.'

'You talked to the doctor too?' Ben exploded. 'Bloody hell, Katy, is there anyone who has not been consulted on our sex life?'

'No, it's not like that,' she said hastily. 'The doctor just asked me about contraception and I told him there's not much call for it at the moment, that's all. I'm sorry.'

Ben looked away. Maybe now wasn't the time to share that Rick and Braindead were also aware of the current sex drought.

He drained his drink, and Katy followed suit. They stared awkwardly at each other.

'Can I ask you a question?' she said eventually, 'without you going mad?'

'Depends on the question,' he replied. He hoped with all his heart it was, 'Do you fancy going to the microbrewery?'

'Are you . . .' she began. She'd gone white and looked upset.

'What is it?' he asked. Unlikely to be a question involving microbreweries, then he thought.

'Are you seeing someone?' she finally said, very quietly.

'What?' he cried.

'Are you seeing someone?' Katy repeated. 'I don't necessarily mean having sex or anything, I just mean, is there someone else?'

'Are you insane?' was all he could think to say. 'Seeing someone? What on earth are you talking about?'

Katy swallowed. 'You're just acting so strangely,' she said. 'There's weird stuff going on. Something's different, and I don't know what it is.'

'So you assume I'm having an affair, do you?' Ben demanded.

'No,' she said, tears appearing from nowhere.

He got up from the stool. 'Don't you ever tar me with your own brush.' He turned away, unable to look at her, and headed for the door.

CHAPTER TWENTY-ONE

Braindead pulled his head out of the fridge, having assessed its contents carefully.

'What is this crap?' he exclaimed, peeling back the lid of a Tupperware box. 'Smells and looks like a cat has honked it up. I swear the only thing worth consuming in here is the beer.' He put the offending tub back in the fridge, then re-emerged with two bottles and offered one to Daniel.

'Want one?'

'No,' replied Daniel. 'I'm not really a beer drinker.'

Braindead unscrewed the top and flicked it towards the shut bin. Daniel gave him a look. Braindead grinned back and retrieved the lid then put it in the bin. Leaning against the counter top, he took a swig.

'Not bad,' he declared, smacking his lips together. 'But not as good as what we would have been drinking down the Brewery Tap. I hope he remembers to try a Midnight Bell. I've been telling him, it just blows your mind, seriously. I hope he likes it. Nothing worse than an overhyped beer that doesn't deliver, is there, Dan? I'd hate Ben to be disappointed.'

'Well, you have no need to worry about that. Where Ben and Katy are going, the drinks certainly don't disappoint.'

'What? They're not going to the Brewery Tap? Ben will have been thinking about it all day. He'll be gutted.'

'There is absolutely no need to worry,' Daniel said reassuringly. 'I've fixed them up with a table at Cocktail Emporium. They are going to have a ball.'

'Cocktail Emporium! Are you insane?'

'I know. They're so lucky. I happen to know the manager.'

'Ben has turned down a night in a microbrewery for a night at Cocktail Emporium? That is a disaster of epic proportions.'

'Oh, don't be so ridiculous, Braindead. Why would it be a disaster?'

'Do I have to spell it out?'

'Yes.'

'M-I-C-R-O-B-R . . . is there another R, or is it just an E next?'

'I know how to spell microbrewery, Braindead.'

'You asked me to spell it out!'

'Not literally. What I meant was, what exactly is the problem with going to Cocktail Emporium rather than a microbrewery?'

'Daniel. I've come to like you, I really have, but sometimes you are the stupidest person I've ever met.'

'No,' replied Daniel, shaking his head vigorously. 'I'm not taking that from you. The Dang Dang Whisky Slider Bombs are the key, you see. If there is any drink capable of being the kind of lubricant that Katy and Ben need to get their love life going again, it's some of those. I am absolutely certain that there is nothing that could get anyone in the mood in a *microbrewery*.' He pronounced the last word as if it had just appeared under his nose and smelt of something terrible.

'Microbreweries are sexy,' claimed Braindead. 'I've taken women there before and had no complaints.'

'How many?'

'Several.'

'Actual dates?'

'Technically speaking, no. We went there for a works night out.'

'Braindead, when did you last have a proper girlfriend?'

Braindead looked back defiantly.

'More recently than you, I'd say.'

'You know very well I don't do girlfriends.'

'Well then, that makes me more of an expert on what women want than you, doesn't it?

'I doubt it somehow,' Daniel sighed. 'So, do you want to help me set up this bedroom or what?'

'Oh yeah,' Braindead nodded enthusiastically. 'I do need help actually getting women from the micro-brewery to the bedroom.'

'So that's it?' said Braindead about twenty minutes later, standing at the foot of the bed in Katy and Ben's room.

'Yep,' Daniel nodded.

'Smelly candles and throw a scarf over a bedside lamp?'

'Looks and feels like a different room, doesn't it?' said Daniel.

'Just looks like a major fire hazard, if you ask me.'

'I've only lit them to show you the effect. We'll blow them out and then Katy's going to text me when they're on their way home so we can get them lit, then we'll melt away the minute they come through the door.'

'I'm not convinced,' said Braindead.

'Well, fortunately it's not you that needs convincing. Katy just wants to show Ben how much she wants him.'

'I don't really get it.'

'Get what?'

'Well, Katy wants to have sex with Ben, right?'

'Yes.'

'And Ben is a bloke.'

'Well spotted, yes, Braindead.'

'Why is she going to all this trouble then? Blokes don't turn down sex, do they? Ever?'

'I can see what you're getting at.'

'Why hasn't she just asked him, or grabbed him or something? To be perfectly honest, putting him through the torture of going to a cocktail bar and then bringing him back here where he could quite literally go up in smoke any minute strikes me as the perfect way to put any poor lad off his stride.'

'Well, I think it's just complicated for them, that's all. Ever since the whole Matthew thing, and since Millie's arrival.'

'I refer back to my previous statement. Ben is a bloke. She's offering sex. Sounds like the most uncomplicated thing in the world if you ask me.'

'I'd like to refer back to *my* previous question, Braindead. When did you last have a girlfriend?'

Braindead closed his eyes to think, then hung his head in defeat.

'Fuck, it is complicated, isn't it?' he sighed.

They stood side by side, both deep in thought about the complexity of love and sex for a few moments before they were disturbed by the sound of Braindead's phone beeping in his pocket. He pulled it out and swiped the screen to reveal what his gadget was demanding. Next minute he was leaping around the room in sheer joy before lowering himself to his knees and raising his arms to the skies.

'Oh, thank you, God. Thank you, thank you, thank you,' he roared.

'Shhhh,' hissed Daniel. 'You'll wake Millie up.'

'But it's brilliant news,' Braindead insisted, making no effort to reduce his volume. 'Ben is at the Brewery Tap and has demanded my company. It's been lovely, Daniel, as always, but it seems as though my night is back on. Thank the Lord.'

Just at that moment Millie gave a wail, clearly wanting to know what all the excitement was all about.

'Now look what you've done,' said Daniel. 'You can't leave now. You need to help me.'

'I'm very sorry, Daniel, but I think you'll find I have a prior engagement,' Braindead whispered loudly.

'You can't go,' Daniel whispered back. 'I won't let you. Katy and Ben need time alone. You *can't* gatecrash. And what the hell is Ben doing in the pub anyway? They're supposed to be getting sozzled on cocktails.'

'He must have made Katy see sense and taken her down the microbrewery.'

'No, this is all wrong,' said Daniel. 'I'm so not happy about this. Text him back and say you can't make it, and then you and me are going to try and calm Millie down.'

'What? You can't make me turn down a night out at a microbrewery twice in one night.'

'I think I can.'

'You can't.'

'I can.'

'Oh no, you can't.'

'Oh yes, I can.'

'What on earth is going on here?' came a shout from the door. They both turned to see Katy standing in the doorway, Millie in her arms and half her mascara down her cheeks.

'Did you wake her up?' Katy demanded.

'Sorry, Katy,' said Braindead, looking at the floor.

'What are you doing here?' demanded Daniel.

'Can I go to the pub now?' said Braindead.

'No,' replied Daniel. 'You can stand there until we know why Katy is here and Ben is at the . . .'

'Microbrewery,' added Braindead helpfully.

'Where did you say?' asked Katy, bouncing Millie up and down on her shoulder.

'He texted me from the Brewery Tap, just now,' replied Braindead.

'Oh,' said Katy.

'I should definitely go and see if he's alright, shouldn't I, Katy?' said Braindead.

'Yes,' she said as new tears emerged. 'You should.'

Braindead slid out of the room like a snake escaping a basket, quickly and silently. Katy slumped on the bed holding Millie close to her chest, rocking gently backwards and forwards in between loud sniffs. Daniel lowered himself gently beside her and put his arm around her. He said nothing. Just waited.

'He was so touchy,' she said eventually. 'He didn't want to talk about anything. Didn't want to tell me anything about what he's been up to. It's just not like him. He's normally so open, isn't he? He'll tell anyone anything.' She shifted a now calm Millie to her other shoulder. 'Then I found a text on his phone.'

'You don't just find texts, Katy. You go looking for them.'

'Okay, so I looked at his phone,' she said guiltily. 'And he'd texted someone called "A" and thanked them for yesterday. He told me he hadn't seen anyone yesterday. He hadn't been anywhere – and yet he had. He must have.'

'It could be nothing, you know,' said Daniel.

'I asked him,' sniffed Katy.

'Asked him what?'

'If he was seeing someone.'

'Oh lordy, you didn't, did you?'

'I had to know, Daniel. But it came out all wrong. I didn't mean, are you seeing someone, as in, you know . . .?'

'Seeing *to* someone?'

'Well yes. I didn't mean that. I just meant, was he seeing someone. Not doing anything with them. But Ben thought I meant he was having an affair or something, and I didn't mean that, honestly I didn't.'

'So what did he say?'

'Oh Daniel, what have I done?' she sobbed.

'What did he say?' Daniel repeated.

She scrabbled for a tissue in her pocket.

'He said that I shouldn't tar him with my own brush,' she blurted. 'Then he left.'

'To go to a microbrewery,' Daniel muttered.

They sat in silence until Katy got up to take Millie back to bed. Daniel waited for her to leave the room, then stood up to blow the scented candles out.

'Don't think you'll be needing these tonight after all,' he said.

CHAPTER TWENTY-TWO

The mobile phone lay there like an unexploded bomb on the crisp white linen tablecloth next to the salad fork, as though it was part of the table setting. A stiff bishop's-hat-shaped napkin sat on top of a plate which would be removed, unused, as soon as a complete stranger who you wanted nowhere near your crotch had laid the napkin awkwardly on your knee. Matthew knew that Alison loved all the unusual etiquette that came with a high-end restaurant. Napkins so rigid they slipped instantly to the floor, multiple sets of cutlery indicating that you would be paying at least a fiver a head extra for additional washing-up, and sombre waiting staff in impossibly fashionable attire who could dampen the mood of anyone who actually intended to enjoy themselves whilst eating in the said establishment.

Matthew was surprised that Alison thought it acceptable to have a mobile phone clearly visible on the table at such an achingly elegant restaurant. Being contactable, should a disaster occur at home, clearly overrode her usual high standards of social etiquette. She was, however, quick to explain her poor table manners to the waiter when he arrived to supply them with water out of a receptacle designed to make you think you'd already spent twenty quid, and you hadn't ordered anything yet.

'I have twins,' she announced to the chisel-faced twenty-something whilst pointing at her phone.

He merely raised his eyebrows, forcing her to continue her explanation as to why she had her phone on the table.

'They're five months old,' she said. 'It's the first time we've left them, so I need to be contactable.' She stared at him, awaiting his approval.

'Of course,' nodded the waiter, clearly baffled as to why she was sharing this irrelevant information when he was used to the daily lunchtime clamour of mobiles ringing and people in suits getting up abruptly from tables to pace the room.

'So our chef's specials today are . . .' he began, standing up straight and mentally preparing himself to reel off a list of dishes that sounded like a shopping list of food combined with spa treatments.

Alison put her hand up to interrupt him.

'We are on rather a tight schedule this evening, so you can dispense with the list of specials and we'll order straight away, if you don't mind.'

'Of course, madam,' said the waiter with a curt bow. 'What would you like?'

'I'll start with the calamari and then I'll have the John Dory, please, but with new potatoes rather than the gratin potatoes.'

'Of course. And you, sir?'

'Calamari for me too, and then I'll have the fillet, medium rare.'

'Very good, sir.'

'And please can I have French fries rather than the thick-cut?'

'Of course. Now I believe you ordered champagne to be at the table,' the waiter said, reaching behind Matthew to draw a bottle out of an ice bucket. He showed the label to Matthew and asked if he would like him to open it.

Matthew glanced up at Alison, who looked stony-faced but gave a barely perceptible nod.

'Yes, please,' said Matthew, grinning at Alison in an effort to get her to reflect it back. She didn't. She looked away and picked her phone up for quick glance at the screen.

'I can't believe you asked for French fries,' she hissed as soon as the waiter had left.

'But . . . but . . . you changed your side order,' he protested, champagne glass in mid-air, ready to raise a toast to their babies.

'To something healthier,' she protested. 'I haven't lost all my baby weight yet.'

'So it's okay to change to something healthier but not something that isn't?'

'Yes,' she hissed back.

He hadn't heard that rule before. He loved French fries. He was in a restaurant and he was having steak. What could possibly be wrong with that?

'Sorry,' he said, deciding to agree so they could get their evening into a better mood. 'Now, can I propose a toast, please, to our beautiful children?'

She blushed slightly and reached for her glass, raising it to his.

'To our family,' he said simply, chinking his glass against hers. They held each other's gaze, suddenly embraced by joy that they had at last become a family. Matthew took a gulp of the fizzing liquid and reached for Alison's hand across the table. This was more like it.

'Our family,' he murmured again, enjoying the sound of it. He watched as Alison bit her lip, trying to keep control of her emotions. He intertwined his fingers in hers and they clung together in a determined grip.

They were still looking intently at each other when the phone sprang to life, buzzing loudly and illuminating the dimness surrounding their candle-lit table in a highly intrusive manner. Matthew's hand was dropped like a stone as Alison gasped and grabbed hold of the phone as though any seconds lost could be a matter of life and death.

He tried to read Alison's face as she furrowed her brow, quickly swiping and tapping in order to access whatever message was coming their way. To his relief, he saw a smile emerge.

'Yes!' she said with a small fist pump. 'I knew he could do it.' She raised her eyes to Matthew, absolutely beaming. Perhaps this poorly timed text wasn't the bad news it might have been.

'Ben managed to get Millie to sleep by seven forty-five. I knew he could do it. He really struggled last night but I told him to hang in there, she'd learn. And lo and behold, there she goes, a whole three quarters of an hour earlier than normal. Brilliant.'

She looked back down at her phone and started to tap back a reply to Ben's message. Matthew couldn't believe his eyes. Before parenthood, if they'd been out for a meal, Alison would have demanded that his phone stay in his pocket at all times. Texting at the table? Alison? This was unheard of.

'Can't you reply later?' he had to ask. If it had been him sitting there texting, he knew Alison would quite likely have grabbed the phone out of his hand and dumped it in the ice-filled champagne bucket.

'Won't be a sec,' she said, without looking up.

Matthew grasped his hands together in his lap tightly. He hadn't planned this whole evening to spend it watching the top of Alison's head whilst she texted some other bloke, least of all Ben. He reached for his glass and downed the rest of his champagne, then lifted the bottle out of the ice bucket, spraying ice-cold droplets of water onto the crisp white linen.

'More?' he said abruptly, in an attempt to divert Alison's attention. She shook her head, still not looking up. He topped his own glass up and slammed the bottle back in the bucket.

'You'll knock it over,' she said, without looking up.

Matthew sat and seethed. Alison put the phone back in its position next to the salad fork and looked up at him grinning.

'I'm so proud of him,' she gushed. 'And he sounds over the moon.' She clapped her hands together in glee. 'What must Katy be thinking? I bet she never thought Ben would take control like this.'

'Harrumph,' Matthew grumped. 'I can't actually believe that Katy is leaving the childcare to that idiot.'

Alison was about to reply when the starters arrived in front of them and her frown disappeared momentarily, morphing into a grateful smile.

'I think that is utterly unfair of you, Matthew,' she said the minute the waiter was out of earshot. 'He just needs guidance, that's all. And he really listens when he knows it's important. Do you know, he actually filmed me on his phone showing him how to purée carrots so he didn't forget how to do it. That's how seriously he's taking it.'

'I'm sorry. What did you say?'

'I said he filmed me puréeing carrots so he could watch it back again and make sure he got it right.'

'You let him film you?' asked Matthew, putting the knife and fork back down again for fear of actually wanting to throw them at something.

'Yes,' she replied, inserting her first mouthful of calamari. Matthew watched her chew and empty her mouth before she continued. 'He actually said I should think about doing some more videos and put them online to help other stay-at-home dads. He said I was really good at it, thanks to my background in training.'

Matthew leaned back in his chair, raking his hands though his hair. Ben had filmed his wife, in his house? There was something very wrong about this latest revelation, but he couldn't quite grasp what it was or how to articulate his displeasure. He took a few breaths, unsure of his next move, whilst an image of Ben leering behind a phone whilst Alison performed in front of him, disturbed his brain.

'You won't be doing it again, will you?' he said rapidly. All he wanted now was for this nightmare to be over. He was even more confused as to what Ben's motivations might be for re-entering their lives. One thing was clear: he needed to eject him as quickly as possible.

Alison was shaking her head and chewing, waiting to empty her mouth before she spoke.

'No,' she said, lifting her napkin up to dab the corner of her mouth. Matthew breathed out. That was all he needed to hear. 'No, I actually think he needs to come back weekly to update me on how he's doing with Millie's routine. He's started well but he has to stay strong, or else he could be back to square one before he knows it. I need to keep him motivated. We also need to go through other weaning foods.'

Matthew stared at her, his eyes wide, his food so far untouched.

'No,' was all he could finally squeak out, shaking his head from side to side.

Alison paused, her fork midway between plate and mouth.

'No,' he repeated. 'He won't want to come back.'

'Why do you say that?' she asked.

'Well, he's probably got his own friends to hang out with, hasn't he? Can't believe he wants to spend his days with you.'

'What are you saying?' she demanded. It was her turn to put her knife and fork down.

'Can't you see he's using you?' he said quickly. 'He'll get what he wants then you won't see him for dust. And anyway, shouldn't he be asking Katy about all this? Not taking up your time. You've got enough to cope with without holding his hand every step of the way.'

Alison looked questioningly into his eyes as he prayed for the unlikely event that she would agree and vow never to see Ben again. She glanced to her side, presumably to check out the proximity of the next table before she let him have it.

'How dare you?' she said through gritted teeth. 'What gives you the right to tell me whether I have enough to cope with?'

'I'm just looking out for you,' Matthew insisted. 'You've just had twins. Surely they need your undivided attention right now?'

'What are you implying?' spat Alison. 'That I can't cope? That I'm not looking after my children properly?'

'No, of course not.'

'Well, it certainly feels like it. All you ever do is interfere. Like you think you can do better.'

'No, I don't!' Matthew said defensively.

'You keep trying to butt in,' she ranted. 'I *know* what I'm doing.' She glared at him, eyes bulging.

'I'm good at it, *really* good at it,' she continued, working herself up into an emotional state and now on the brink of tears. 'And at least *Ben* can see that. At least he makes me feel like I know what I'm doing even if my own husband doesn't.'

Matthew gasped. The last thing he wanted to hear was that Ben was doing something he wasn't.

'But you don't even like Ben,' he protested weakly. 'You used to think he was an idiot too.'

'He needs me, Matthew. He listens. He appreciates what I'm doing.' She paused for a second before blurting out, 'He told me I was eye candy.'

She stood up and thrust her napkin onto the table, then picked up her mobile phone and ran towards the door.

He stared after her, her last words going round and round his head, oblivious to the stares of the adjacent tables. His phone beeped in his pocket. Perhaps it was her.

He lifted it out and read the new text. It was from Ian.

Have you shagged her yet?

CHAPTER TWENTY-THREE

'I cannot believe the Brewery Tap closes at midnight,' declared Braindead as they marched through the damp, drizzly streets of Leeds. Their hands were thrust deep in their pockets and their shoulders hunched, as though rigidity would keep out the biting chill of the bleak January night. The Christmas cheer of December had well and truly disappeared, leaving the city feeling hollow and naked, leading to thoughts of hibernation rather than joy and goodwill to all men.

'I just don't understand the licensing laws in this country,' Braindead continued. 'I thought it was all sorted. You could stay open as long as you wanted. Seems to me the rubbish places can stay open as long as they like, whereas it's the quality pubs still shut early. What's that all about?'

'I don't know,' replied Ben. He'd drunk too many pints of Midnight Bell to really care. Still, he was disappointed too that time had been called, as he knew he wasn't ready to go home and face Katy. 'It's probably down to customer demand or something,' he offered Braindead.

'Well, I'm a customer and I demand that only the decent pubs are allowed to stay open late and the crap ones have to shut early. That way the crap ones are incentivised to improve. Actually, that's genius. Why has no-one thought of that?'

'I think because it depends on how you define decent and crap. Your crap could be someone else's brilliant.'

'My crap could be someone else's brilliant?'

'Yes.'

'You're just trying to confuse me now.'

'No, I'm not. Bloody hell, it's cold.' Ben pulled his arms in as tight as he could to his body.

'You're telling me,' said Braindead, shivering beside him. 'Why couldn't I have been born somewhere like Spain? A country where you never need a coat, that's where I'd like to live. You can go straight out at night without agonising for hours on end as to whether you want to spend all night freezing your tits off or all night worrying about where to put your coat. And to think, in Spain you never have to lose your coat. How brilliant would that be? I would save a fortune.'

'You're right, Braindead, you should move to Spain,' Ben muttered.

'And all the bars open all night, don't they? You go there on holiday and everything's open. The crap bars *and* the good bars.'

'But they all sell crap beer,' Ben reminded him. 'Last time we all went to Spain you didn't stop moaning because all you could get was weak lager.'

'Oh yeah,' said Braindead, his shoulders sagging slightly. 'I'll just have to put up with this country then.'

They turned right, down another street, and both came to an abrupt halt.

'Jesus!' exclaimed Ben. 'What on earth is going on in there?'

They surveyed the long line of short-skirted, vest-topped young women who were jostling two or three abreast in a long queue to get into the Pink Coconut nightclub, located halfway up the street.

'Oh my days,' declared Braindead, his eyes lighting up. 'Christmas has finally arrived. Will you look at that? Women. Everywhere. I don't care what's going on in there, *we* are going in.'

'Seriously?' exclaimed Ben. 'What on earth do you want to go in there for?'

'Er,' said Braindead, pulling a face. 'To meet a woman, of course. It's my one criticism of the Brewery Tap that your chances of meeting an unattached woman in there are slim. But look at this,' he said, spreading his arms wide. 'Surely I can't fail amongst all this?'

'I'm not going in there,' said Ben, shaking his head.

'Oh come on,' replied Braindead. 'I can't go in on my own. No-one will come near me.'

'You won't pull anyway. Not anyone decent. No-one ever pulls anyone decent in a club.'

'You did,' replied Braindead.

Oh yeah, Ben remembered. He'd forgotten that he'd actually met Katy in this very club.

'It was a theme night, though,' he defended. 'Don't you remember? You were with me. It was one of those stupid school discos.'

'And theme nights are different, are they?'

'Yeah. Non-clubbers go to theme nights. Neither me nor Katy would have been there if it hadn't been a theme night. In fact, we were both there under duress because other people had begged us to go. It was pure chance that we met in a club really.'

It seemed like a whole other lifetime ago. Ben had hated every minute of seeing grown women run around in school uniform, given that he was a teacher and predisposed to find nothing at all attractive about it. Katy had been there with some new, younger mates, as all her real mates had long since married and had kids. Ben had accidentally thrown a pint of lager down her front when she'd bumped into him whilst storming off the dance floor because one of her party claimed never to have heard of Paul Weller. He'd offered her the compensation of an escape route and a kebab, and the rest, as they say, is history.

Was that really only two years ago? Unbelievable. And here he was, back again outside the Pink Coconut. He could see the same kebab shop at the end of the street, a steady stream of revellers already partaking of post-alcohol comfort food.

'Let's just go for a kebab, eh, mate?' he said.

'Noooooo,' said Braindead. 'Heeeeeelp me find a wooooooooman?'

Ben considered his options. He could go inside the club with Braindead, have a few more drinks then end up sitting on his own feeling miserable whilst Braindead tried to chat someone up, or he could go home and just be miserable whilst having a difficult conversation with his fiancée.

Fifteen minutes later they were in the club. They'd handed over an exorbitant amount of money then queued another ten minutes to hand over yet more money and their coats through a dark cubby-hole where the likelihood of ever getting anything back seemed negligible. Finally, when they emerged into the main area of the club, Ben wished with all his heart he was home, even if he did have to face Katy.

It was all wrong. He didn't belong here any more. He felt like he was visiting a zoo. When he'd last been here at least he'd felt like part of the zoo, albeit an animal that wasn't quite sure why it was there and hoped to be released as soon as possible. Memories of awful music, sticky floors, stinking toilets, under-staffed bars and terrible drinks came flooding back, and for the second time that night he was relieved that being in such a grim establishment was no longer a necessity. He was a father and fiancé, which had secured him a Get out of a Nightclubs free card.

'Need a slash,' said Braindead, tapping him on the arm and diving off into the crowd. Ben wondered how long he would have to wait for Braindead to return before he could decently claim he'd searched high and low then assumed it was Braindead who'd gone home.

'You came. Oh my God, you came!' came a shriek in his left ear accompanied by a pumping of his left arm.

Ben looked down to see Charlene grinning like a Cheshire cat whilst sucking on a straw inserted in a bottle full of some hideous bright pink liquid.

'Hi Charlene. I'm not really here,' he boomed at her. Charlene wasn't listening; she'd turned away and was waving her arm wildly.

'Abby. Abby!' she was screaming. 'Look who's here! Ben's come. Look, he's here. Bring everyone over.'

'I'm not really here,' he shouted again at her. 'I'm just here for Braindead. I'm going in a minute.'

'What?' said Charlene. 'You can't go now. You have to stay and meet everyone, and Zack McFrank hasn't even been on yet.'

'Zack McFrank?'

'Yeah. The DJ has just said he'll be on stage any minute.'

'Who's Zack McFrank?'

Charlene's mouth dropped open and she pulled the straw away from her mouth for the first time since he'd bumped into her.

'Six-Pack Zack McFrank from *Britain's Got Talent.*
He's doing a special appearance.'

Ben had no idea who she was talking about.

'What's special about it?' he asked.

'He's getting his six-pack out.'

He was starting to understand why the crowd
appeared to be ninety-five percent women.

'We had no idea,' Ben shouted back. 'Braindead
just saw all these women and demanded we come in.'

'Beeeeeeeeeen!' came a squeal and Ben found
himself face to face with Abby.

'Is it really him?' asked another girl who had
appeared next to Abby. Then another three girls
materialized, all in their late teens and early twenties,
and stared right at him

'It so is,' said Abby, looping her arm through
his. 'This is our friend Ben, otherwise known as
Stay-at-Home-Super-Hero-Dad.'

'Oh my God,' said one of the other girls. 'Wow.
Here, can I have a selfie?' she asked as she pushed
Abby out of the way to get close to Ben and thrust a
phone out in front of them.

'What's she doing?' Ben asked Abby, disturbed
by all the bodily contact and phone being thrust in
his face.

'She wants a picture of you,' she replied.

'Why?'

'Because of your video, of course.'

'What video?'

'You remember. The one of you at the music class, that Charlene put on Facebook.'

'Fucking brilliant,' one of the other girls shouted in his ear. '*I'm going home to listen to the Arctic Monkeys very loud.* Just genius. We all get together now on a Thursday morning and turn Kanye West on full blast. The kids love it. The neighbours aren't too happy, though.'

'See,' cried Charlene. 'You are an inspiration.'

Ben was just standing with his mouth open.

'I thought I'd told you to take it down?'

'Oh my God, girls, look,' shouted Charlene, distracted by something over Ben's shoulder. 'Zack McFrank is coming on. We have to get down to the stage *right now.*'

And they were all gone. Pushing him out the way to get to someone trying to make the most of his fifteen minutes of fame. All apart from Abby, who snaked her arm through his again.

'I knew you'd come,' she breathed before lifting a straw to her mouth and sucking on it suggestively through glistening lips.

He was just about to tell her he was leaving because this was all too weird when he spotted Braindead over her shoulder, searching for him.

'Heeeelp,' shrieked Ben over Abby's shoulder. 'Over here, Braindead.'

Braindead turned around and caught sight of Ben just as Abby raised her hand and laid it on his cheek. Assessing the situation, he gave Ben a quick thumbs up and a grin, then turned his back to leave Ben to it.

'Fucking Braindead,' muttered Ben under his breath, as Abby loomed closer and closer.

He grabbed her hand from his cheek and ducked under her arm.

'You remember Braindead?' he shouted at Abby as he dragged her over to where his friend was standing. 'In the coffee shop?'

Braindead winked at Ben as they approached.

'Nice one, son,' he said in appreciation of Ben's achievement at attracting a crazy lady within five minutes of entering a club.

'Getting married. Have a daughter,' said Ben, pointing to himself.

'Oh yeah,' said Braindead, as though it had just occurred to him. 'What the fuck are you doing, man?'

'Nothing,' replied Ben. 'She's . . . aggressive.'

'Really?' said Braindead. 'Would you mind if I . . . I quite like the look of her.'

'Be my absolute guest,' replied Ben. 'Abby, you do remember Braindead, don't you?' he shouted in Abby's ear.

'Shots?' Braindead shouted at Abby.

Ben gasped. No *hello*. No *good to see you again*. Was it any wonder that Braindead couldn't get a girlfriend? To his amazement, Abby grinned back at Braindead and then at Ben.

'Don't mind if I do,' she replied, and headed off to the bar, leaving the two of them to follow.

Half an hour later after four shots each at the bar, Ben was starting to feel his legs wanting to go in an entirely different direction to his body. The sniff of potential woman had turned Braindead from a dedicated worshipper of craft beers to the happy round buyer of various luminous liquids at Abby's request. Zack McFrank had attracted all but the totally hammered or male to swarm around the stage, leaving the bar clear to allow the three of them to line up in front of Kevin, their own personal barman. Behind them Zack teased his audience in the build-up to him revealing a jaw-dropping six-pack, but Abby no longer seemed interested. She'd dropped Zack like a ton of bricks, apparently more attracted by Braindead with his nervous, pathetic chat-up lines and open wallet.

'You suit orange lips,' he told her, commenting on the bold tone of lipstick she was modelling. 'Not many women can carry off orange, but you do it amazingly. It's like, wow, I have never seen orange look so good on a face. You have a face for orange. Did you know that?'

'I had no idea,' said Abby flatly, raising her eyebrows at Ben.

'Braindead is the funniest man I know, Abby,' said Ben, draping an arm around his buddy.

'And we all know what funny men are . . .' began Braindead.

'Really sexy,' Ben finished off for him, not trusting Braindead with what his conclusion might be. 'Women find funny men really sexy, don't they, Abby? It's a well-known fact.'

Abby giggled then downed another shot.

'Doesn't mean I have a big cock, though,' continued Braindead. 'Just so you know. I mean, it's not small or anything, just not enormous, if that's what you're thinking. I don't want you to think that just because I'm funny and sexy that I have a massive cock. Wouldn't want to disappoint you. Because that can happen, can't it? And I'd rather this conversation continued with you knowing I have an average-sized cock, then we all know where we stand.'

Abby giggled, and Ben's mouth dropped open.

'Mate,' he said, gently pulling Braindead to one side. 'Too much information. Not sure Abby's ready for that yet.'

'Oh,' said Braindead. He glanced at Abby then put his mouth close to Ben's ear to attempt a whisper.

'I was just trying to manage expectations,' he hissed. 'I think that's where I'm going wrong. I seem to disappoint women so I thought if I start by lowering expectations that might work in my favour. Besides, it seems really unfair that she doesn't know how big my cock is but I can see exactly how big her tits are.'

It was like an automatic reaction, he couldn't help it. Braindead mentioned Abby's tits and Ben found himself staring at her overflowing black sequined vest top which failed to hide the contrasting turquoise bra desperately trying to restrain her bust. As soon as he realised what he was doing he flicked his eyes away. Abby trapped his gaze and he felt helpless to look elsewhere in case he looked in the wrong place again.

'Another round?' said Braindead, somewhere to his left.

'Yes,' replied Abby, refusing to release Ben's gaze.

'Back in a mo,' said Braindead, and he made for the other end of the bar to attract Kevin's attention. He was only ten yards away, but he was gone, and Ben felt naked and vulnerable.

'Like what you see?' Abby said, smiling and snaking her hand over his arm.

'No!' he cried. 'I mean yes. I mean, I'm sorry, I didn't mean to do that. I'm so sorry.'

'I liked it,' she said, leaning forward so that he could feel her hot breath on his ear. 'You can look anytime.'

'No,' he said again. 'I don't want to. Not that you're not lovely to look at and everything but . . . I'm engaged, Abby. I have a baby.' The music was throbbing around in his head, the shots were making him feel weak in more ways than one and the proximity of Abby's breasts was breathtaking. He looked longingly at Braindead, who had his back turned to him at the bar. *Please turn round*, he thought. *Please come back now and then we'll go and this will all be over.*

Then things went a bit hazy. Abby was kissing him, holding his head firmly between her hands as she ground her lips against his. *Stop!* his head was screaming as his legs started to buckle under him. He raised his hands to grasp her arms in an attempt to free his head, but she just tightened her grip. Ben thrust his hips outwards, as though any contact at waist level would spark spontaneous combustion. Suddenly someone grabbed his shoulder and yanked him out of Abby's grasp.

'What the fuck are you doing?' shouted Braindead.

'Thank God,' muttered Ben, wiping his lips as he staggered backwards.

'I'll get my own drink, shall I?' enquired Abby, looking slightly smug. She headed off to hunt down a barman.

'I can't believe you!' said Braindead. 'I leave you for five minutes and she was all over you? You've got Katy, you wanker. Why do you have to go and steel my bird?'

'I didn't! She jumped me.'

'Oh yeah,' said Braindead sarcastically. 'Women do that all the time, don't they? Do you think I'm an idiot or something?' He looked Ben up and down in disgust, then turned and walked off.

CHAPTER TWENTY-FOUR

'They fancy each other,' shouted Matthew.

'What?' Ian shouted back.

'I said, they fancy each other,' Matthew repeated, right in his ear.

He had sat alone in the restaurant for some time, trying to get over the shock of Alison's proud announcement that Ben had described her as eye candy. He'd sat sipping the rest of the champagne, staring into space and mulling it over, while the rest of the restaurant bustled around him. It was just such an odd response from Alison. She was the last person to be happy to be on the receiving end of such a label. The thought that she would ever enjoy being appreciated merely for her looks was unimaginable.

'Eye candy,' he kept muttering to himself in disbelief. He was certain that if he'd ever called her eye candy, she would have blown a gasket and accused him of some kind of hideous demeaning behaviour. But no, apparently being called eye candy by the likes of Ben – a young, fit, footie-playing, ex-PE instructor, super caring stay-at-home dad – well, that was a major compliment. She was seriously chuffed. He thought she might even have been blushing as she flung it in his face as her parting shot. Matthew was angry with Ben for saying such a thing to his wife, and even angrier with Alison for liking it.

They'd actually been flirting, he suddenly realised when he'd nearly polished off the whole bottle of champagne. That's what it was. In his own house. How dare they! And they were both parents of newborns. Absolutely disgraceful!

Having ascertained Ian's whereabouts via text, he paid the bill to a bewildered waiter, who cheered up dramatically when he saw the size of the tip. Matthew fled the restaurant to download the latest development to his mate.

It was now after ten, and what Ian had described as Becki's local did not look like the type of place that a man in his forties could frequent without looking like a bit of a loser. Matthew soon found Ian in Cocktail Emporium, standing alone at a high table, ogling his girlfriend on the dance floor whilst trying desperately to look as though he was twenty years younger. His shocking pink and yellow designer shirt could have been carried off by a long, toned torso, but Ian's slight beer belly and too short arms meant the colourful garment made him look like a children's TV presenter. An attempt at using hair wax to hone a more youthful style had failed, due to lack of hair. What was left was unpleasant, greasy-looking strands. However, he still had a massive beam on his face when Matthew walked in, and he welcomed him with a bear hug and a cocktail.

'Seriously?' said Matthew. 'You drink cocktails now?'

'Sure,' Ian shrugged, taking a sip. 'No big deal.'

'And what are you wearing?'

'Becki took me shopping today. She says I look ten years younger.'

'You look like someone desperately trying to look ten years younger. Is this really all necessary, just for her?'

'Who is the one in a happy, sexually active relationship here, and who is the one running to me because his wife fancies another bloke and they haven't had sex in months? If it makes her happy if I wear a pink shirt, mate, I'm gonna wear a pink shirt.'

Matthew felt his shoulders sag. If only this problem could be solved by wearing a pink shirt. Somehow he didn't think it would have the necessary impact on Alison. He picked up the drink bought for him by Ian and took a sip. It tasted disgusting.

They didn't talk for a while, just stood together watching the clutch of women on the dance floor, who were tottering and writhing against each other, displaying their young bodies to the various groups of men loitering around the edge. They were no doubt waiting for the point when they would be drunk enough to step onto the dance floor themselves and chance their arm at trying to pull. Becki was contorting her body into ridiculous positions, causing

Matthew to look away at one point as it seemed inevitable that any minute he was going to see a flash of knickers.

'So tell me again exactly what she said,' Ian asked eventually, turning his back on the dance display to avoid distraction.

'She said Ben told her she was eye candy.'

'Right,' Ian nodded.

'That's a come-on, right?' said Matthew. 'He fancies her?'

'You can't be sure,' said Ian, shaking his head.

'But she liked it,' urged Matthew. '*Alison* liked being called eye candy!'

'You never can tell with women, mate. When I was married I'd tell Caroline that she looked gorgeous and she'd fly off the flipping handle – tell me I was after something, or ask me what cock-up I was covering up. Women's reactions to compliments are one of the most mystifying things known to man. Throwing a woman a compliment is like throwing meat into the lions' den. You may get a big fat lick, but more than likely you'll get your hand bitten off.'

All Matthew could do was nod in agreement. Just that evening he'd told Alison how much her dress suited her. He'd realised his mistake when she had pointed out that it suited her because it was an old maternity dress she'd bought in the early stages of her pregnancy and was now, to her horror, the only dress in her wardrobe that actually fitted.

'What really worries me is what motivated Ben to say that,' Matthew continued. 'Why would he say that to Alison?'

'It's an odd choice of phrase for your wife, I have to admit,' said Ian. 'To me, eye candy is long legs, a penchant for pastel miniskirts and candyfloss for brains. Having said that, I think you're thinking about this way too deeply. Just knock the bugger out. Whatever he said, whyever he said it, it's time to get rid, my son. You can stand for this no longer.'

'I know,' Matthew agreed. 'I told Alison she shouldn't see him again, that he was taking advantage and she didn't have time, and she went mental. Told me I couldn't tell her what to do, and at least Ben appreciated what a good mother she was – not to mention that he called her *eye candy*.'

'It's alright, mate,' said Ian, putting a hand on his shoulder, 'I hear you. Calm down.'

'*How can I calm down?*' said Matthew, his eyes bulging. 'He's in my house, with my wife, and I can't do anything about it.'

'You have one other option,' replied Ian. 'But you're not going to like it.'

'Anything,' gasped Matthew. 'Tell me what to do.'

'Well,' said Ian agonisingly slowly. 'The way I see it is, if you can't get Alison to stop seeing Ben then you have to get Ben to stop seeing Alison.'

'How do I do that? Alison's practically bringing up Ben's daughter at the moment. He's not going to give up that lifeline easily.'

'Fair comment,' Ian nodded. 'So I think really your only option if you want to shut this entire thing down is to . . .' He hesitated.

'Do what?' demanded Matthew.

'Tell Katy.'

'Are you fucking insane?'

'What would Katy do if she found out Ben was spending time with Alison behind her back?'

'She'd have a heart attack.'

'Correct . . . and then what would she do?'

'Make him stop.'

'Exactly. She knows as well as you do that them two together is a disaster waiting to happen. Between you, you must be able to make it stop before someone gets hurt.'

Matthew stared back at Ian. He knew there was sense in what he was saying but there was one major flaw in his plan.

'I can't contact Katy,' he stated.

'Why not? It's all over between you. So you had a one-night stand. Big deal. It was ages ago, but it'll come back to haunt you if you don't sort this mess out.'

If only it had been just a one night-stand, thought Matthew. It should have been, but then he'd even managed to screw that up. In a moment of panic and madness he'd declared his love to Katy in the labour ward whilst she'd been having contractions. He'd even offered to leave Alison if Katy would have him but she'd turned him down, choosing to marry

Ben instead. It had been left to Daniel of all people to talk Matthew down and make him see sense – that he didn't love Katy; he was just hankering after their carefree teenage romance, which could never be recaptured. So Katy's last impression of him would be of a desperate, pathetic man professing his undying love for her. How could he ever face up to her again, let alone try and convince her that her fiancé had been flirting with Alison?

'There must be another way,' he pleaded.

Ian thought for a moment then shook his head.

'Call Katy. Get it over with.'

CHAPTER TWENTY-FIVE

There was crying coming from somewhere. She turned over in bed and caught sight of a red flashing light on the baby monitor on her bedside table. It was Millie crying. What time was it? The corner of the duvet obscured the clock. She pushed it out of the way to reveal it was 6.32 a.m. Not bad. She'd take that. Now whose turn was it to get up? She and Ben had a loose agreement to take it in turns at the weekends, but there was no rule as to who took Saturdays and who took Sundays. Usually it was whoever broke first on Saturday at Millie's wails. *I'll get up today*, she thought, *seeing as Ben has had her all week*. He could have the first lie-in. She turned over to tell him that he could stay in bed. He wasn't there. It was obvious he hadn't been there all night. No dent on the pillow, no watch on the bedside table. Katy gasped as the memory of their fallout the previous evening came flooding back. She'd stayed awake until midnight waiting for him to come in so she could apologise. But she must have fallen asleep and now it was morning. She shot up in bed, desperate to find evidence of his existence. For the first time in her entire life she longed to see a stray sock or pair of boxer shorts strewn on the floor. But there was nothing. The bedroom was eerily neat as though Ben's existence had been scrubbed entirely.

She jumped out of bed, threw on a dressing gown and made for Millie's room, a million different options running through her head. Perhaps he'd gone home with Braindead. Perhaps he'd forgotten his key and slept out on the landing; it had been known before. Or perhaps she'd driven him away for good with her accusation the previous night. Would he ever forgive her? Perhaps he was with her, whoever she was. Perhaps he was in a ditch? At what point should she start ringing hospitals? All these thoughts paraded through her brain as she performed the mundane early-morning rituals surrounding a baby. Clean nappy, feed, clean clothes. Millie wouldn't wait for Katy to decipher the small incident of her father going missing. Essential activities needed to be performed, and only after that could Katy start to have a meltdown.

Having dressed Millie in a pink outfit, as Ben seemed to be avoiding handling any pink clothing, she took her into the living room to lay her on a blanket with some toys. She nearly dropped Millie when she discovered a large, barely moving object lying on the sofa, which on closer inspection turned out to be a fully clothed Ben, sound asleep. His drool had created a dark wet stain on the cushion and there was an indecipherable smell that required the immediate opening of windows despite the sub-zero temperatures.

Katy pulled the curtains open roughly and let in fresh air. She picked up the remote control from the floor and pressed some buttons, eventually settling on *Peppa Pig* in order to cause maximum irritation. She glanced back at Ben, who hadn't moved, then pressed another button, which increased the volume to beyond staying asleep or even pretending to stay asleep level.

The big lump heaved and sighed before it turned over awkwardly. Ben blinked his eyes open to see Katy sitting on the floor next to Millie kicking on a play mat.

Neither of them said anything as the sound of humans pretending to be animals behaving like humans filled the awkward space between them.

'Why is kids' telly so sexist?' Ben muttered eventually after Peppa Pig had jumped in another muddy puddle. 'We are not letting Millie watch this when she's older and can understand what's going on here.'

'I think you're reading too much into it,' said Katy, staring at Millie, not knowing how to communicate how mad she was that he'd given her a scare by sleeping on the sofa and how sorry she was for what she'd said the night before.

'I'm not,' said Ben. 'Daddy Pig is an idiot, hasn't got a bloody clue, and yet Mummy Pig is so wise and brilliant.'

'Well, it's just one show,' replied Katy with a shrug of the shoulders.

'Dipsy,' said Ben.

'What?'

'I take offence at a male Teletubby being called Dipsy. And he's actually named after a Dipstick. Just wrong and rude.'

'How do you know he's named after a dipstick?'

'Wikipedia.'

'Oh.' She stared back down at Millie. *Where the fuck have you been?* she wanted to scream at him. *Why did you stay out so late? Who were you with?*

Another whole episode of *Peppa Pig* passed by in silence until they reached plastic toy advertising hell, and Katy was forced to speak. She looked up to see that Ben had closed his eyes again.

'I'm sorry,' she said. He didn't move. 'I'm sorry about what I said last night, it all came out wrong. I didn't mean it to sound like that.' He moved, emitting a tiny snore. Katy groaned in frustration. She was trying to apologise and he was fast asleep, and he hadn't even told her where he'd been. Just moaned about gender inequality in children's animation. She reached over and threw a cushion at him.

'Whassup?' he said, opening his eyes with a start, then batting the cushion away.

'I need to know where you were,' she said. 'I was worried.'

Ben blinked back at her wordlessly. Either he was trying to remember where he'd been, or he was trying to think of where he was going to tell her he'd been.

'I didn't want to wake you when I came in,' he muttered eventually. 'We ended up in the Pink Coconut.' He heaved himself up, rubbing his eyes.

'Oh,' she said. That was weird. Ben hated the Pink Coconut.

'See anyone?' she asked, as casually as she could muster.

His palms stopped mid-rub, hiding his eyes completely for a moment, then he gripped the edge of the sofa and hoisted himself up.

'Not really,' he said.

'I'm so sorry about what I said last night,' she blurted out, unable to let him leave the room with everything hanging over them. 'It came out all wrong. It's just . . . it's just been such an odd time with us swapping like this, getting used to different roles. I think the guilt of leaving Millie has just made me a bit paranoid, that's all. I'm so sorry. It was a stupid thing to say. I know you'd never do anything behind my back. Please forgive me.'

She wished he'd look at her, but he was just staring into space and she had no idea what he was thinking.

'Ben,' she said miserably. 'I really am sorry.'

He scratched his head and looked down at her.

'Let's just forget about last night,' he said.

'Okay,' she whispered, feeling relief sweep over her.

He dropped to his knees and knelt down next to Millie, bending forward to give her a kiss. He raised his head and gave Katy a peck on the cheek.

'I think I need a shower,' he said, with a small smile. He hauled himself up and went out of the room, leaving Katy in shock at the sight of bright orange lipstick marks all over his left ear.

CHAPTER TWENTY-SIX

'What exactly are we doing here?' asked Daniel, as he sat down next to Katy on a damp wooden bench later that afternoon.

'I needed to get out,' she muttered, blowing on her hands. 'Thought I'd bring Millie here to see the excitement to come in a few months' time when she's ready for swings and slides.'

Daniel gazed around the soggy playground. What he saw was immensely depressing and not remotely aesthetically pleasing.

'What are these morons doing?' he asked, nodding his head towards a dad who was challenging the laws of physics by seating himself opposite a very young child on a see-saw. The child was dangling at the top, unable to descend, whilst the father desperately tried to fling himself up from the ground. On the other side of the playground a woman sat at the top of a slide with a toddler on her knee, clearly struggling to get her ample bottom to force itself down the slide.

'Being parents,' said Katy.

'So being a parent generally involves sitting in uncomfortable, awkward positions?' asked Daniel, adjusting his coat under his bottom.

Katy cocked her head on one side and thought for a minute.

'Basically, yes, she replied. 'You seem to spend a lot of time sitting on the floor, or in little kid chairs that aren't meant for adults, or on play equipment also not meant for adults. As a rule, parents are uncomfortable most of the time.'

Daniel tutted. 'I genuinely have no idea why we have the growing population problems we have.'

'He came home last night with lipstick on his ear,' Katy blurted out.

Daniel didn't reply.

'Did you hear me?' she asked.

'Yes,' he nodded. 'I'm just trying to process the implications of lipstick on an ear.'

'I think you'll find the implications are that some-one had their lips on my fiancé's ear.'

'I know,' said Daniel slowly. 'I'm just trying to work out what that means.'

'It means that he's a lying hypocrite.'

'Not necessarily,' replied Daniel, turning to face her. 'You just saw lipstick on the ear, you say. Were there lipstick marks near any of his other organs?'

Katy stared back for a moment, incredulous.

'If you mean his you-know-what, then I have no idea, since I can't say I've had the opportunity to inspect that particular area, but now you've mentioned it, I can't get the image out of my mind.'

'All I'm saying is that lipstick downstairs would be conclusive, but lipstick on the ear, well, I'm not sure that's enough evidence to go throwing further accusations around. Any chance you can do a further inspection?'

'No!' she exclaimed.

'Would you like me to?'

'No! You're not really helping.'

'Sorry. Let's start again. Did you ask him where he'd been after he left you?

'He said he ended up in the Pink Coconut with Braindead. He hates the Pink Coconut.'

'Mmmm, I see,' said Daniel, nodding wisely. 'With Braindead. Right, we'll soon have this sorted. Have you got Braindead's number with you?'

Katy read out the number off her phone whilst Daniel tapped it into his. He held it up to his ear and waited patiently for Braindead to answer.

'Hey, it's Daniel here,' he said eventually. 'Yes, gay Daniel,' he sighed, raising his eyebrows at Katy. 'I was just calling as I hear you ended up in a nightclub with Ben last night and I wanted to find out if you'd had any luck with the ladies. It sounds like just the sort of place where you might be successful.'

Daniel paused, listening intently.

'You met someone? But that's fantastic, Braindead.'

Daniel gripped Katy's hand reassuringly as he listened to Braindead. 'Snogging Ben! Are you sure?'

'What?' said Katy, leaping up. '*What?*' she screamed.

'Hang on, hang on,' said Daniel, waving her down. 'Of course I won't tell Katy, Braindead. I'm very surprised at Ben.'

'Abby!' Katy exclaimed suddenly, her eyes bulging. 'It's that bitch Abby.'

'It wasn't Abby, by any chance, was it, Braindead?' Daniel enquired.

'It was. Oh, just a lucky guess. I hear a lot of Abbys go to the Pink Coconut. So what did you do?'

Daniel nodded at the phone as Katy paced in front of the bench.

'I see. Well, if I see him I'll pass the message on that he owes you fifty quid for drinks. I'd better go now. Okay. See you. Bye.'

'He kissed that slapper!' Katy exclaimed. 'I might have known. She was all over him right in front of me at the registry office, so goodness only knows what she would have been like with me out of the picture. Bloody hell!' she shouted, getting up and kicking the roundabout, causing the two other parents to look over at her in disgust. 'What am I going to do?'

'Describe Abby to me,' Daniel ordered.

'Er, I don't know, young.'

'How young?'

'Maybe twenty. Why? Do you think that's it? I'm old and decrepit and a bit saggy because of the baby. He doesn't fancy me any more, does he? He wanted something younger, firmer, bouncier.'

'Probably,' replied Daniel, nodding.

'Really? Is that what you think?'

'Well, it sounds good to me.'

'He's doing it to get back at me, isn't he?' Katy gasped. 'For sleeping with Matthew. He's had a one-night stand because I did. It's all my fault,' she wailed, putting her head in her hands. 'I knew it was too good to be true, him forgiving me.'

'He did forgive you,' said Daniel. 'He asked you to marry him.'

'Yeah, well, we're not married yet, are we? We haven't even set a date.'

'And why is that exactly?'

'You try planning a wedding when you've got a baby in the house.'

'Really? Is that all that's stopping you?'

'And we can't afford it, and I'm back working full-time and my fiancé might be having an affair, for goodness' sake.'

Daniel shook his head and took her hands in his.

'It just doesn't make sense,' he said gently. 'Look, I know it's painful to remember the mess you got yourself into before Millie arrived, but when it comes to Ben you have to remember this. He came back for you. He found out the truth and yet he still came back for you and proposed. He's overcome a lot to be with you and I really don't think he'd throw that all away for the sake of a twenty-year-old who wears questionable lipstick. Do you?'

Katy looked away and bit her lip.

'Do you want to believe he's having an affair?' Daniel asked. 'Would it help get rid of some of this guilt you're carrying around with you because you cheated on him?'

Katy could feel the tears pushing their way to the surface. Perhaps Daniel was right. Perhaps she wouldn't hate herself so much if Ben cocked up too. Was she just looking for him to fail?

'Ben has totally put his faith in you,' said Daniel, wiping a tear away from her cheek. 'Maybe you need to do the same.'

Chapter Twenty-Seven

For the second time in twenty-four hours, Ben dug his hands deep in his pockets and braced himself against the biting Leeds wind. He was late, so he was walking fast. He was also worried that someone he knew might see them together, but he figured he didn't have a choice. He had to see Alison today and dig himself out of the situation he'd got himself in. Even if it did mean meeting her in broad daylight in the middle of Roundhay Park on a Saturday afternoon amongst all the other parents of young children, desperate to get out of the house. Katy had headed off with Millie to do some shopping in town, so at least he hadn't had to lie to her as to where he was going. He was done with lies and he needed to see Alison to put a halt to this one.

He spotted her before she saw him, perched neatly on a painted green bench, double buggy parked at a perfect right angle next to her. She'd insisted they meet at three p.m. sharp so that she could walk there and Rebecca and George could enjoy some fresh air. Matthew would be down at the driving range, so he would be none the wiser. Ben saw her glancing at her watch so he picked up speed, knowing she would be getting frustrated at his slight delay.

'I don't think we should see each other any more,' he announced, plonking himself next to her on the bench, hands still stuffed deep in his pockets.

Alison's perfectly made up face furrowed as she turned to look at him.

'You're late,' she said.

'I know. I'm sorry. We can't carry on doing this.'

'Why not?'

'I can't lie to Katy any more,' said Ben. 'It's all getting out of hand. She thinks I'm having an affair because I'm acting all weird.'

'An affair!' exclaimed Alison. She looked around nervously in case anybody had overheard her. 'With me?' she hissed.

'No, of course not. She doesn't know about you, does she? She doesn't know who with. She's just suspicious because of all the sneaking around.'

'Oh,' said Alison, with a confused expression.. 'So just tell her – you're not having an affair, you're just coming to see me.'

'No,' said Ben quickly.

'But why not?'

He stared back at her blankly. What could he tell her? Certainly not that if he told Katy, they definitely wouldn't be seeing each other again.

'She'd be jealous,' he lied.

'Really?'

'Yeah,' he said, looking away. 'Keeps me on a short leash, does Katy.'

'But jealous of me . . . with you?'

'Oh yeah,' Ben nodded. He pretended to watch a couple of lads kicking a ball about on a lawn in front of them. 'Anyone, really. Must be the age gap thing.'

'But we're nowhere near finished,' Alison protested. 'There's still so much I need to tell you. Millie's not in a reliable sleep pattern yet, and I know you think you're handling it really well, but what happens when she has a blip? When she's getting more teeth, for example, and waking up four or five times a night and you're so tired that you don't know which way is up – what will you do then? Ask Katy what to do? Will she know what to do with a constantly crying, teething baby?'

Ben stared back at her. He knew Katy wouldn't have a clue and neither would he.

'I'll work it out,' he said, trying to sound more confident than he felt.

'But I can help you,' said Alison. 'Why wouldn't Katy want you to have help, just because of some stupid jealousy? She's as bad as Matthew, honestly she is.'

'What do you mean, as bad as Matthew?' Ben asked.

Alison looked down and clasped her leather gloved hands together. 'Well actually, we did have an argument about you on Friday night.'

'What do you mean? Are you saying he knows we've been seeing each other?'

'Yes,' replied Alison. 'Didn't I tell you?'

'No, you didn't.'

'Must have slipped my mind,' she continued, not noticing Ben's horror. 'He was concerned for my safety, having a strange man in the house, so I had to tell him it was only you.'

'And what did he say?'

'Oh, he was fine with it. Couldn't understand why Katy wasn't helping you, but as I said to him, Katy didn't seem to have many maternal instincts.'

'So why did you argue, then?'

'It was when you texted to tell me you'd managed to get Millie to sleep early. He got all silly about it, tried to tell me that I shouldn't be helping you. He even demanded that I shouldn't see you again.'

Ben sank back against the bench. Matthew had known all along. What on earth must he be thinking?

'I told him, it's got nothing to do with him,' Alison went on. 'He's not the one at home all day, is he? He hasn't a clue. You have to find your new tribe when you have a career change like we both have, and often they're the last people you'd expect them to be.'

'Is that supposed to be some kind of compliment?' asked Ben.

'It is.' Alison looked down at her hands. 'I've actually really enjoyed seeing you.' If Ben wasn't mistaken there was a hint of colour in her cheeks. 'It's been so good to be with someone who doesn't judge you. I hate the relentless scrutiny of the other mothers –

just waiting for you to slip up, make a mistake, show any kind of weakness, all so they can feel better about their own shortcomings.'

'I'm sure they're not really thinking that,' said Ben.

'Believe me Ben, they are. They'll all cut you some slack because you're new and a man, but you just wait. Give it a couple of weeks and you'll hear them whispering behind your back about the state your car seat is in or your inability to dress yourself and care for a baby.'

Ben tucked his shirt in, his brow furrowed.

'Actually, I think you're wrong,' he said. 'The mums I've met so far have been quite sceptical of me to start with, but I've never felt judged. In fact . . .' He leapt up so he could fish his phone out of his trouser pocket. 'Take a look at this.'

He searched on his phone and eventually managed to locate the Teenage Mums Facebook group page. Charlene had sent him the link, and he'd watched the film of his Music, Mummy and Me experience several times now and managed to see the funny side. He was also secretly quite proud of the comments that had been left underneath.

'*You are an inspiration,*' he read out to Alison. '*I've ditched baby music class and me and Alfie are having a much better time hitting saucepans at home really loud.* This next one's my favourite,' he said, pointing at the screen. 'Listen. *Thanks for showing you should just enjoy being with your baby. No longer being tortured by tambourines and stupid tunes. Turns out Chelsea LOVES One Direction.*' He turned and grinned at Alison. 'Obviously I'm not proud of the One Direction bit, but not bad, eh?'

'I don't understand.' Alison stared at him, open-mouthed. 'What have you been doing?'

'Oh, sorry, I never told you, did I? It was our first day and me and Millie got barred from Music, Mummy and Me. Can you believe it? I was mortified. Turns out I just happened to say what everyone else was thinking. Look, watch this.' He tapped on the play button and let Alison watch the film of his first and only experience of baby music class. When it was finished she looked up at him speechless with shock.

'You don't approve, do you?' he said. He should have known that Alison would be a supporter of anything that the so-called experts suggested would further her children's development.

'Well, say something,' he urged. 'Tell me I'm an idiot if you want. You know more about these things than I do. Was it a massive mistake? Have I scuppered Millie's chances of being the next McCartney?'

Alison shook her head in a daze, then looked over to her two babies.

'I've got it wrong, haven't I?' said Ben, panicking at Alison's lack of response. 'I should have stuck with it. Millie's going to be deformed or something because I couldn't stand sitting in that class with her like I should have done.'

'No,' said Alison at last, gripping his arm in her hand. 'You haven't got it wrong. I'm just thinking that perhaps . . .' She swallowed as if she couldn't quite believe what she was about to say. 'Perhaps it's me who's got it wrong.'

Ben gasped.

'Maybe I have got it wrong,' Alison continued, looking pale. She stared at her children as if she was seeing them for the first time. 'I'm raising my children by the book because I'm petrified that if I don't I'll be a bad mother.' She looked like she might cry any minute.

Ben looked around awkwardly. He didn't want to be sitting next to a crying mother of twins. You could get locked up for that. He put his arm around her to try and prevent any further upset.

'I'm doing it all wrong,' she said, tears brimming.

'No,' said Ben, as a rejection of both her tears and her statement. 'You're not. If it wasn't for your organisational prowess I would still be at the super-stressed, super-stupid, dipshit stage, and hating every minute of it. I need you to tell me all that practical stuff so I *can* enjoy myself with Millie.'

Alison sniffed and raised her head to look at her babies again.

'I've taken it too far,' she said, shaking her head. 'All I think about is planning and organising. It's all I ever dreamed of for so long, and I'm not even taking the time to enjoy it.'

'You just need to chill out,' Ben shrugged. 'Enjoy being a family, not conducting a military operation.'

Alison bit her lip and nodded.

'Who'd have thought it, eh?' Ben gave her a cheeky grin. 'I end up giving *you* advice on childcare. If we were together we'd make the perfect parents.'

Alison blushed again.

'And we both make a mean video. There's you with your top-quality carrot puréeing and me with my harassment of childcare professionals – we should have our own TV show.'

Alison managed to raise a smile.

'Speaking of which, I showed Charlene the clip of you doing your cooking demo, I hope you don't mind. She wants to put it on her Facebook page too, but I said she had to ask you first. She said you were so much better than the health visitor, who's a complete arse . . . in her words. She said you did it like they'd do it on *Blue Peter*, like anyone could understand.'

Alison stared back at him wide-eyed, still looking a little shaken at the unexpected revelations that the afternoon had brought.

'No,' she said eventually. 'They're not very good, really.'

'Alison, they are brilliant. You should do more, seriously.'

'No, I don't think so,' she said.

'Go on,' said Ben. 'Think of all the parents you'd be helping to get the basics right so they can spend the rest of the time enjoying their kids. And,' he said, slapping his hand against his head as he made an epic realisation. 'If you carry on doing your videos then I can get your advice without us having to see each other. Genius.'

Alison looked away quickly.

'No, I'm sorry, I didn't mean it like that,' Ben said hastily. 'It's not that I don't want to see you, it's just . . .' He tailed off. He couldn't explain that their unlikely friendship was doomed by the secret he had to keep from her. 'It's just that, you know, I can't explain it to Katy.' He stared at her, praying she could understand something of the utter gibberish he was talking.

Alison slowly raised her eyes to meet his.

'I can understand why Katy feels maybe a bit threatened by me,' she said.

'*Yes*,' said Ben. Why hadn't he thought of saying it like that? 'That's it. She'd be so threatened by you. You've got this mother thing licked and I'm not sure she'd cope well with that at all.'

Alison nodded slowly.

'Perhaps I could do some more videos,' she said. 'If you really think they're that helpful.'

'Totally,' said Ben. 'I would be a gibbering mess without you. And like I said, I'm sure there are other stay-at-home dads who would be only too happy to get your help as well as a bit of *eye candy*.' He smiled and gave her a nudge.

She gave him a weak smile back.

'And the other people on YouTube *are* terrible,' she said. 'I did actually watch some after you said that's where you'd learned how to use your steriliser. Those women make the rest of us mothers look like idiots.'

'So you'll do some, then?' asked Ben.

'Okay,' she agreed. 'I will if you think they're helpful. I'll need you to give me a hand me, though.'

'Why?' he asked, panicking. This was all about not seeing each other again, not inventing another reason to be together.

'Well, I can't film myself, can I? And I've no idea how you put these things on the internet.'

'Of course you can film yourself. You just need a mini-tripod or something, and uploading is easy.'

Alison looked back at him blankly and helplessly.

'Do you want me to come and show you?'

Alison nodded.

'Alright, then.' How could he say no? He'd see her one last time, sort her out with video sharing, then that would be it. Sorted. It would finally all be over.

Chapter Twenty-Eight

Matthew hovered.

Matthew paced.

Matthew stopped pacing, dived into a coffee shop and drank a double espresso.

Matthew stood outside the door of the advertising agency and felt his heart beat extremely fast. *Calm down*, he told himself. *This is a simple exercise.* He would go in. Ask to see Katy. Calmly and clearly explain what had been happening and request her assistance in preventing Ben from spending any more time with his wife. Easy. What was there to be nervous about? The fact that the last time he'd seen Katy was on the labour ward when he'd offered to leave his wife for her was all water under the bridge. Surely Katy would have taken enough drugs during childbirth to be inclined to think it had been a hallucination of some sort. It was all in the past and they were on to another catastrophe now, which just needed some attention and then everything could go back to normal. Couldn't it?

He took a deep breath, pushed through the door and headed towards the receptionist.

'Hello.' He coughed, trying to rid his voice of the nervous squeak. 'Could I see Katy Chapman, please?'

The woman wrinkled her brow. 'Are you here for a meeting?'

'No, it's a personal matter. I just need to tell her something. It won't take long. I know where her office is; I can wait in there if she's busy.' He turned to head for the lift.

'I can't allow that,' the receptionist shouted after him. 'You can only go up there if it's an emergency and you're a close friend or relative.'

Matthew turned on his heel and faced her stern gaze.

'It's an emergency,' he said finally. 'Death in the family.'

'Oh, I see. Are you her partner?'

He stared back at her.

'Yes,' he muttered.

'But I thought Katy's partner was a PE teacher?' She frowned. 'You don't look like a PE teacher.'

Matthew looked down and gulped. He felt weedy. He always felt weedy when compared with Ben.

'I've just come from the funeral directors, and I need to talk to Katy about something really quickly.' He looked down at his shoes, hoping the reception-ist would read this as a signal that he was struggling with his emotions and she really should let him do whatever he needed to do.

'Okay then. You can go up now,' was all he heard.

He nodded, then turned to walk towards the lift. He pressed the button and stood waiting, keeping his buttocks taut in case the receptionist spotted any further evidence he wasn't the sports-mad Adonis she'd envisaged.

He emerged from the lift on the second floor, praying it would come flooding back to him where Katy's office was. It didn't. He prowled the corridors hoping for some sort of reminder but none came. Instead he found himself peering into offices then having to avert his eyes quickly from the cool-looking 'creative' types inhabiting them, who eyed his boring suit with disdain.

Having done two laps and convinced he'd looked into every office, he found a stairwell and traipsed up to the next floor, hoping he would have more luck there. He did. Immediately. He opened the door to the main corridor and slammed straight into Daniel.

'Steady, watch where you're going,' Daniel said as he expertly swerved a cup of coffee out of harm's way.

'Sorry,' Matthew muttered.

'Oh my God!' exclaimed Daniel. 'Matthew?'

Bloody hell, thought Matthew. Daniel was a complication that he didn't need right at this moment.

'I just need to tell her something, that's all,' he blurted out. 'Just tell me where she is and I'll be gone in ten minutes, I can assure you.'

'Oh no,' said Daniel, shaking his head vigorously. 'We are not going through that again. Leave,

Matthew. Whatever it is you have to say, it's not welcome. You and her, in the same room? In the same building? Are you insane? Think of your family.'

'I am thinking of my family,' he said, stamping his foot like a child. 'And Katy's. We have to stop him before it's too late.'

'Stop who?' asked Daniel, 'What are you talking about?'

'Ben,' said Matthew in desperation. 'He's taking advantage of her and it will all end in tears, I know it will.'

'You know about Ben?' asked Daniel, incredulous. 'How do you know about Ben?'

'*You* know about Ben?' Matthew questioned in amazement.

'Yes.'

'How?'

'Katy told me. And for the record, I think it's probably just a storm in a teacup and I've advised Katy to let it blow over.'

'Are you some kind of idiot?' Matthew exploded. 'This relationship is toxic. It could all blow up in our faces at any point.'

'And what on earth has it got to do with you?'

'Because he's flirting with my *wife*! It's got everything to do with me.'

'Who is?'

Matthew stopped. There was something off about this whole conversation, but he wasn't sure what it was. The two men stared at each other, confused.

'Ben has been spending time with my wife and I need Katy to help me put a stop to it,' said Matthew emphatically.

Daniel continued to stare at Matthew, his eyes widening.

'KATY!' he bellowed.

'WHAT?' came a shout from somewhere down the corridor.

'I need you in the conference room, right now,' he shouted back.

Two minutes later Katy bustled into the conference room. Daniel sat at the head of the long boardroom-style table, his elbows resting on the arms of his chair, his fingertips drumming together. Matthew stood with his back to the room, staring out of the window over the concrete spires of Leeds.

'This had better be good,' said Katy as she closed the door behind her. 'Crispy Bix will be here any minute.'

'Katy,' said Matthew, turning around.

'Matthew!' she exclaimed. She glanced over at Daniel, horrified, then fixed Matthew with a glare. 'What are you doing here?'

'Hear him out,' said Daniel, getting up. 'I'll be in my office,' he added as he made for the door.

'No!' shouted Katy, moving to block his path. 'You can't leave us alone together. It's . . . it's not right.'

Daniel looked down on her and smiled.

'I was so hoping you'd say that.' He sat back down in his chair with a grin and motioned Matthew to carry on. 'I really didn't want to miss this.'

'It's Ben,' Matthew began.

'Ben!' exclaimed Katy. 'What about Ben?'

'Well, he's been spending a lot of time with Alison, and I need you to put a stop to it.'

Katy didn't say anything for a good few seconds, then she burst out laughing.

'Is this your idea of a joke, Daniel?' she said eventually, once she had calmed down.

'No,' said Daniel. 'I admit that a teeny-weeny bit of me wishes it was, but no. This is nothing to do with me, I can assure you.'

Katy turned back to Matthew. 'You're not serious, are you? There's no way Ben would be spending time with Alison. He doesn't even like her. He thinks she's, well, a bit stuck-up.'

'Stuck-up!' cried Matthew. 'That's rich, that is.' He began to pace the room. 'Well, he's not calling her that any more. She's on bloody cloud nine because he called her eye candy.'

'Eye- candy!' Katy exploded. 'Ben called Alison eye candy? Don't be so ridiculous!'

'Yes, he did. I believe it's what's known as flirting.' Matthew threw a questioning glance over at Daniel, who nodded his agreement.

'I would concur that yes, calling someone eye candy constitutes flirting.'

'No,' said Katy, shaking her head violently. 'I don't believe you. You've got him mixed up with someone else, hasn't he, Daniel? Ben's been acting strange, but that's because there's something going on with Abby, not Alison.'

'Abby?' asked Matthew. 'Who's Abby?'

'A friend of Charlene's that Ben kissed on Saturday night,' Daniel replied helpfully.

'What?' cried Matthew. 'He's stringing two women along as well as you, Katy?' He turned to face her in bewilderment.

'No, it's not like that,' Katy said defensively. 'You've got it all wrong about Alison. He hasn't been seeing her. He wouldn't go within a million miles of her, or you, after what happened.' She looked away, embarrassed, unable to hold his gaze. 'Alison must be making it up. Why on earth would Ben want to spend time with your wife?'

'Because of you,' spat Matthew. 'Because you left Ben right in it. She's been helping him learn how to look after your baby whilst you're at work. Got himself in a right mess, apparently. Alison stepped in and offered to help, and ever since then they've been getting together so Ben can learn all about babies.'

Katy stared back at him with her mouth open.

'No,' she muttered eventually. 'He wouldn't do that. He wouldn't turn to Alison. Anyone but her. Why didn't he ask me?'

'You said yourself, you were pretty clueless,' offered Daniel.

'You are allowed to be present but *not* heard,' shouted Katy.

'Okay,' said Daniel, sinking down in his seat.

Matthew took a step forward and placed both his hands on the back of a chair.

'He's been to our house, Katy. He . . . he . . .'

'He what?' demanded Katy, starting to panic.

'He filmed my wife,' Matthew paused, struggling to get the words out, 'p-peeling . . .'

'Oh my God,' gasped Daniel, unable to contain his excitement. 'Sorry,' he said when Katy gave him a glare. He clapped his hand over his mouth to prevent himself saying anything else.

'Carrots,' said Matthew, glancing at Daniel. 'Peeling *carrots.*'

'Carrots!' exclaimed Daniel. 'I thought . . .' he stopped. 'It doesn't matter what I thought, does it?' he said meekly.

'And he called her eye candy,' declared Matthew again. 'He had the gall to call her *eye candy.*'

'I have to ask if this was whilst she was peeling the carrot?' enquired Daniel quietly.

'I don't know,' boomed Matthew.

Katy had sat down. She replayed the last few weeks' events in her mind and realised it made perfect sense that Ben had been getting some outside help with Millie. It explained why he'd been so resistant to filling her in on anything he'd been up to during the long daytime hours spent with Millie. What made no sense at all was that this assistance had come from Alison, a woman whose complete lack of sense of humour Ben had barely tolerated during their antenatal classes and whom Ben had hoped never to meet again once the truth about Katy and Matthew's liaison had been revealed.

She looked up at Matthew and shook her head again.

'It doesn't make any sense,' she said quietly. 'Why Alison, of all people?'

'He's with her now,' said Matthew. 'Alison told me this morning he's coming round. She said something about a steriliser.'

'Steriliser!' gasped Katy and Daniel.

'That's right. And sleeping routines.'

'Oh,' said Katy.

The term 'sleeping routine' had not been in their vocabulary, since Millie appeared to be one of those babies who didn't have one. That was until this past week, when sleeping routines had been mentioned several times by Ben, out of nowhere. The phrase smacked of the uber-organised Alison, who had shared her military-style preparations for the arrival of her twins with everyone at the antenatal classes they'd attended together. Katy, on the other hand, had remained in denial that there was a human being on the way right up until the eleventh hour.

'Alison is A!' she exclaimed suddenly.

'What?' asked Matthew.

'Ben's been getting texts from someone called A. It must be Alison.'

'Well, she was certainly texting him on Friday night whilst we were trying to have a civilised dinner at Grants.'

'Ben and I were out on Friday night,' said Katy, her head snapping up. 'They were texting each other *then*?'

'They were indeed. She actually – and I cannot believe I'm saying this – but Alison actually texted him *at the dinner table*.'

Katy stood up abruptly.

'They're together at your house now, you say?' she demanded.

'Yes,' Matthew confirmed. 'You realise that we have to put a stop to this, don't you, Katy? We cannot let this continue.'

'Well, what are we waiting for, then? Let's go.'

'Now?'

'Yes, now.' Katy turned to Daniel. 'Tell Crispy Bix I had a family crisis. You can handle them, can't you?'

'Can't I come?' whined Daniel.

'No,' Matthew and Katy replied simultaneously.

'I think you're making a serious mistake if you don't let me come with you.'

'We don't *need* an audience,' said Matthew. 'Come on, Katy. Let's sort this out right now.'

'Are you sure that's wise?' questioned Daniel. 'I mean, think about it. Do you seriously think it's a good idea to arrive at your house alone together, given your history? It won't be them looking like the guilty party, but you.'

Matthew and Katy looked at each other. Matthew shrugged.

'I suppose he has a point,' he said.

'Yes,' said Daniel, giving a small fist pump. 'Sean can handle the meeting. I'll get my coat.'

'I'm sorry for your loss,' the receptionist shouted over to Katy and Matthew as they emerged from the lift.

'What?' asked Katy.

'She's in shock,' said Matthew, hurrying Katy past the receptionist. 'I'm just taking her out for some fresh air.'

'Hold all calls,' waved Daniel, skipping after them. 'We are in the midst of crisis.'

CHAPTER TWENTY-NINE

There was a loud noise coming from inside Alison's house. This was unusual. Normally it was an oasis of calm and serenity, but as Ben stood on the doorstep carrying Millie in her car seat, he could hear something thumping really hard inside. In fact the noise was so loud that he had to ring the doorbell several times before anyone came to get him.

'Come in,' Alison shouted at him when she eventually opened the door. 'We're playing the Arctic Monkeys VERY LOUD,' she continued with a grin, 'to get ourselves in the mood for doing the next video.'

'Okay,' Ben shouting back, wishing she would turn it down.

'Come on through,' she yelled. 'We've been waiting for you.'

Ben bent to get Millie out of the car seat then traipsed after Alison into the kitchen, where she thankfully turned the music down so they could at least hear themselves think.

'I phoned Charlene yesterday,' she announced, as Ben laid Millie carefully on a rug next to Rebecca and George.

'Did you?'

'Yes, I told her she could use my video, and she was really pleased. Then she had a brilliant idea.'

'Really?' said Ben, standing up. 'Charlene?'

'I'm going to do a proper website,' Alison said, beaming. 'For people just like you. With clear, simple instructions about looking after a newborn. Nothing complicated, just the basics, like you said. So you can get on with enjoying having a baby.'

'Sounds brilliant,' said Ben, amazed at how excited she seemed and delighted that his cunning plan to keep getting advice from Alison might actually work.

'And Charlene suggested a name,' she continued. 'But I'm not quite sure about it.'

'Okay,' said Ben. 'Hit me with it.

'The Dummies and Daddies' Guide to Babies,' she announced.

There was silence as she scrutinised Ben for a reaction.

'It's brilliant,' he declared.

'But does anyone really want to be branded a dummy?' she asked uncertainly.

'Of course they do. Being branded a dummy allows you to declare you know absolutely bugger all. Everyone assumes you simply know how to look after a baby, don't they? We're all dummies when we start, and no-one should be afraid of admitting that.'

'Right.' Alison nodded thoughtfully. 'Well, that's that then. The website has a name.'

'Wow,' said Ben. 'Get you.'

'I know,' said Alison. 'Who'd have thought you coming back into my life would have led to this?'

'Life is very weird,' agreed Ben. 'Now, shall I teach you how to make your first film for your very own website?'

'Oh yes,' she grinned. 'Please do.'

After Alison had taken a full twenty minutes to determine how to lay Ben's steriliser out in the most helpful fashion and when Ben had finally worked out how to attach Alison's phone to a small tripod he'd acquired for the purpose, they were ready to roll.

'So how do I look?' she asked, just as they were about to start.

He glanced over at her. She did look different, somehow, but he couldn't work out why. She seemed younger, more relaxed.

'Charlene said I needed to look less like Mary Poppins,' said Alison. 'I needed to appear more approachable, less threatening.'

'Just like a *Blue Peter* presenter,' declared Ben. That was what was different. Her shirt was fitted but open at the collar and was a vivid aqua blue. She was wearing jeans that he'd never seen her in before and her blonde hair was in a ponytail rather than her usual super-sleek, shoulder-length bob.

'It suits you,' he told her. 'Really it does.'

'Still a bit of eye candy?' she asked with a small smile.

'Oh, most definitely eye candy,' he confirmed. When she relaxed like this, Alison really wasn't half bad. He'd actually quite miss her. If it hadn't been for the fact that it was all too complicated, then it was entirely possible they might have become friends.

'Right,' he said, standing up straight. 'Are we ready? Shall we shoot a rehearsal and see how it comes out? Then you can have a go at setting it up yourself. Ready?'

Alison cleared her throat and nodded, smiling into the camera.

'So in three, two, one, ACTION.'

'I don't fucking believe it!' came a gruff voice from the doorway into the hall.

'Matthew!' exclaimed Alison. She looked up, her pink, glossy lips forming a perfectly shocked circle shape. 'What are you doing home?'

Ben froze, his back to Matthew. *Fuck*. It was happening. His worst nightmare.

'Katy! Why are you here?' was the next thing he heard Alison yelp. Ben spun round to see Katy's head poking out from behind Matthew's shoulder in the kitchen doorway.

He gasped at the sight of them together. He'd never expected to be confronted by that vision again.

'Filming my wife, in my own home. What kind of weirdo are you?' said Matthew, advancing towards Ben.

'What are you doing here together?' Ben asked, searching Katy's face for an explanation as Matthew loomed over him. He looked over to Alison. What did she see? *He* saw a disaster waiting to happen. Did she see it? This could not, would not, end well, and the most likely casualty was going to be her, given that she was the only person in the room who had no idea of the secrets and lies compiled between the other three.

The image of Matthew in the labour room came flooding back to him, fighting him tooth and nail to convince Katy that she should ditch Ben for him. Was that his plan? He was back again to battle for Katy, but right in front of Alison this time?

'Don't do it,' he said instinctively.

'Don't do what?' challenged Matthew. 'Tell you to stop harassing my wife, to stop taking advantage of her?'

'Oh, that's brilliant coming from you,' he couldn't help but throw back. 'I have absolutely nothing to feel guilty about, unlike . . . unlike . . .' He petered out, realising he was entering dangerous territory. 'And you haven't answered my question. What are you both doing here *together*?'

'We have Daniel with us,' said Katy, standing on tiptoe to be seen over Matthew's shoulder. 'He's here in the hall,' she said directly to Ben.

'Hello, one and all,' came a high-pitched shout from somewhere out in the hall.

'We weren't . . . nothing . . . is going on,' Katy continued, glancing nervously at Alison. 'But quite clearly there is something going on here.'

'Hang on a minute,' said Alison, stepping out from behind the island to stand beside Ben. 'I'll tell you exactly what's going on here, Katy. We are two stay-at-home parents pulling together in Ben's hour of need when his fiancée couldn't be bothered to be there for him.'

'Excuse me,' said Katy, pushing past Matthew to square up to Alison. 'Is that what Ben's been telling you?'

'He didn't have to,' said Alison. 'You ran back to work as fast as you could and left him stranded.'

'You don't have to defend me,' said Ben, laying a hand on Alison's arm.

Katy stood in shock at the contact between them.

'I didn't just leave him,' she said. 'He *wanted* to do it.'

'Well, it's just a good job I was there to do what you should have been doing,' said Alison, putting her hands defiantly on her hips. 'I'm sure Ben will agree with me.'

Katy felt her jaw drop slightly. Sickening thoughts were pouring into her head. Do what exactly? Be a mum, a partner? Or a lover? Surely not? She looked at Ben. He was studying the floor, failing to defend her.

'Ben?' she said. He looked up but didn't say anything. 'What's going on?' she asked.

'Yes, *Ben*,' said Matthew. 'What *has* been going on?'

'Nothing,' Ben shouted back, almost speechless. 'How can you two even think . . . how can you even dare to . . .'

'You called her *eye candy*!' accused Matthew.

Ben gasped.

'No, I didn't. Not really,' he protested.

'You did,' cried Alison, turning to Ben.

'I didn't mean it like that,' he said to her, then turned back to Matthew. 'I was just trying to make her crack a smile, relax a bit, that's all. Make her feel good. Alison isn't . . . I wouldn't . . . isn't *really* what *I'd* call eye candy.'

There was a sudden flash of movement as though someone had turned the lights off and on really quickly, and the next minute both Alison and Katy were screaming as Ben fell to the floor, luckily onto the floral patterned rug, avoiding babies lying under baby gyms.

'You hit me,' exclaimed Ben, his hand flying to his lip and finding a smattering of blood.

'Yes, I bloody well did,' said Matthew, his jaw set and fists clenched at his sides. 'Nobody insults Alison like that,' he said firmly. 'I think you'll find that my wife *is* actually eye candy.'

'Oh Matthew,' gasped Alison, turning her attention away from Ben lying on the floor to gape at her husband. 'I . . . I . . .'

'But you are not *his* eye candy, nor anyone else's for that matter. You are *my* eye candy,' said Matthew, stepping forward and grasping Alison by the shoulders and staring deeply into her eyes.

Alison's hands flew up to her mouth, her eyes wide in surprise.

'You're *my* eye candy and *my* wife too,' he continued, 'but I need you to *just* be my wife sometimes. Not a mother, not a teacher, not a helper, just my wife, Alison. Because I need her. I *want* her. I *love* her.'

Alison blinked back at him.

'Will you be my wife, Alison?' he urged, shaking her slightly by the shoulders.

'I will,' she whispered. 'Oh Matthew,' she said, stepping forward and falling into his arms.

Matthew closed his eyes and embraced her as silence fell on the room. When he opened his eyes again he fixed Ben with a glare over Alison's shoulder then pushed her gently away from him and looked her in the eye.

'So I think you should go now,' he said to her.

'What, me?' she asked, startled.

'Go on. You're going out. I'm looking after Rebecca and George today.'

'What, now?'

'Yes. I presume your spreadsheet is on the desktop of the laptop?'

'Yes, but—'

'No buts. All I do all day is look at spreadsheets. I know spreadsheets. Breast milk in the fridge?'

'Yes, but . . . that's for emergencies.'

'This is an emergency. I'm going to have the most stunning eye candy in Leeds on my arm tonight when we go out for dinner, so you'd better get down those shops and buy something to wear. Now off you go.'

'Okay, okay, but you'll—'

'No buts. *Leave*,' said Matthew, pushing her through the kitchen door. He ushered her out into the hall, closing the door behind them.

'Take as long as you like,' he continued, reaching for her coat. 'I'm staying home all day.'

'Don't forget to—'

'I am going to enjoy my children,' said Matthew firmly. 'I'll be fine. *We'll* be fine.'

Alison hovered for just a moment, looking quizzically into his eyes.

'Of course,' she nodded. 'Actually, you're right. You should enjoy them, that's a really good idea. I don't need to be in control of my children all the time, do I?'

'That's right, Alison,' said Matthew. 'Go and relax, and then we'll try and have an entire meal at Grants tonight, shall we?'

'I'd like that,' she said, reaching up to kiss him on the check.

'And then we'll come home to bed,' he said, catching her hand and squeezing it.

'Matthew,' she giggled, turning slightly pink. She turned to put her coat on and pick up her bag, then blew a kiss to her husband as she walked out the door.

Matthew closed the door behind her and turned to lean against it, heaving a great sigh.

'Boy, was that a close shave,' said Daniel, still sitting patiently on a chair in the hallway. '*You* could have lost everything there.'

Matthew looked up with a start.

'Are you still here?'

'I've been sitting quietly, not causing any trouble,' Daniel said. 'Would you like me to go with Alison? I think she could do with some styling tips.'

'No,' said Matthew just as the door flew open from the kitchen and Ben strode out. He looked at Daniel and Matthew, then took his coat from the rack and headed towards the front door.

'Where are you going?' cried Katy, running after him.

Ben stopped inches from the door and breathed in and out slowly. He turned to face her.

'What were you thinking?' he said. 'Coming here with . . . him?' He didn't even look at Matthew, just gave him a cursory nod.

'Because you were here, Ben,' she whimpered. 'Because you were with Alison and we couldn't let it continue. We had to put a stop to it.'

He stared back at Katy, saying nothing.

'Why would you do this?' she asked. 'Why turn to Alison? I don't understand.'

Ben looked from Katy to Matthew then back to Katy.

'That much is obvious,' he declared.

He turned and left.

'Go after him, then,' urged Daniel, after the door slammed. 'What are you standing there for looking like a Disney World cast member? Really, Katy, primary colours on a day like today. What were you thinking?'

She turned to look at Daniel, still trying to process exactly what had happened over the last few minutes.

'Daniel's right,' said Matthew. 'I think you've got some work to do with that one.'

'I really don't think you are in any position to offer me relationship advice,' she said through gritted teeth.

He shrugged. 'I think you'll find that I handled the situation with Alison pretty well.'

'I have to agree, actually,' said Daniel. 'Who'd have thought that all Alison wanted was for a caveman to claim her, pick her up, throw her over his shoulder and run into the woods with her. Genius move, Matthew. I commend you.'

Matthew nodded briefly. 'Thank you. Wish I'd realised that about five years ago, though.'

'I don't care what Alison wants,' stormed Katy. 'What am I going to do?'

'Go after him!' Matthew and Daniel shouted in unison.

'Right,' she said, heading for the door. 'I'm going.' And then she was gone, door slammed behind her.

'Three, two, one,' said Daniel just as the door was flung open again.

'How?' she cried, poking her head around the door. 'We got here in Matthew's car.'

'Well, I can't go anywhere. I'm looking after my children,' said Matthew.

'What am I going to do?' she asked in despair.

'There's a bus that goes from the end of the street into town,' Matthew suggested.

'Great, let's go.' Katy grabbed Daniel by the arm.

'Are we seriously going in hot pursuit of someone on a *bus*?' he complained. 'Have you lost your mind, Katy?'

'Well, have you got any better ideas?' she asked. 'I don't see you whizzing round the corner on a motorbike with a side car so I can hop on and chase a Vauxhall Corsa round the streets of Leeds.'

'I was quite enjoying that little scenario until you mentioned the words Vauxhall and Corsa,' replied Daniel.

'So have you got any better ideas?' she demanded.

'Why don't we call a cab?'

'I'm not going to stand here waiting for half an hour for a cab to turn up,' she said furiously. 'Not exactly what you'd call *going after him*, is it? More like letting him get as far away as possible before I get my arse into gear.'

'Look, there's no need for you to take your frustration out on me,' said Daniel. 'Let's get a high-speed bus into town, then, in the absence of any other means of pursuit.'

'Right,' she said. 'What are we waiting for? Let's go.'

Matthew held up his hand. 'You can't go,' he said.

'Why not?' she asked fearfully.

'What about Millie?'

'Oh my God!' Katy's hand flew up to her mouth. 'I forgot all about her. I can't believe it!' She dashed into the kitchen to find Millie quite happily chewing on a plastic ring. 'I'm so sorry,' she said, kneeling down to touch her. 'I didn't mean to forget you, honestly I didn't.'

'Are we seriously going in hot pursuit, on a bus,' said Daniel, appearing behind her, 'with a *baby*? It's hardly *CSI: Miami*.'

Katy looked up at him. 'The hot pursuit will have to wait. I need to be a mum now. I think I'd better just take Millie home.'

'You do realise you won't be able to call it a hot pursuit, then, don't you?' he enquired. 'Not after a delay of some hours when you do precisely nothing to catch up with him.'

'I think Katy's right,' said Matthew, walking in with Rebecca in his arms. 'She needs to act like a responsible parent.'

'Oh fuck off, Matthew,' said Daniel and Katy together.

CHAPTER THIRTY

Katy stood outside the Brewery Tap and peered in through the window. She'd never been inside a microbrewery before. She wasn't really sure what one was. Did they serve very small pints? Was the beer brewed by midgets? Probably not, because then it would be called a midget brewery, wouldn't it? But would a midget brewery just be for midgets? The thoughts spun around in her head until she had to tell herself to stop because she was sounding like Braindead.

She really hoped Ben was in here. She'd been round all his other haunts and drawn a blank until she'd resorted to sitting and having a coffee to warm up and try and rack her brains as to where she might find him. A bizarre experience in a pub at eight o'clock at night, sitting alone with a coffee surrounded by middle-aged men supping bitter. It had been the quickest cup of coffee she'd ever drunk as she tried desperately to think of any places he'd mentioned recently. He wasn't answering his phone and she was thinking of resorting to Braindead when she suddenly remembered him harping on about a microbrewery. Two possibilities in the city had been offered up by Google, and after drawing a blank at one where she'd been openly stared at by a scruffy-looking pair of heavy metal fans, she'd come literally to the last chance saloon: the Brewery Tap.

She pushed the door open and surveyed the room, conscious that she was overdressed for a microbrewery on a Monday night. She'd wanted to look nice for Ben, attractive, borderline eye candy, perhaps. She was wearing make-up and long sparkly earrings along with a vivid red wool jacket. Her long legs had now fully recovered from childbirth and were set off nicely by a very short black velvet skirt and knee-high suede boots.

She'd felt foolish, however, the minute she'd stepped into the first pub. No-one dressed that way on a Monday night in a back-street pub in the centre of Leeds. By the time she walked into the Brewery Tap she still wasn't used to being appraised at the door. A loud wolf whistle greeted her and she was just about to turn and run when it was followed up by a familiar voice.

'Fuck, me Katy. Microbrewery, *not* micro-skirt.'

Katy had never been so happy to hear Braindead. She scoured the room until she saw him and Ben sitting in the corner nursing their pints. Ben was looking at her expressionlessly. He lifted his pint and downed it as she walked towards them.

'May I join you?' she asked as she reached their table.

Ben nodded slowly as he placed his glass on the table.

She eased herself down onto a chair.

'You had a good day, Katy?' asked Braindead.

Katy and Ben slowly raised their heads to stare at him.

'No, right, course not,' said Braindead, nodding his head.

Silence descended.

'Good news is that me and Ben are mates again,' Braindead piped up. 'You know, after the fracas with that mate of Charlene's. What was her name?'

Ben and Katy continued to stare at Braindead.

'What *was* her name?' Braindead repeated.

'Abby,' Ben whispered.

'That's it, Abby,' Braindead nodded. 'Can't believe I forgot. Anyway, do you think I should call her? You know, now you've told her the score, Ben? Now you've told her to never pounce on you again because you are totally in love with Katy and would do anything for her. And you mean anything, not just stuff like watching what she wants on the telly, even if it's crap, or pretending to like drinking wine. No, the kind of anything you mean is giving up your job to look after Millie so she could go back to the high-flying job she loves and you can have enough money to move to the suburbs and have a fancy wedding that she wants and you don't give a shit about. That is the kind of love you are talking about.'

Ben and Katy continued to sit very still, staring at Braindead.

'So should I?' asked Braindead.

'Should you what?' muttered Ben.

'Call Abby! Haven't you listened to a word I've been saying?' Braindead paused, swivelling his eyes between the two of them. 'Sod it,' he declared. 'I'll go home and call her now. What have I got to lose, eh? Nothing, that's what. You don't mind if I go now, do you, mate?'

Ben shook his head.

'Good to see you,' Braindead said to Katy. 'Just like old times, eh? Same time next week?'

Katy nodded mutely as Braindead got up from his chair and left.

Katy and Ben continued to stare awkwardly ahead, neither knowing what to say.

Eventually Katy swallowed, knowing it really was down to her to make the first move.

'Thank you,' she said.

Finally Ben looked at her. 'What did you say?'

'Thank you,' she repeated, feeling her hormones start to swell and the first indication of possible tears.

'What for?' he muttered, looking back down at the floor again.

'For giving up your job for me,' she said, to the top of his head. She felt utterly ashamed. 'I don't think I ever said thank you.'

Ben didn't look up. His shoulders moved up and down to indicate he was still breathing, but that was it. When eventually he did look up, to Katy's astonishment he had tears in his eyes.

'I just wanted you to be proud of me for a change,' he said. 'Instead of being some hopeless layabout PE teacher, I wanted to be someone you could be proud to call your husband. Someone who was being a great dad to your daughter whilst you could concentrate on your career. Turns out I couldn't get that right either.' He looked down again and she watched his hand reach up to wipe something away.

'We got thrown out of Music, Mummy and Me,' he said, looking back up.

'What? Why didn't you tell me?'

'I thought you'd think I was a failure,' he said. 'I didn't get it. It was just too . . . weird. I couldn't make any sense of why we were doing what she said so I got arsey with her and she threw me out. Told us never to come back.'

Katy was just to about to interject when he launched into his next confession.

'Then I couldn't get the sodding steriliser to work. I know you'd shown me, but I just thought it would be a piece of cake so I didn't really listen. I couldn't make it do its thing, and I was panicking because we had no bottles sterilised and I thought I was going to murder Millie because of dirty bottles, so I did the unthinkable, well, actually, I did two very stupid things.'

'What?' said Katy, wide-eyed. What else hadn't he told her?

'I roped in Braindead and Charlene to help me. What was I thinking?' He made his hand into the shape of a pistol and pretended to fire it into his own head. 'Braindead nearly totalled the damn thing with a screwdriver and Charlene . . . well,' he stopped, biting his lip. 'To start with she just told me to watch videos on YouTube to help me work baby stuff out.'

'YouTube?' Katy echoed.

'Yeah,' Ben nodded. 'Melissa from Minnesota showed me how to use a steriliser.'

'You'd rather ask Melissa from Minnesota for help than me?'

'I just didn't want you to think I was an idiot. Then when I had a bit of a meltdown because I wasn't coping, Charlene said she had the answer to all my problems, only I didn't realise she meant Alison. She just arrived on my doorstep with her . . . and Abby.'

'Oh,' said Katy. 'I see.'

'I didn't invite them, I swear I didn't, but once she was there Alison made it seem all so simple, somehow. She knew exactly what to do. She could even make me look like I knew what I was doing.'

'But why didn't you just ask me? Talk to me, tell me you were struggling?' asked Katy.

Ben shrugged.

'You succeed in life, Katy,' he said. 'That's what you do. I thought at the very least I could succeed at this.' He shrugged again and she thought she saw the hint of tears coming back. 'But it's so *hard,*' he said, a single tear spilling down his cheek. 'It's . . . it's just so *relentless,*' he gasped. 'They need you *all* the time. You think they're only small, they can't make you jump through hoops, but they do. Constantly. And then they cry and you have no idea why, so there's nothing you can do but ride it out until they finally stop because you've given them a different-coloured spoon to suck. None of it makes any sense!' He drew breath, staring wildly at Katy. 'And then there's all this stuff you should know, like out of nowhere. Like when to start giving them proper food, so you panic and you Google it and then you get fifty different opinions so you ask the health visitor, who talks complete and utter gibberish, so *you*, a complete and utter novice, have to decide which one to believe. What the hell is that all about? I mean seriously. How long have we been raising children as a civilisation and we still can't decide when to start weaning? It's utterly ridiculous. We've abolished many life-threatening diseases, cloned a sheep, put a man on the moon, but deciding if apple or carrot is the best first food for our kids . . . no-one is brainy enough to work that one out.'

Katy knew exactly how Ben felt. She'd spent most of the first few weeks with Millie feeling bewildered, confused and like she'd landed on a different planet where she understood nothing.

'No-one appreciates how hard it is,' Ben went on. 'There're all these people out there doing this job which is fucking impossible, quite frankly, and yet no one realises, no-one appreciates it. No-one.'

'I'm so sorry,' said Katy, grabbing his hand. '*I* appreciate it, I really do.'

'And to top it all,' said Ben. 'Do you know what the worst of it is?'

'No,' said Katy, bracing herself.

'I've turned into my bloody mother. *No-one appreciates me, no-one knows what I do for this family*,' he said in a mock girly tone with his hand on his brow and a hint of a smirk on his lips.

'I cannot tell you how much I appreciate you,' said Katy. 'I know I didn't show it when you first offered to look after Millie. But . . . but I was where you are now, at the end of my tether, failing every day, thinking I was a rubbish mum.' She hesitated, wondering whether to make her next confession.

'I guess a bit of me didn't want you to succeed because that would make me feel less terrible about my failings.'

Ben didn't say anything, just breathed out slowly.

'I shouldn't be surprised you ended up asking Alison for help,' she continued. 'It would have been pretty pointless asking me. I just wished you'd told me, so I didn't have to go and get all jealous that someone else was sniffing round you.'

'You were jealous, were you?'

'Of course,' said Katy. 'I know that you wouldn't ever do anything like that and I feel absolutely terrible for thinking you might.'

'I never would, you know.'

'I know,' she replied. 'But it would have been no less than I deserve, wouldn't it?'

Ben didn't reply.

'Daniel reckons I've been waiting for you to punish me for what I did. That's why I found it so easy to believe you were having an affair.'

'I don't want to punish you,' said Ben. 'That's all done. It's in the past. That is until I stupidly got myself involved with Alison again.'

Katy gave him a watery smile.

'Then why won't you have sex with me?' she asked quietly.

'What do you mean, I won't have sex with you?'

'Well, we haven't done it since . . .' She paused, finding it difficult to get the words out. 'Since you found out about Matthew.'

'Really!' he exclaimed. 'Is it that long? Why didn't you just ask me?'

'I tried,' she said. 'Remember? With the Dang Dang Whisky Slider Bombs, but that all ended very badly.'

'You should have just said. You didn't need to go to all that trouble. You should have just talked to me.'

'What, like you just talking to me about the fact you weren't coping looking after Millie?'

They both looked at each other in silence.

'Shall we try just talking to each other in the future?' said Ben eventually.

'What a novel idea,' said Katy.

'Very mature of us, I reckon.' Ben grinned and took her hand. 'Shall I start?'

'Fire away,' she replied. 'Whatever you want to get off your chest.'

'Before I start, can I just ask where you've put our daughter?'

'Oh, she's at your mum's. She's having a sleepover.'

'Great,' he replied. 'So here's the first thing I want to say.'

'Hit me with it.'

'What on earth are we doing sitting in a microbrewery when we have the flat all to ourselves? We should be having sex.'

CHAPTER THIRTY-ONE

Six weeks later

'Really?'

'Yes.'

'You really think I need to wear a tie for a christening?' asked Ben for the fourth time that morning.

'It's not a christening, it's a naming ceremony,' Katy told him.

'I know. Amounts to the same thing, though, doesn't it?'

'Not really, given that a christening is religious and a naming ceremony isn't.'

'What I mean is that it's just an excuse for a party. The ceremony bit is something to be endured so you can have a right old rave-up.'

Katy stopped applying her lipstick and turned to look at Ben.

'And it's an excuse to buy a new outfit,' he added. 'Am I right?'

She looked down at her Fifties-style dress. It was pale blue lace, mid-calf length, and she'd spent every lunchtime for a month searching it out. It looked amazing, and in normal circumstances she might have been upset if it hadn't been immediately obviously she'd bought a new frock. But then he was a man, after all, and today of all days she refused to be upset.

'Oh, I've had it a while,' she said, waving her hand dismissively. 'Just never got round to wearing it.' She decided to change tack. 'Actually, I picked this up yesterday. Thought you could do with a new tie. Why don't you try it on with your white shirt and smart trousers?' She handed him a bag and held her breath as he pulled out the tie, which was exactly the same colour as her dress. She prayed he wouldn't notice. He shrugged and dropped it on the bed, then reached for the ironed white shirt she'd left hanging on the back of a chair. In fact, he would wear pretty much whatever she wanted provided he didn't have to put any thought into it.

'I'll go and get Millie ready,' she said as she gave herself one last check in the full-length mirror. She looked just how she wanted to on this important day. Pretty and happy. Perfect. She checked her watch. It was all about timing now. Being late would ruin everything, and given that she'd not tackled getting Millie into her outfit yet and Ben was only half dressed, then anything could happen to cause a delay.

'Come on then, you,' she said to Millie, pulling her out of her baby seat and easing her into an abundance of white taffeta. Ben hadn't asked what Millie would be wearing today. Clearly her outfit hadn't registered as important. Katy hoped again that he wouldn't notice that the wide sash around her belly was the same colour as his tie and her lace dress. She lifted Millie up once all buttons were secured and held her tight to her chest, looking in the mirror at the pair of them. She should be nervous, she realised, but she wasn't. She was just happy. Her only worry was whether Millie would throw up over her before they made it to the ceremony.

Ten minutes later they all stood in the hall waiting for the taxi to arrive.

'You look fit,' said Ben.

'As a mother approaching forty way too rapidly, I take that as a massive compliment.'

'That's how it was intended,' said Ben, tugging his tie loose. Katy fought the compulsion to tighten it back up again.

'Remind me who's coming,' he said.

'Oh, the usual, you know,' she replied. 'Just close friends and family.'

Ben nodded. Katy had offered to organise everything for today's ceremony and that suited them both.

'Do you not think this tie is over the top?' he asked, taking another tug at it.

'No,' said Katy, trying to stay calm. 'Why don't you keep it on until you get there and if you're not comfortable, take it off then.'

'Right, I'll do that,' Ben agreed. 'We could drive, you know. We don't really need a taxi, do we?'

'Look, it's all organised. Just try and enjoy it, okay?'

'Okay.'

Ben was making Katy feel nervous. Where was the bloody taxi so they could just get on with it?

'Shall we wait downstairs?' she suggested. If she watched Ben bobbing around on one foot any longer she might throw up.

'Good idea,' he said, picking up Millie.

Katy went to pick up the nappy bag, which weighed a ton.

'I can take that,' Ben offered, taking it from her. 'Bloody hell, what have you put in here? The changing table?'

'Just stuff we might need,' she said.

'You need some lessons on nappy bag efficiency,' Ben declared. 'Me and the Millster have it down to a five-item maximum these days. And we've agreed that by puberty she'll have it down to just two. Wet wipes and spare pants, that's it. No messing.'

'I'm impressed,' said Katy. 'Seriously. Now that's the taxi. Let's go, shall we?'

'You remember we've just got to call in at the registry office on the way,' said Katy, once they were all secure in the back of the cab after a few minutes' grappling with the seat belt and Millie's seat.

'I know, I know,' said Ben. 'It's still bothering me that I can't remember the registrar handing me the birth certificate when we left.'

'I'm not blaming you,' said Katy. 'It's my fault. I'm sure she handed it to me, but I've no idea where I put it. It doesn't matter anyway. They've got us a copy and that's all we need.'

'Quite surprised they even need a birth certificate for a naming ceremony,' said Ben. 'If parents are going to go through all that palaver, I think you'd be pretty certain that they managed to register the baby at birth.'

Katy shrugged.

'I guess it just helps to make it official, doesn't it?'

'But to who? God?'

'Clearly not, as it's non-religious.'

'Well, who then?'

'I don't know,' said Katy, trying not to lose her cool. 'They just said we needed to take it, that's all. In any case, we needed another one, didn't we, given we'd lost the first one?'

'S'pose,' Ben shrugged. 'Eh up, there's Braindead,' he cried, leaning towards the window as they drew up outside the registry office. 'Bloody hell. He's got a tie on. You've got Braindead into a tie, Millie, can you believe that? Who'd have thought it? I bet you're the first woman he's ever worn a tie for,' he continued, squeezing her toes.

'He's not wearing it for her,' said Katy as the taxi drew to a halt.

'Eh,' said Ben, jerking his head to look at Katy. 'What do you mean?'

She felt herself go hot and then cold with pure nerves. Suddenly she couldn't speak. She swallowed repeatedly until finally she managed to squeak, 'Will you marry me . . . today?'

Ben went white.

He's going to say no, she panicked. She thought she might be sick.

'Today,' he murmured.

She nodded.

He looked through the window at Braindead, who was clapping wildly and pointing to the top of the steps. He looked up and saw his mum first, dressed top to toe in pink, including pink shoes. She was busy tugging his dad's tie into place while he protested by keeping one finger firmly inserted in his collar. Then he saw Rick next to his new wife, who must have been having top-ups by now as she still had a deep tan. Next to them stood Katy's mum and dad, who Daniel was keeping entertained. Katy's dad was clearly in awe if a little scared of Daniel's lime-green suit and the fact that he was holding Katy's bouquet as naturally as if he were about to become a new bride himself.

'I don't need some big fancy wedding,' said Katy, taking his hand. 'All I need to know is that you and me are in this together . . . forever.'

Ben's jaw had dropped and he showed no sign of being able to speak.

'There's no naming ceremony,' she continued. 'Just someone in there waiting to marry us.' She glanced down at her watch. 'In ten minutes' time.'

Dazed, Ben looked back up at the small crowd of their nearest and dearest then back down at Millie, then finally at Katy.

'My tie matches your dress?' he murmured.

She nodded vigorously.

'That's it,' she said. 'You're catching on. Look, Millie's ribbon is the same colour.'

He looked down and gasped, his hand flying to his mouth.

'Our wedding, today!' he exclaimed.

'That's right,' said Katy. 'Everyone's here for us. I even had to invite Abby because Braindead insisted.'

Ben looked back out the window. Braindead was standing on the kerb, attached to Abby by the mouth.

'Yuck,' said Ben, looking away fast.

'So will you?' said Katy, catching both of his hands. 'Will you marry me,' she said slowly, 'right now?'

'I will,' said Ben, welling up. 'Of course I bloody will.'

Katy thought she might burst into tears before she remembered she had to tell Ben one more thing.

'And I've organised a honeymoon,' she announced. 'Just a couple of nights. Your mum said she'd have Millie. I've booked us into a little cottage on the moors.'

'You are amazing,' declared Ben. 'A wedding and a honeymoon in an empty house. You know what that means, don't you?'

'What?

'We're going to have sex.'

'Yes,' nodded Katy, grinning.

'And more than once.'

'Oh, most definitely,' she laughed. 'Most definitely.'

EPILOGUE

From the website
www.dummies&daddiesguidetobabies.com

NEWS – 1 JUNE

Please accept my apologies for not having posted any updates for the last two weeks. I will be filming the promised video on how to treat minor injuries resulting from babies learning to walk later on today, as well as updating the suggested list of first words to teach your ten-month-old.

The reason I haven't been able to post recently is due to the fact that I am overjoyed to announce that I am three months pregnant! It has come as an enormous surprise to me and my husband as our twins arrived after many years of IVF and we never expected to conceive naturally. However, as we now understand, apparently it's quite common after a successful IVF pregnancy. It will, of course, be a lot of hard work having three babies in the house under two, but it's something both my husband and I are really looking forward to. He has also promised to take his fair share of parental duties so that I can carry on with this website, so watch this space.

Alison

Leave a comment:

Dipsey Daddy Daycare:

WOW, ALISON!!!! I know I don't normally leave comments on your website, just avidly watch all your videos to keep me up to date, but I had to say a mahoosive congratulations. I can only imagine how happy you are. This website saves my life daily, by the way – promise me you won't stop doing it . . . I need you. Just don't tell anyone I said that.

Alison:

You don't really need me – you are perfectly capable and you know it. We are beyond happiness – you?

Dipsey Daddy Daycare:

All good. I'm coping, which is a huge step forward. Millie gets cheekier by the day and so it's a lot more fun. There are moments when I really enjoy myself!

Oh, and I started a Music, Daddies and The Arctic Monkeys group with other stay-at-home dads I met through this website. We meet every Friday lunchtime, listen to some tunes and play poker with the kids sitting on our knees. Millie has a great poker face.

Alison:

That's just . . . so you, Ben. Glad you are enjoying yourself, though.

Dipsey Daddy Daycare:
Oh, and I'm a married man now. I wear a ring and every-
thing. We are definitely not pregnant. We listened to the doc-
tor's advice about contraception, unlike some I can mention!
Having fun practising, though!

Alison:
Please – I don't need details.

Dipsey Daddy Daycare:
Ha ha – you'd better get some more practice yourselves,
because you'll have no time when the next one arrives!

Alison:
Enough now.

Dipsey Daddy Daycare:
Okay. Bye then. Keep up the good work. That's the website, I
mean, not the practising! Right, I'm really going now. Bye.

THE END

Acknowledgements

This is the fourth book I've written and published. Can't quite believe that. So much has happened since I first put pen to paper and fingers to keyboard back in 2007. There have been times when waiting for something to happen has nearly killed me and times when so much has been happening it has nearly killed me! I've been lucky enough to experience the utter thrill of writing my first novel, getting my first agent and then my first foreign publishing deal. Then nothing happened for a while until I decided to take the matter in my own hands and had the most brilliant time self-publishing my first book, which led to my first number one, which led to my first UK publishing deal.

So I'd like to take this opportunity to thank the people who were right there at the beginning and those who are here at what feels like sort of the end of the beginning.

Thank you to Jordan Pecile, Jeff Hutton and my fellow students at the Manchester Community College, Connecticut who first made me write. It's so important to just start and that's what you all did for me.

Thanks as always to Bruce, my husband, who made me believe I could finish. That I was capable and not insane. You have no idea how important that is. And to all my friends and family for being the inspiration behind many of my words and thoughts.

Now, eight years later, my people are not just classmates and tutors and family and friends but agents and publishers and publicists and marketeers and distributors, who all make up the world of publishing. My biggest thank yous must go to Araminta Whitley and Peta Nightingale for their support and honesty, and to Jenny Geras and Selina Walker for their belief and sharing some of the journey with me.

But mostly I have to thank every single person who ever bought and read one of my books. Thank you. You made me very happy.

Who knows what the next phase holds, but whatever happens, I feel very lucky to be here.

About the Author

Hi everyone. If you're reading this you've either just finished *No-One Ever Has Sex in the Suburbs* or you're thinking about starting it but thought you'd check me out first to see if you think I could write a book you'd enjoy. So here's me – see what you think. I always wanted to be a writer and I got my chance when my husband's career moved us to America for three years. In a bid to avoid domestic duties and people who didn't understand my Derbyshire accent I wrote *No-One Ever Has Sex on a Tuesday*, which went on to be successfully published internationally and became a number 1 best-selling ebook in the UK. I'm now on my fourth book and back living in the UK where my joy is my family and my writing. Achieving my dream as an author has lead me to think about pursuing other goals, which currently include spontaneous dancing on a table without collapse (me or the table) and meeting a real live moose.

If you have just finished reading *No-One Ever Has Sex in the Suburbs*, thank you so much and I really hope you enjoyed it. It would be wonderful if you felt you could write a review – it doesn't have to be long, but will always be appreciated.

If you would like to get an email when my next book is released please sign up here: http://goo.gl/75JPbV. Your email address will never be shared and you can unsubscribe at any time.

I love hearing from my readers so do please come and visit my website: www.tracybloom.com, find me on Twitter @TracyBBloom or join me on Facebook where I am Tracy Bloom Author.

Printed in Great Britain
by Amazon.co.uk, Ltd.,
Marston Gate.